Steady and Slow

Tales from Grace Chapel Inn

Steady and Slow

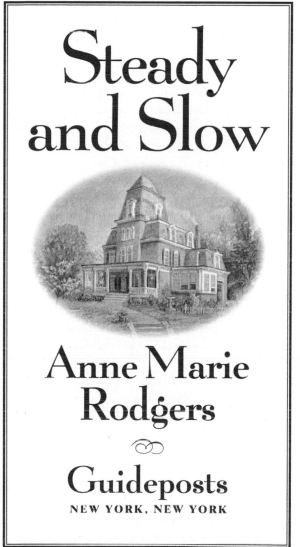

Anne Marie Rodgers

Guideposts
NEW YORK, NEW YORK

Acknowledgments

All Scripture quotations are taken from
The Holy Bible, New International Version. Copyright © 1973,
1978, 1984 International Bible Society. Used by permission
of Zondervan Bible Publishers.

Guideposts.org
(800) 932-2145
Guideposts Books & Inspirational Media
Series Editors: Regina Hersey and Leo Grant
Cover art by Edgar Jerins
Cover design by Wendy Bass
Interior design by Cindy LaBreacht
Typeset by Nancy Tardi
Printed in the United States of America
10 9 8 7 6 5 4

Acknowledgments

For Squirt, the real "M.P.," and with thanks to Centre Wildlife Care, Robyn Graboski and Karen Kuhn for all you have taught me.

—Anne Marie Rodgers

Chapter 🐢 One

The Howard sisters were enjoying a glowing sunset. It was not long after supper, and the days were growing shorter as summer weather ended and October set in. There would not be many more opportunities to view the stunning, cotton-candy sunsets, as autumn soon would bring a chill to the air. Already, the temperatures were becoming cooler, and all three sisters had added an extra layer over the lighter clothing they had worn earlier in the day.

Louise, Alice and Jane sat on the front porch of their spacious Victorian home, which they had converted into a bed-and-breakfast establishment after their father's death. Louise, the eldest, wore a pale blue sweater set beneath her lightweight ivory jacket, but instead of the skirt she usually preferred, she had put on a pair of black trousers as a concession to the brisk air. She sat in one of the white wicker chairs around a matching table, her short, silver coiffure shining where the sun's rays still touched it. A sturdy woven basket stuffed full of yarn sat on the floor beside her, and she was knitting industriously, her lips moving as she counted.

"What are you making, Louise?" asked Jane, the youngest sister. Jane had a flair for coming up with eye-catching outfits even when she wasn't trying. This evening, she was dressed in a simple pair of blue jeans with straight legs, but over her white top she had donned a soft green sweater with an unusual, flared collar and bell-shaped sleeves. Her long, dark hair was pinned up in a French twist, which her sisters knew was easier than it looked. If it took Jane any time at all to fool with her hair, she would abandon the effort and scrape it back in a ponytail.

"I'm beginning a new afghan," Louise reported, her fingers slowing as she looked up over the top of her silver-framed reading glasses. "It's not for anything special, but I like to keep a completed item on hand in case I am asked to donate something for a charitable raffle or auction."

Alice chuckled, ruffling a hand through her easy-care bobbed hair, which was a pretty, subdued rusty shade. "Trust you to be thinking ahead, Louise. I wish I were that organized."

"I'm not 'that organized,'" Louise protested.

"It was a compliment, not a criticism," Alice assured her older sister. She half-rose from the porch swing where she had been sitting idly, using her sneaker-clad foot to move the swing gently back and forth. She had worked that day and still wore navy pants with white nursing shoes and a smock, over which she had tossed a gray sweatshirt that zipped up the front. "That's beautiful yarn," she said, craning her neck for a better look. "And I like that combination of colors."

Louise smiled, fingering the soft creams and pinks in varying shades. "I thought they were lovely too. The yarn wasn't on sale, but I just couldn't resist it."

Alice sat back, pointing into the yard. "Your yarn almost matches the color of the chrysanthemums, doesn't it?"

"It is a very close match," Jane said, admiring the fall blooms she had planted to extend the colorful look of the inn's autumn landscape. "I was thinking—"

But the rest of her sentence went unfinished as she sat bolt upright, peering intently into the yard. "What on earth . . . ?" she said out loud.

Alice followed the direction of her gaze, and Louise did the same, peering over the top of her spectacles.

Behind Jane's chrysanthemums and asters was a line of taller, bushy astilbe that had bloomed early in the summer. Jane had not deadheaded them because the tall, airy spires were an attractive accent later in the year. Although the bloom stalks had faded gradually to a soft buff, the foliage of this particular cultivar was beginning to turn a deep crimson color. But that wasn't what riveted the sisters' attention.

Right in the middle of the section with the most densely branching plants, something was disturbing the tranquil garden. The tops of the flower stalks waved wildly in one section, while in another the plants appeared perfectly undisturbed.

"There's no breeze to speak of," said Louise in a puzzled tone.

"And Wendell is inside," added Alice, referring to their cat, a gray tabby who once had belonged to their late father Daniel. "He was lying on my bed when I went up to get my sweatshirt."

Jane felt a slight shiver dance along her spine. It was unrelated to the temperature of the air. "Then what is it?" she asked in a hushed tone.

Alice and Louise were staring at the vigorously waving tips of the plants. "I don't know," Alice admitted. "Maybe it's a stray cat or dog."

"Maybe," Louise said doubtfully. "But the movement seems awfully slow and deliberate for a—"

Jane blinked as something began to emerge from the leafy haven. "My heavenly stars, it's a turtle!"

"A very big turtle," Louise stated, as if they couldn't see the obvious.

Alice cleared her throat. "Actually," she said, "I believe it's a tortoise."

"What's the difference?" Jane asked curiously, still watching the creature as it trundled slowly out of the tall leafy plants and onto the front walk.

"Tortoises don't have webbed feet," Alice said. "And

most of them are desert-dwellers, or at least they live where it's very warm."

Louise arched one eyebrow as she and Jane both turned and looked at Alice. "That," Louise pronounced, "is an odd piece of trivia. Where did you learn that?"

Alice shrugged. "I have no idea. I'll bet each of you has funny little nuggets of information tucked away in your head. You know, useless tidbits that you have no idea how you acquired?"

Louise simply shook her head. "A *very* odd piece of trivia," she repeated.

"Ladies!" Jane said in exasperation. "Something a lot odder than that trivia just invaded our front yard. Am I the only one who thinks this is extremely strange?"

Alice rose from the swing and moved down the steps past Jane, who obligingly pulled her long legs out of the way.

And indeed it *was* strange. The tortoise was quite the largest turtle-type creature Alice had ever seen outside of a zoo. She remembered a visit to some kind of animal park from her childhood, where she had seen an enormous Galapagos tortoise; this, while far smaller than that one, looked very similar in many ways.

The animal had stopped once it got onto the concrete walk. It had a highly domed shell that looked to be at least eighteen inches from side to side, and it was close to two feet from the front edge to the back. Walking, it had an odd gait, both bowlegged and pigeon-toed as its two front legs turned out at the knees and then in the opposite direction at the ankles, so that the claw-tipped feet were turned slightly inward. It had abruptly withdrawn into its shell at Alice's approach, the large head completely disappearing, while its two front legs slid together, fitting partially into the shell to form a solid wall of protection. The legs looked like small tree trunks and were covered with horny scales of various sizes, ending in blunt-tipped claws as much as an inch in length.

There still was enough light left for Alice to see that the

tortoise shell was composed of platelike pieces in shades of brown and tan, similar to the colors of the skin and legs.

"That thing is huge," Louise said. "I've never seen one like it around here before."

"They're not native to the scorching deserts of southeastern Pennsylvania," Jane said, grinning.

"No," Alice agreed, paying her sister's teasing no heed. "I imagine he is someone's pet that got away."

"Well, let's hope it skedaddles right on back home," Jane said.

"I don't think tortoises have a homing instinct as pigeons and some mammals do," Alice said seriously. "I think we're going to have to give it a little assistance to get it home."

"What kind of assistance?" Jane asked suspiciously. She stood and went down to the walk, cautiously circling the tortoise.

"We're going to have to take it in, at least overnight," Alice said.

"Take it in?" Louise sounded aghast as she put down her knitting and joined them on the sidewalk. "In where? In the house? Alice, we are *not* bringing that creature into the house. Who knows what diseases it might be carrying."

"If it's a pet, it's probably had veterinary care and is as healthy as you and I are likely to be," Alice said. "Besides, I'm not asking you to touch it. I just want to provide shelter for it until I can call someone in the area who might be able to help."

"I'm with Louise," Jane said. "I don't want that thing in the house. But if you really think it needs help, you could keep it in the shed overnight."

Alice shook her head. "If it were still summer, that would be a fine idea, but it's autumn. There is a frost warning out for tonight, which means it will get too cold out for a tropical creature." She gave her sisters her very best pleading-puppy-dog eyes. "Could we put it in the laundry room tonight? Just for one night?"

Jane and Louise were silent.

"Look at it. I bet it's staying on the walkway because the concrete is still warm from the heat of the day. But it will cool down quickly now that the sun is going."

Neither of her sisters spoke.

"Okay," said Alice, "if it lives through the night, I'll take it somewhere else tomorrow."

"What do you mean, *if* it lives through the night?" Jane looked quite taken aback. "It looks perfectly healthy to me. Do you really think it could die?"

"I don't know," Alice said. "I know reptiles can't control their body temperatures, but I don't know anything about this kind of tortoise."

"Except that it lives in the desert and it's not really a turtle," said Jane sotto voce to Louise.

"Except that," Alice agreed.

"Odd piece of trivia," Louise announced once again. But she was weakening. "Just for *one* night?" she asked Alice.

"One night." Alice nodded earnestly. "I'll call the vet tomorrow. He may know who owns it. After all, there can't be many of these running around out there."

Jane snorted inelegantly, choking back a chuckle. "That's for sure."

"Well," said Louise, looking at Jane, "I couldn't live with myself if something happened to this tortoise because I wouldn't let Alice bring it into the laundry room *for just one night.*"

Jane sighed. "Nor could I." She looked at Alice. "All right. One night. It stays in the laundry room and anyone who even breathes the same air it does has to wash every exposed inch of skin before getting anywhere near my cooking."

"Oh gracious," said Louise. "The last thing we need is a guest getting sick with some turtle disease."

"Tortoise, Louie," corrected Jane, tongue in cheek.

"All right," Alice said. "It was funny once. Now stop."

Both her sisters looked at her, detecting the faint note of hurt in her tone.

"Oh, Alice," Jane said, putting a hand on her sister's back and massaging in a comforting circle. "We're only teasing you."

"I know." Alice smiled at each of them. "I'm just a little worried about this animal. Where in the world could it possibly have come from?"

Jane and Louise exchanged a look, each longing to blurt out, "the desert," but they knew their levity would not be appreciated.

Louise turned back to the porch to hide the smile on her face. "It's getting too dark to see well. I think I'll go inside and find a cozy place to knit a little longer before I turn in."

Jane looked at Alice. "Are you going to need help with that thing?"

Alice looked down at her new charge. "I don't know. It's a pretty big creature, isn't it?"

"It is, indeed." Jane watched as Alice knelt by the huge shell. "I can hold the doors for you, at least," she offered.

"Thanks, Jane." Alice moved around behind the tortoise and got her hands firmly under the shell on each side. "Holy cow," she said as she lifted her burden. "You must weigh over thirty pounds." It certainly was larger than the twenty-pound sack of potatoes she had carried into the house for Jane the day before.

The muscles in her arms felt strained as she carefully walked around the side of the house, following the pathway to the back of the inn, where her father had enclosed part of the former porch to create a laundry room.

Jane scurried ahead of Alice and opened the door into the laundry room.

"Maybe I should put down papers," she suggested, looking doubtfully at the tortoise. "We don't have any kind of container big enough to keep it in."

"I'd think it would just make a huge mess with papers on the floor," Alice said. "Besides, I'd be afraid it might try to eat them. I'll clean up very thoroughly in here after it's gone tomorrow."

"Do you think we should give it something to eat and drink?"

Alice shook her head. "No. Reptiles don't eat three squares a day as you and I."

Jane chuckled.

"It should be fine overnight," Alice went on. "I'd rather wait to talk to someone who knows more about it before I give it anything to eat or drink."

"All right." Jane opened the door that led from the laundry room into the kitchen. "Don't forget to scrub your hands before you touch anything."

Alice laughed. "What are you, the bacteria police? I'm a nurse, remember? I know a lot more about sterilizing and cleaning than most people. Believe me, I won't forget."

"Sorry," said Jane with a grin. "I guess I'm just a little paranoid about teeny little details like, oh, salmonella, for instance."

"I know, and I don't blame you for worrying," Alice replied soothingly. "I'll scrub until I take the first layer of skin off my hands. I promise."

"I may hold you to that." Jane grinned again and vanished into the kitchen, closing the door behind her.

Alice knelt on the floor in front of the tortoise. It was closed as tightly into its shell as it could get, and she had not seen it move a lick since she had frightened it on the front walk.

"I'm sorry, my friend," she said to the tortoise. "Tomorrow we'll figure out how to help you. For tonight, this should be a lot more comfortable than the sidewalk."

As she knelt there, she realized she had forgotten something important. "Dear Lord," Alice said, "please fill me with

Your wisdom as I care for this, Your creature. Help me to treat it properly and guide me to people who have the knowledge to keep it healthy and safe. Help me get it back to its family, or wherever it came from. And Lord, thank You for softening my sisters' hearts and letting Grace Chapel Inn respond to this tortoise in its time of need. Guide my hands in all that I do. In Your name I pray. Amen."

Chapter 🐢 Two

On Monday, Jane had no breakfast to prepare since all the weekend inn guests had left midday on Sunday. It was a rather nice treat. Over the past month, there had been such a steady stream of guests that she hadn't had a morning off in quite a while.

She hummed as she folded towels. She sang softly while she double-checked the room she had prepared for the guest scheduled to arrive that afternoon. She did a little twirl on the path as she headed out to the garden for a few late tomatoes. One vine, bearing small yellow fruits the size of ping-pong balls, apparently had not gotten the memo that autumn was coming, and it still was producing tomatoes by the bowlful.

As Jane came back into the kitchen after storing her garden gloves in the shed, Alice was just setting the cordless telephone back into its cradle. She looked unusually somber for Alice, who usually had a ready smile for everyone.

"What's wrong?" Jane asked her sister.

"The turtle—sorry, tortoise—will have to stay until tomorrow." Alice said it fast and low as if perhaps that would make it more palatable.

"Really?" Jane sighed as Alice nodded. She set down the basket of tomatoes. "Why?"

Alice pulled out a chair and flopped down into it, resting her arms on the table. "I called the veterinarian's office. She does not treat any kind of reptile."

"Well, rats," Jane said. "I guess maybe some other vet, perhaps one in Potterston, does?"

"Perhaps, but this vet referred me to a wildlife rehabilitator named—" Alice consulted a piece of paper she'd been clutching in her hand. "Dane Rush. He's the director of a place called Wild Creatures Rehabilitation. He gave me directions. It's located just outside Potterston."

"But you said this tortoise isn't really a wild animal," Jane said. "It's a pet, probably."

"True, but the vet felt that the rehab expert would have more knowledge of an exotic species, and our new friend certainly qualifies as that."

Jane laughed ruefully. "It does, indeed."

"So I called Mr. Rush," Alice said, "and he will be happy to see the tortoise, but he is not available until tomorrow."

"All right." Jane felt relieved. "I can live with tomorrow. I just don't want it staying as long as some of our guests."

"Speaking of guests," Alice said, "the woman who is arriving today called while you were outside. She's going to be earlier than she had originally planned. She will arrive around eleven."

"That's not a problem." Jane began to wash the tomatoes, already considering how she might use them in a meal. "Her room is ready, and I have tomorrow's breakfast planned."

"Do we know how long this guest is staying?"

"Almost three weeks," Jane said happily. "She is an evaluator for the state education commission, and she's going to be traveling to a number of schools in the local area each week."

"I wonder what she evaluates."

"That I can't tell you," Jane said. "I'm afraid my

sleuthing efforts were somewhat limited during our telephone conversation. But she'll be here a long time. I imagine we'll know quite a bit more in short order."

At that very moment, the sisters heard someone come into the entry hall through the front door.

"I bet that's our guest," Jane said.

She left the kitchen and walked forward through the house. A woman stood near the reservation desk tucked beneath the stairs, looking around with interest. When she heard Jane coming, she turned with a friendly smile, extending a hand.

"Hello. I'm Eva Quigley. I have a reservation." Their new guest looked to be somewhere in her upper thirties, with very fair skin and beautiful copper hair cut in a short, simple style.

The woman was slight of build, far shorter than Jane, and she looked as if a good gust of wind would take her sailing right along with it. Something about her made Jane think of a pixie or a leprechaun. She wore slacks in an earth tone and a pretty blouse beneath a vest embroidered with acorns and leaves.

"It's nice to meet you, Ms. Quigley. I'm Jane Howard. Grace Chapel Inn is run jointly by my two sisters and me."

"You, Alice and Louise, right? And please, call me Eva," she said, handing Jane a credit card.

Jane was surprised. "How did you know my sisters' names . . . Eva?" She tacked on her guest's first name with a grin.

The woman ticked off her talking points on her fingers as she spoke. "Louise answered the phone when I called for general information weeks ago. Then I spoke with Alice earlier today when I called. And now here you are."

"You have a good memory," Jane told her as she completed the registration and picked up the proper room key. "I'm not sure I would have remembered the names unless I had committed them to memory for a specific reason."

Eva smiled modestly. "I've always been good with names."

"It's a useful talent." Jane stepped out from behind the desk. "Let me give you a very brief tour and then I'll show you to your room. We serve breakfast starting at eight unless you need your meal earlier. If that occurs, just let me know the day before."

Eva followed Jane as she indicated the living room, and behind it the dining room where guests' meals were served. The parlor, across from the living room, featured Louise's piano; and the library, which once had been Jane's father's office, still held his mahogany bookshelves and lovely old desk.

"This is all so pretty," Eva said as they entered the library. "Oh, Scrabble! Do you play?"

Jane followed her guest's gaze. There, nearly hidden on one of the bookshelves, was a Scrabble box. Jane had dusted around it many times without really paying much attention to it.

"Not in a very long time," Jane confessed. "I played occasionally with friends when I was in college."

"We must have a game," Eva said enthusiastically.

"I don't even know if all the pieces are there." Jane walked to the bookshelf and slid the Scrabble game out of a stack of game boxes that included backgammon, checkers, chess and Parcheesi. Thankfully, it was not dusty. The sisters were scrupulous about keeping the inn in tip-top shape, but she could not recall the last time the box had been opened.

Setting the game on her father's desk, Jane removed the lid. Eva leaned forward eagerly. "The game board and letter racks all are here. Let's see if the number of letters is correct."

The two women took a couple of moments to sort each letter of the alphabet and compare them to the list on the side of the game board.

"They're all here," Jane said as she began to scoop them back into the bag.

"Wonderful!" Eva looked pleased. "Perhaps you'll have time for a game sometime soon?"

"I would enjoy that," Jane said. She wasn't much of a

games person, but Eva seemed pleasant, and Jane had no objection to a friendly game with their guest. "Tomorrow, perhaps? I'll set it in the dining room and we can use the table in there."

"It's a date," said Eva. "I adore games. I have to do two school visits tomorrow, but I should be back here by three or so."

"All right," Jane said. Then she thought of the question Alice had asked her. "What will you be doing on your school visits?"

"I am an evaluator for the state's Title Nine program for exceptional children. I visit schools to see how well their programs mirror our state standards."

"That sounds interesting," Jane said, "although I imagine there are times when you don't see the things you hope to."

"Not very often," Eva said. "In most instances, our educators are doing a very good job. I often make suggestions for improvements, but rarely do I have to report that a school is not meeting students' needs."

"That's good to hear." Jane smiled. "Now why don't I show you to your room?"

∞

Tuesday morning, Jane served Eva a honey-nut fruit salad and a Florentine omelet. Toasted French bread with blackberry preserves and coffee rounded out the meal. Their guest left with a happy smile.

"You must give me the recipe for that fruit salad—it was scrumptious. We'll have our game when I return this afternoon," she called to Jane as she went out the front door.

"All right," Jane answered. "I'll look forward to it."

"What game is that?" Louise asked. Both she and Alice were in the kitchen as Jane carried Eva's dishes in from the dining room.

"Scrabble," Jane said. "We're going to play a game this afternoon. Would either of you like to join us?"

Louise shook her head, thinking of her afternoon. "I can't. I have two piano lessons this afternoon." She grimaced. "I'll be sure the door to the parlor is shut so you don't have to listen to our fits and starts. Both of these children are . . . perhaps the best way to describe them is 'reluctant learners.'"

"I can't join you, either," Alice said. "I am helping with the hospital auxiliary's Care Package Program this morning, so I'll have to take the tortoise to the wildlife place this afternoon."

"Oh good," Jane said. "I'll be glad when that thing is gone. Are you sure it's still alive? I peeked at it earlier, and it was as frisky as a stone. I don't think I've see it even twitch since you brought it in."

"It's alive," Alice said mildly. "It's just that every time you open the door to the laundry room, it gets frightened and draws its head into its shell."

"How long can it go without eating?" Louise asked. "Or even more importantly, without water?"

"The rehabber said it will be fine for the day or two it would be with us. Apparently, tortoises don't eat or drink at the same rate mammals do."

"That makes sense," Jane said thoughtfully. "Snakes don't need to eat every day, and they're reptiles too."

Louise shuddered. "I'd prefer not to discuss snakes at the table, please."

Jane grinned. "Sorry."

"I'll be gone this morning, as well," Louise said. "I'm sorry to run off and leave you with the dishes, Jane, but I promised Aunt Ethel that I would take her to the library. She wants to have a look at the Friends of the Library's book sale, and I suspect I shall be needed as a pack mule for the return trip."

Alice laughed. "Suddenly, the hospital auxiliary is looking pretty good."

"As is making beds," Jane said, joining in Alice's laughter.

Louise smiled at her sisters' mirth as she rose to begin cleaning up her dishes. "It could be worse," she said. "I certainly can guarantee my morning will not be boring in any way."

"Not as long as you're hanging out with Aunt Ethel," Jane said.

Louise returned to her room to exchange the blue house flats she had worn to breakfast for a sturdier pair of walking shoes and to pick up her light khaki-colored jacket, as she expected the morning might be cool. She already had dressed in a long, slimming brown skirt with a pretty ivory twinset that she had bought two weeks earlier, and she had fastened her pearls about her neck as she had done every single morning since before she could remember.

She was right, she thought a few minutes later as she walked toward the carriage house. It was cool enough that she was glad she had thought to wear the jacket. While southern Pennsylvania often experienced a halcyon Indian summer in October, it was not unusual for cooler weather to set in first before people were teased with one final blessing of warmth before winter.

Louise and Ethel met in front of the carriage house and exchanged greetings before setting off in Louise's white Cadillac. Ethel also had dressed for cooler weather, in a pair of brown tweed slacks with a brown corduroy jacket. Her red hair looked as if it was aflame in the sunlight as she walked toward Louise along the path from the carriage house, and Louise had to smile to herself. Ethel must have gotten her color touched up recently, if the vivid shade was any indication.

The two women chatted, exchanging the latest local news until they reached Acorn Avenue, where the library stood.

Upon entering, they were greeted by the young, energetic librarian, Nia Komonos. Nia wore a burnt-orange skirt and blouse set that looked wonderful with her dark hair and olive skin tones.

She was outgoing and friendly, and her big dark eyes

sparkled as she said, "Ethel! Louise! Hello, hello. Ethel, did you get my message? *Preparing the Feast* is available and you are at the top of the list."

Preparing the Feast was a novel told from the point of view of Leah, a fictitious servant in the house of Pontius Pilate who came to be an unlikely helper at the Last Supper, and how she was changed by the role she played in Jesus' final hours. Louise had read and enjoyed it when it first came out some years before.

"I did get your message," Ethel responded. "Thank you for holding it for me. I can't wait to read it. Everyone says it's a wonderful book."

"I thought so," Nia said as she produced the book and scanned Ethel's library card. "And if you need more recommendations when you finish that one, I'll be glad to offer some suggestions."

"I would appreciate that," Ethel said. "There's so much available that I only want to read the most interesting things. After all, at my age, who knows how many more books I might have the chance to read?"

Louise rolled her eyes. "Oh, Aunt Ethel, I suspect you'll be able to read a great, great many more books in your lifetime."

A man approached the desk. He had entered through the front door, and he carried a thin manila folder beneath one arm. His face was weathered and tanned, and he wore a farmer's cap with a tractor company's logo emblazoned on it. His blue denim overalls covered a belly that looked as if he had enjoyed a few too many biscuits. As he approached the women, he removed his hat to reveal dark brown hair shot with silver. Louise estimated that he was somewhere between her age, sixty-five, and Ethel's, about ten years older.

"Good morning, ladies," he said.

"Good morning," all three women chorused.

"I'm Herb Hoffstritt. Two *F*s, two *T*s." He smiled broadly at Nia. "You must be the librarian."

"I am," Nia said. "Can I help you with something, Mr. Hoffstritt?"

"Oh, you finish taking care of these lovely ladies first," he said, gesturing toward Louise and Ethel.

Ethel batted her eyes at him. "Well, aren't you the charmer? I'm Ethel Buckley and this is my niece, Louise Smith."

"Pleased to meet you," the man said, smiling as he shook each woman's hand.

"Hoffstritt . . ." Ethel said thoughtfully. "I knew a Malcolm Hoffstritt in school. Would you be any relation?"

"My eldest brother," he said. "He lives over near Philly now."

"Ah. No wonder I haven't seen him in years." She bobbed her head toward Nia. "If you need her help, please go ahead. We were only chatting."

He hesitated.

Louise began to turn away, but Ethel clutched her elbow in an unshakable grip and stood firm. Louise could not move off without creating a stir.

She cast her aunt a rueful look. Could her aunt be trying to eavesdrop?

"Thank you," Mr. Hoffstritt said. He turned to Nia. "I found something odd when I was going through a box of old family papers yesterday. It was written by my great-grandfather to my great-grandmother during the time he fought in the Civil War."

"Which side?" asked Ethel.

The man turned, apparently not minding the intrusion. "Union. He was a local fella. I found his discharge papers, dated in 1865, along with a couple of letters. And this one letter said something odd. I thought you might know what it meant," he said to Nia.

"Perhaps," she told him. "If not, I'm sure I can find someone who can help you. What is it?"

"In this letter, there is a mention of something that

happened here in Acorn Hill. I never heard of any action occurring around here. I thought it all happened west of us, around Gettysburg."

"Fighting, you mean?" asked Nia. "No, I have never heard about action around Acorn Hill, but I'm new to the area. Ethel, are you aware of any battles that took place here?"

"No," said Ethel. She looked at Louise, who also shook her head.

"What, exactly, does the letter say, if you don't mind sharing it?" Ethel asked Herb.

"Not at all." He opened the folder and took out two sheets of paper. "I made copies of the letter so I wouldn't have to keep handling the original. It's pretty fragile."

"An excellent idea," Nia told him approvingly.

Herb laid the papers side by side on the library desk. He pulled out a pair of reading glasses and donned them with a sheepish expression. "Can't see anything up close anymore without these durned things."

"You're in good company," said Ethel with a chuckle.

"Let me find it," he went on. "I won't read you the whole letter, just the part about Acorn Hill. It's dated October 2, 1863. That would be three months after the Battle of Gettysburg.

"'. . . As I came off my picket, I have seen all the boys are busy writing. A man from Potters Town is discharged and in the morning, he intends to start home and has offered to carry this to you and the others who are doing such a fine job in our unfortunate absence. I was one of my company who went on a raid into Maryland—'

"Oh bother," said Herb. "Where is that part about the fighting? Here we go:

"'. . . Please include in your next letter a bit more about the dustup at Acorn Hill. When we returned from Maryland, several of us boys were very amused to hear about that recent fracas and it does confirm our opinion that the traitorous gray backs are not so well-governed as those of us in Uncle Samuel's service . . .'

"And that's it," he concluded, looking over his spectacles at the women.

"*Potters Town?*" asked Nia, looking at the letter and emphasizing the break between the two words.

"The *w* was dropped and it was revised into one word when the town was incorporated, I believe," Ethel, who was well-versed in local history, told her. "Your letter is just fascinating," she went on, addressing Herb. "I have never heard anything before about a battle at Acorn Hill."

"It didn't say it was a battle," Louise felt obliged to point out. "I can't imagine that he would have used the term *amused* if he was referring to combat."

"I don't know about that," Ethel said. "A soldier's sense of humor would have been quite different from a civilian's, I suspect."

"It sounds as if whatever happened involved Confederate troops," Nia said. "Mr. Hoffstritt, straight ahead on your left is the history section, which has a sizable collection of information about the town and the surrounding area. Unfortunately, I am still not familiar enough with local history to be of much assistance. We could research for a long time without coming across anything."

"The historical society over in Potterston might have some information," Ethel suggested. "They have an extensive historical collection that covers the whole county."

"Thank you," said Herb. "I think maybe I'll check the history section and look around for a bit. I'm not sure I want to drive all the way to Potterston just to satisfy my curiosity."

"I'd be happy to help with your research," Ethel told

him. "I am not going to be able to rest until I find out about the Battle of Acorn Hill."

"If there was one," Nia said.

"Well, if there was, it is certainly a significant piece of this town's history and we should embrace it," Ethel said grandly. "Let's do some research, Mr. Hoffstritt."

"Oh please, call me Herb," he said.

"Aunt Ethel," Louise said, "what about the book sale?"

"Oh pish-posh," Ethel said, waving a hand in dismissal. "I'll come back tomorrow and look at the books. This is much more important."

Louise wanted to remind Ethel that her time, which she graciously had given up, was valuable, but she bit her tongue. One rarely prevailed in an argument with Ethel, who seemed to have an amazingly facile memory when it came to recalling events as she liked to remember them.

"All right," she said. "I guess I'll just drive home again."

"Thank you for bringing me in, dear," Ethel called over her shoulder. "I'll find my way home. You may help me with my books tomorrow." She already was hurrying toward the history section, with Mr. Hoffstritt following sedately behind.

Taken aback, Louise did not have a ready reply. By the time she opened her mouth, Ethel had vanished from sight. Louise turned to Nia, shaking her head. "Do you suppose she considered for one moment that tomorrow may not suit me?"

Nia's dark eyes were dancing. "Not for a minute."

Louise nodded glumly. "That's what I thought."

Chapter Three

"Jane, I need your help." Alice came into the kitchen early in the afternoon. She was wearing a pair of her oldest dungarees and a light blue sweatshirt, with sneakers on her feet. "I'm taking the tortoise to the wildlife rehab person."

Jane continued to knead a ball of dough she had mixed up for biscuits, feeling the stretchy, elastic dough roll beneath the heels of her palms. Past experience told her that she nearly had succeeded in incorporating enough air into the dough.

"All right," she said to Alice. "Just give me a minute." Quickly, she shaped the dough into a ball and set it in a bowl. After covering it with a piece of cheesecloth, she carried it to a sunny spot on the table, where it would absorb some warmth. "There," she said as she washed her hands. "That needs time to rise, anyway. Now what can I do?"

"Hold the door," Alice said. "I need both hands. That animal weighs a ton."

Jane obligingly opened the laundry room door as her sister approached the tortoise. The animal had retreated to a corner, and it had not moved since the evening before. But when Alice drew near to pick it up, it gave a startled hiss and barricaded itself more tightly in its shell much as it had the day before.

"Gracious," said Jane. "That's a scary sound. Will it bite?"

Alice smiled as she got a good grip on the sides of the shell and lifted the tortoise into her arms. "I don't think so. But until I talk to the wildlife expert, I'm not prepared to find out. I'll keep my hands well away from its head."

"Well, I won't be getting close enough to test it either," Jane said. She scampered to hold open the outer door off the porch and followed as Alice carted the animal out to her car, which she had brought close to the inn's back path. Moving around her sister, Jane pulled open the back door of the car.

"Other side," Alice gasped.

Jane rushed around and opened the other back door.

Alice had laid a blanket on the floor in the backseat after pushing the front passenger seat as far forward as it would go, and the tortoise just fit in the space created.

"Thanks, Jane," Alice said, still breathing hard from her exertion. "I'll be back as soon as I have delivered our 'guest.'"

"Shall I sign the visitors' book for this one?" Jane asked. She chuckled and waved as her sister climbed into her Toyota. When Alice drove away, Jane returned to the kitchen with a sense of relief. Every time she looked at that tortoise, she still had had visions of salmonella poisoning befalling a guest at the inn.

♋

The wildlife center was on the other side of Potterston. After Alice arrived, she followed the discreet signs up a long lane to a small red brick house.

Parking the car, she glanced over the back of the seat. The tortoise did not appear to have moved one inch during the drive, so she felt safe leaving it in the car for a few moments.

She climbed out and approached the small front porch. A sign greeted her, PLEASE RING THE BELL AND ENTER, so she pushed the small lighted button to the left of the door and stepped into a front room that appeared to be a combination reception area and office.

A counter had been built across half the room. On the side where she stood were a battered couch, three low tables and several chairs. On top of one table was a large television with a built-in DVD unit. A couple of enlarged photos had been framed and hung on the walls. In one, a young woman wearing a T-shirt with the same logo that appeared on the wildlife center's sign wore a falconer's glove on her left arm, which was raised to create a perch for a large brown and white owl. In a second photo, a bear cub sat on a blanket on the floor, and in a third, a baby raccoon sucked at a bottle held by a gloved hand.

Across the counter stood a desk supporting a large computer. In addition, there were several file cabinets and a table piled with what looked like educational literature on the wildlife center and a variety of animal species. In front of the window on that wall was a tiered wrought-iron stand containing an array of leafy plants and several African violets bursting with pink and purple blossoms.

A Dutch door with its top half open led into what looked like a hallway beyond the reception area. A man came into view. He wore a T-shirt with a silk-screened sea turtle on it. Jeans and sneakers completed his outfit. Tall and slight of frame, he had curly blond hair and pleasant features. She estimated that he was somewhere in his early forties.

He smiled at Alice, blue eyes crinkling at the corners as he opened the closed bottom of the Dutch door and extended his hand. "Hello. I'm Dane Rush. Are you the lady with the tortoise?"

Alice smiled, nodding as she shook his hand. "Yes. I'm Alice Howard. The tortoise is in the backseat of my car."

"Well, let's go get him. I'm eager to have a look." Dane Rush opened a gate in the counter and walked outside as Alice preceded him.

"He's in here," she said, opening the back door.

"What a beauty," Dane said reverently. He lifted the animal out without any apparent effort, and Alice realized that while Dane might have appeared thin, he was certainly fit. "It's a sulcata," he told Alice.

"A what?" She shut the car door and hurried behind him as he strode back into the house with the tortoise.

"An African spurred tortoise," he tossed over one shoulder. "Follow me. I'll give you the nickel tour." He passed by the counter and led Alice back into the center. "On your left is the room where we keep our permanent residents," he told her. "They are all handicapped in some way that makes it impossible for them to survive in the wild. The second door on the left is our storage and laundry room."

A quick glance showed that the door of the animal area was closed. The second stood open, revealing a washer and dryer, shelf after shelf of towels, sheets and bedding, three chest-style freezers and a whole wall of foods and medicines.

"At the end of the hall is a small kitchen and lounge area. For humans," he added with a smile. "I get a lot of volunteer help."

"And on the right," he continued, stepping into the room he indicated, "is the exam and treatment room. We had a wall knocked out to create a larger space. This is where most of the action around here takes place."

Alice looked around with interest. A stainless steel surgical table extended from one wall, with a sink and a floor-to-ceiling arrangement of shelves and drawers within easy reach. Another wall held more storage, two more double sinks and a dishwasher, broken up by counter space. On the remaining walls were shelves full of cages, kennels and aquariums of all sizes. There were a number of birds, a few rabbits, two squirrels, a red fox and a possum, and several cages of snakes and turtles. A larger kennel was covered with sheets and had a prominent sign—RED-TAILED HAWK. BITES HARD! USE GLOVES. A young man and a young woman were engaged in cleaning and feeding. They glanced up and smiled as Alice came in.

"Outside, we have pens for larger animals, release cages

for the ones we are rehabilitating to go back to the wild, and a shed with more storage," Dane told her. He set the tortoise in the middle of the table. "Now let's take a look at our friend here."

Alice watched quietly as Dane examined the tortoise's shell and appendages. The tortoise remained closed tightly in its shell, its two front legs drawn together to protect its face, and Dane smiled. "Let's see how much you weigh," he said to the motionless creature. He set the tortoise on a scale and waited until the digital numbers remained stationary. "Thirty-seven pounds," he told Alice. "Hey, Juls, would you get me a handful of timothy and some cabbage?" he asked.

The young woman nodded. "Sure."

While she complied, he turned over the tortoise to examine the bottom shell. "Hey, look. Initials."

Alice peered at the marks on the shell. "*M.P.* I imagine those are the initials of the owner."

"Or maybe the tortoise's initials," Dane said, chuckling. "Miss Piggy?"

"My Pet?" Alice said in return.

The young volunteer who approached with the hay said, "Mighty Pretty," and they all laughed.

Dane set the tortoise on the floor. "Let's see how interested you are in food," he said to the animal as he placed the hay and cabbage leaves on the floor in front of it. Then he leaned back against the counter and looked at Alice. "You're lucky it's autumn," he said.

"Why is that?"

He grinned. "I actually have time to talk with you. In the spring and summer, we are inundated with orphaned babies. Every cage in here is filled, some with entire litters of squirrels, possums, rabbits and other little orphans. I need twice the number of volunteers just to keep up with the feeding, much less to do the daily cleaning. And we get more injured animals during those seasons too, simply because there are more animals out and about when it's warm."

He glanced down at the tortoise, which was still motionless. "I guess you want to know about this fair lady."

"So it's a female?" Alice asked. "At the risk of being indelicate, how do you know?"

"Male adults have a concave plastron—that's the bottom shell—and a longer tail than females," Dane told her. "Males also have a wider opening between the scutes back here than females."

"Scoots?" Alice repeated. "As in *scooters?*"

"*S-c-u-t-e-s*. Scutes are these platelike sections of shell." He ran a gentle finger across the tortoise's shell. Then he pointed to a section at the base of the upper shell in the very back. "It's much more difficult to determine the sex of juvenile sulcatas. That's true of nearly all chelonians."

"Chelonians?"

"Tortoises. Members of the class of reptiles called Chelonia," he explained. "The sulcata is the third largest tortoise in the world and is widely used in the pet trade. Few people realize that a cute little tortoise the size of a baseball is going to grow more than two feet long and weigh as much as one hundred pounds. And they can live as long as eighty years too."

"How old do you think this one is?" Alice regarded the tortoise. It still had not moved.

Dane reached for a tape measure on a shelf behind him. Moving slowly around behind the tortoise, he measured its shell and said, "It's difficult to determine age, because size is affected by their diet and care, but she's probably a young adult. I suspect she's thirty or so. Maybe—I'm no tortoise expert."

Next, he picked up a small digital camera. "I'll take some photographs and send them to all my contacts, including the area veterinary offices," he told Alice. "Perhaps someone will recognize her."

"I hope so."

Dane photographed the animal and then the two of them

watched her for a little while. The tortoise did not appear to be interested in the hay.

"I wish she would eat," Alice said. "I don't want her to starve. I didn't even know what to feed her, so I didn't feed her anything."

"Dark leafy greens like bok choy, collard and mustard greens," Dane said promptly. "Cabbage, grass, alfalfa, tiny amounts of strawberry and carrot. You also should purchase a complete tortoise diet. They are available at most pet stores. Don't worry if she doesn't eat for a while. Turtles and tortoises can go a long time between meals, and she might be too stressed to eat for a bit." He reached for a small container. "This is calcium. You should sprinkle it over her food to promote healthy shell growth."

"Oh no," Alice said hastily. "I can't keep her. I thought that you . . ."

Dane's eyebrows rose. "I can't take her right now," he said. "I'm leaving on Saturday to go to South Africa for three weeks. All of my animals are going to other facilities. There wouldn't be anyone here to care for your tortoise."

"But I can't take her home," Alice protested. "She needs to live inside, doesn't she?"

He nodded. "It's too chilly outside now."

"I have no place to put her except for our back porch."

"Is it insulated and warm?"

Alice nodded. "Well, yes. It's our laundry room as well. But my sisters and I run an inn. We have guests coming and going all the time and—"

"I bet a tortoise would be a big hit," Dane said enthusiastically. "Tell you what. I'll lend you a large heat pad and a basking lamp. I'll send along a bale of hay and some tortoise food with this calcium, and I will give you the number of a friend of mine who will be your resource person if you have questions. If you haven't found her owner by the time I get back, I'll look for a place that might be able to take her."

"My sisters are going to kill me," Alice predicted. "Couldn't one of your volunteers take it?"

"I'll ask, but most of them are college-age kids who live in apartments," he told her. "A landlord would not be too thrilled with a tortoise this size living in one of his rental units."

Alice's shoulders slumped. "All right." She accepted the calcium. "Exactly when did you say you would be returning?"

In the car a few minutes later, she sighed heavily as she began the drive back to Grace Chapel Inn. "Lord," she said, "please help Jane and Louise to accept our temporary tortoise guest. Help them see that we need to be good Samaritans to all, no matter their species. And please," she added, "guide me to M.P.'s owners quickly, if you don't mind."

Jane glanced at the waterproof watch on her left wrist as she set up the Scrabble board for the afternoon game with their guest. She had recently purchased the timepiece after ruining a couple of others with water damage, mostly in the kitchen. The purchase was proving to be worth every penny. The watch showed three-thirty, which meant that Jane had a little more than an hour and a half before she would have to stop the game and get dinner.

"Hello," called Eva from the stairs. "I'm on my way."

"No rush," Jane called back.

A moment later, Eva strode into the dining room. She was breathing a bit fast, and she still wore the clothes she had worn throughout the workday. Jane particularly recalled the gorgeous gray pantsuit because it was both trendy and practical. She wished to find something like it.

"Let's get started," Eva said, sliding into a chair.

Jane laughed. "Would you like to have a drink first? I think the game can wait a few minutes."

"Just water will be fine." Eva poured herself an icy glass of water from the pitcher Jane had set on the table beside a small plate of vegetables, cheese and crackers. "Really fine," she said, as she took a second drink. "I must remember to carry a bottle of water with me each day. I get terribly dry and thirsty by the time I get home."

"I can chill one for you each day," Jane offered.

"That would be lovely." Eva picked up the pad and pencil Jane had set nearby, clearly assuming the role of scorekeeper. Then she reached for the bag of letter tiles, shook it thoroughly, and held it out toward Jane with the drawstring top open. "Shall we draw to see who goes first?"

"Would you like to change your clothes?" Jane asked.

"I'm in no hurry."

"No, I'm fine," Eva said. "I like to pack light, so I don't bring a lot of changes of clothing with me."

"All right." Jane reached into the bag her guest extended and captured a letter. She waited a moment until Eva had done the same. Then each revealed the letter she held.

Jane held an E; Eva opened her palm to show an N.

"Looks like you get the honors," Eva said. "Make it good."

Jane grinned. "I'll do my best."

Both women put their tiles back into the bag. Jane shook it and pulled out seven letters, which she arranged on the small easel in front of her.

"*Hmm.* Give me a minute," she said, looking at her selections with dismay as she set them in alphabetical order, the way she preferred to work. Her tiles were D, G, I, I, N, N, S.

Eva drew her own seven tiles while Jane puzzled out the best word she could form to earn points. Finally, Jane began picking up her letters and laying them down on the board. Her first letter, a D, covered the pink star in the center of the board and the word moved horizontally right from there. The board had a plastic surface with small indentations into which the tiles fit, making it far more difficult for the tiles to slide out of place. The game board also was on a swivel base so that either player could rotate it to face herself during a turn.

"*Dings*," said Jane. She began to count, although she had counted silently a moment earlier. "The S is on a double-letter space, and I also get a double-word score since I covered the pink star in the center when I opened the game. I believe that gives me sixteen points."

It was a respectable score, she thought, especially given the paucity of vowels. Then she glanced again at her letters and thought, *Well, shucks.* D-I-N-I-N-G would have given her eighteen.

"It's a start," said Eva. "I absolutely love this moment in the game, don't you? It's so full of possibilities."

Jane drew an E, another I, another N, an O and a blank tile, which could represent any letter she chose when she used it. All one-point values. *Hmm. Pretty limited possibilities,* she thought to herself.

Eva swiveled the board to face herself, studying it with pursed lips. "I have some difficult letters," she said. Jane was just about to utter some words of encouragement when Eva began to lay down her letters. She started with Jane's D, and placed letters down vertically. And down. And down.

"There," she said a moment later. "*Detoxify.* The X is on a double letter and the Y is on a triple word. And I used all seven of my letters, which gives me a fifty-point bonus. So my total score is . . . one hundred forty."

"You're joking." Jane chuckled. She leaned forward to check out the board, and her laughter died as she counted. With sixteen points for the X, the word garnered thirty points, which then was tripled. Once the bonus was added, Eva leaped into triple-digits. "Wow," Jane said weakly after a long moment of silence. "Congratulations. That's excellent."

"Thank you," Eva said cheerily. "I try to get in at least one of those per game. Your turn," she added, picking up the bag to draw seven new letters.

She studied her letters. E, I, I, N, N, O and the blank tile. No matter how she looked at it, she could not see any big scoring opportunities.

Finally, she laid down her best offering, N-O-T-E placed vertically next to the O-X-I-F from Eva's turn. "*Note*," she said. "The blank tile will act as a T. It also makes *no, ox, ti* and *ef.* Twenty points."

"So you're up to thirty-six."

Eva barely paused once the board turned back to her. Rapidly, she laid down tiles vertically upward from the G in Jane's first word, *dings.* One of the O's was on a double-letter space, Jane noticed.

"*Quohog*," Eva said with satisfaction. "That's thirty-six more points for me. Hey, look at that! My score just in this round is equal to your total score. Isn't that odd?"

"Very," Jane said, sitting up straight as inspiration struck. "But Eva, I'm afraid I have to challenge you. The word is *quahog*, spelled Q-U-A-H-O-G. The rules say that if you lose a challenge you have to lose a turn."

"Oh no," Eva said. "*Quohog* is an accepted alternate spelling for *quahog*. It's in the Scrabble dictionary." To Jane's astonishment, Eva picked up a fat paperback book from the chair beside her. "I found it in the inn's library and brought it out in case we had questions," she said.

"I didn't even know we had a Scrabble dictionary." Jane was dumbfounded. She took the book and quickly opened it to the page with the *q*'s. And just as quickly, she found *quohog*, large as life. *Stupid clam!*

"So you lose a turn, as the rules say," Eva announced. She sounded so perky and pleased that Jane began to regret having sat down to the contest.

While Jane sat irritated during her lost turn, Eva laid down A-S-T-U-T-E across the U in *quohog* for fourteen points. "A modest score, but the only one I could see," she said.

Jane gritted her teeth.

On her fourth-round turn, Jane had a B worth three points, plus an N and five vowels all worth a paltry point each. It was hard to make big points with a hand like that, she thought, looking at the ten-point Q and the eight-point X on which Eva had capitalized so handsomely.

Jane studied the board. She was tantalized by a triple-word space at the top of the board but could not make a single combination. The letters she had drawn were pitiful. She sighed in frustration, then used the E in *astute* and laid down her word. "*Bean*. Twelve points."

"Very nice." Eva's sing-song tone sounded as if she were speaking to a child. "That brings you up to forty-eight points. My turn."

Eva quickly laid down C-H-U-N-K, which earned her thirty points. "It probably is not the biggest score I could have found," she explained earnestly to Jane, "but I don't want to be stuck with that K. They're hard to get rid of, you know."

Jane winced. She had yet to see thirty points in her score column.

While Eva had been considering her options, Jane had picked out three new letters to round out her complement of seven letters again. She drew an E, an I and an O, which gave her seven vowels.

When her turn came again, she turned her tile rack around and showed Eva her selection. "I have all vowels. I'd like to discard two of them and pick two new letters."

As she reached for the bag, Eva said, "But that's not in the rules."

"Are you sure?" Jane clutched the bag tightly. "That's the way my sisters and I always played the game—"

"Oh no, no, I am sure that is not in the rules." Eva reached for the rule book, which they had set to one side with the game box. There was a pause of a few moments, then, "The rules say that you may forfeit your turn if you would like to discard your letters and draw all new ones. You could do that," she added helpfully, extending the rule book to Jane opened to a page on which, no doubt, were written the words that backed her up.

"No," Jane said, ignoring the rule book. She was not about to lose another turn. "Never mind. I'll just play with these."

On the fifth round, Jane added T-I-E, but even with a triple-letter space, it was worth only five points. Eva then created W-E-A-V-E-R horizontally and A-R vertically, using a double-word space with *weaver* to get to twenty-six points.

Was that really how the letter *R* was spelled? Jane wasn't sure, but if she challenged and lost, she would lose another turn. No thanks, she decided. She had had enough humiliation for one day, and it appeared she was going to get plenty more before the sun set.

And she did.

Jane got sixteen points; Eva got twenty-one.

Jane made R-O-B and T-I-E-R for fourteen points, but Eva laid down Z-I-L-L-A-H on a double word for thirty-six.

Jane nearly blurted out, "What's a zillah?" and challenged, but there was no way she would give Eva that satisfaction. She almost could *hear* the other woman willing her to display her weak vocabulary. Again.

By round eight, Jane still had three I's among her seven tiles, and was thoroughly sick of trying to find ways to use the annoying letter *I*.

Round nine came, and Jane laid down an F and an N across the I in Eva's *zillah*, a word Jane was determined to look up—later, when Eva wasn't around.

"You know," Eva said, pointing at the lower left corner of the board where a triple-letter score was just waiting for someone to use it, "it's too bad you didn't have an *I*, because you could have made *jin*, and used that triple letter. But I'm sure you've thought of that."

Jane gave in, her curiosity momentarily getting the better of her anger. "I thought *gin* was spelled with a *G*," she said, carefully omitting the fact that she had a trio of tiles with the letter *I* now having a great laugh at her expense.

"The drink is," Eva told her. "But J-I-N is in the Scrabble dictionary as an alternate spelling for J-I-N-N, which is short for J-I-N-N-I, a supernatural being in Islamic mythology. Interestingly enough, J-I-N is *not* listed anywhere in Webster's Third New International Edition. Unabridged, of course."

"Of course," Jane murmured, but Eva prattled on, unaware of any sarcasm in Jane's tone.

"Webster's Third has more than four hundred fifty thousand words in it, many of foreign extraction and many slang. You would think J-I-N would be there if it was anywhere, wouldn't you? But since it is listed in the Scrabble dictionary, we can use it."

"Of course," said Jane again.

"And it's my turn again," Eva announced as she toted up the score. "And I—oh look, Jane! You're finally in triple digits. One hundred nine. Very good."

"Thanks," said Jane "so much."

Finally, in the tenth round, Jane outscored Eva thirty-nine to twenty eight. But by then, Eva's overall score had raced so far ahead of Jane's that there was little satisfaction.

"The score is three hundred ninety-eight for me and one hundred forty-eight for you," Eva announced after completing her turn. "Are there still tiles left in the bag? Oh, I do hope I can break four hundred. I'll never be able to hold up my head in public if I don't."

Two rounds later, Jane's goal had changed. Her single burning desire now was to get over two hundred points before the game ended. Eva, across the table, was almost giddy with relief. She had shot over four hundred on her last turn.

By round twelve, Jane had one hundred ninety-six points. She had laid down C-U-R-D-S, twenty-eight points, near the bottom right corner in such a manner that it would be impossible to use the triple-word square in the corner to rack up a huge score. *Ha*, she thought. *So there!*

Unfortunately, when Jane picked up the bag to draw again, she took the last four letters in the bag. That signaled the end of the game, since Eva would be unable to draw letters again. So after Eva's final turn, both women stopped perusing the board and counted up the points on their unused tiles. Jane had eight points, having gotten letters worth more than one point, and she watched in dismay as Eva subtracted the eight to put Jane's final total at one hundred eighty-eight points.

Eva herself had only five points to deduct. "So our final score is four-twenty-four for me and one-eighty-eight for you," she said in a chipper tone. "Very nice effort, Jane."

Jane's jaw was clamped so tightly shut that the joint ached. She could not even reply. Instead, she stood and started replacing the tiles in the bag.

"Shall we play again tomorrow?" Eva asked brightly as she leaned forward to help gather game pieces.

Are you serious? was Jane's first reaction, but good manners prevailed. "Sorry," she said, consciously relaxing her jaw. "I'm going to be too busy tomorrow."

"Oh well, perhaps another day, then."

"I'm pretty sure I'm busy most of the time for the next few weeks." Jane slapped the lid back on the box and strode from the room.

Behind her, she heard Eva say, "Too bad. I suppose it's lucky that we got a game in today."

Chapter 🐢 Four

Quickly, Jane stuffed the game back onto the library shelf from whence it had come. Then she escaped to the kitchen, where she could be fairly sure she would not be pestered by their gloating guest.

She slipped the lid off the slow cooker of beef stew and stirred it with short, angry strokes. *Honestly. How overly competitive could one person be?*

It was nearly time for dinner, and as Jane was setting the table, Louise came into the kitchen. "Hello, Jane. Wait until I tell you what happened at the library today." She assessed Jane's progress with their dinner, then turned and opened a drawer. "How many trivets will we need on the table?"

"Two," Jane said. "And if you think you have a good story, you'll never believe how I spent my afternoon."

Louise cocked her head. "Oh?"

Just as Jane opened her mouth to air her annoyance with their guest, Alice came through the back door. "You're both going to kill me," she announced, shucking off her coat. "The wildlife person is going to be away and couldn't take the tortoise. So we're stuck with her for a couple of weeks."

"A couple of *weeks?*" Louise echoed. "Goodness gracious, Alice. Where on earth will we put it?"

"I plan to put her back in the laundry," Alice said.

"Are you *sure* we couldn't keep it in the shed or in an outside enclosure?"

"It just isn't warm enough at this time of year. Besides, predators might be able to get at her. Mr. Rush, the wildlife rehabilitator, thought she would be fine on the porch until he gets back from his vacation. He gave me food and supplies," she said, eyeing Jane nervously.

Jane positioned the last fork precisely with the final place setting and walked back across the kitchen. She took the lid off a pot on the stove and stirred it as steam billowed up.

"Jane?" Alice said.

"Yes?" Jane did not look up. She stirred a bit more, then tapped the excess liquid off the wooden spoon and set it on a spoon holder placed next to the stove.

"I'm really sorry," Alice said. "I just didn't know what else to do. There was no place else to take the tortoise. Is it all right with you?"

Finally Jane looked up. Her finely arched, dark eyebrows were drawn into an uncharacteristically forbidding straight line, and below them, her blue eyes were stormy. "I don't really have a choice, do I?" She picked up the wooden spoon and wagged it repeatedly at Alice to reinforce her point as she addressed her sister. "You can't put it outside or in the shed because it's getting too cold. Please just keep it away from me and from this kitchen. Heaven only knows what kind of diseases it might be carrying."

Alice's face was stricken. She opened her mouth, then closed it again. "I'm sorry," she said, nearly whispering. "Tomorrow, I'll try to find someone else to take it."

Louise glanced from one sister to the other. "No, Alice," she said. "We can manage to deal with one tortoise for a few weeks. And who knows? Maybe you'll find the owner sooner than that." She crossed the room in her no-nonsense fashion and placed an arm around Jane's shoulders. "Jane had a rough day, I believe, and she was just getting ready to tell me about it when you came in."

"I'm sorry, Alice," Jane said as her expression softened. "Louise is right. It isn't really you or the tortoise. I just had a most humiliating afternoon, and this seemed to be the last straw." She leaned her head against Louise's shoulder.

"What happened?" Alice asked in concern. "I thought you were going to play a game with our guest this afternoon."

"So did I," Jane said in a disgruntled tone. "But it was more like hand-to-hand combat than a fun and friendly pastime." She sniffed. "Would you check those biscuits in the oven, please? They should be about done."

Alice went to the range and flipped the light switch. "Golden-brown," she reported. "Shall I get them out?"

Jane nodded.

Alice picked up a potholder and slid the cookie sheet containing the beautifully puffed up buttermilk biscuits out of the oven. She grabbed a spatula and transferred them to the basket Jane had set on the counter, then covered them and brought the basket to the table.

"Why don't you tell us what happened during your game," Louise suggested. Behind Jane's head, Louise gestured for Alice to bring the rest of the meal to the table.

Jane sighed as she allowed Louise to lead her to a seat. "We were supposed to play a friendly game of Scrabble. Or so I thought. But during the first round, Eva scored one hundred forty points, and let's just say she's very good at rubbing her opponent's nose in the dust she leaves behind her."

"My goodness," Alice said, setting the food on the table. "I didn't even know it was possible to get a score that high in Scrabble. She must be really . . ."

Jane studied Alice for a tense moment, and Louise winced before Jane went on to summarize the game, mentioning the way Eva had appeared so sweet even as she was gloating. She told them about the special dictionary and the *quohog* challenge, and about how she was afraid to challenge the word *zillah*.

"It's a good thing you didn't," Louise said. "It really is a word. It has something to do with India's governing system. A zillah is a specified area, like a school district or county." Alice stared at her. "That's an odd piece of trivia." She used the same words that Louise had used in regard to her knowledge of tortoises two days earlier. She looked at Jane, and together they said, "A very odd piece of trivia."

All three of them started to laugh and their shared mirth seemed to defuse some of Jane's frustration and anger. Louise and Alice took their seats, and after Louise offered a prayer, Jane finished recounting the Scrabble story with a wry sense of humor.

"Heavens!" Alice said. "She sounds extremely competitive."

Jane nodded. "Exactly. I never thought I was a very competitive person, but all I have been able to think about is some way I can show her up. Isn't that terrible?"

"It's human," Louise said. "So what have you come up with?"

Jane had to laugh, even as she shook her head at her own lack of talent. "Nothing, unless I challenge her to a bake-off."

Both her sisters laughed.

Then Alice said, "I feel for you. I am not much of a games person. I just don't care enough."

"Oh, I care enough," Jane said feelingly. "I'm just not very good at most of them."

Louise leaned forward. "What you need is a game our guest is not familiar with, something that depends on more than words and logic."

"Sounds good to me," Jane said gloomily. "But I can't think of anything like that except for golf, which would require a lot more time and practice than I've got."

"What about quoits?" Louise asked.

"Quoits?" Jane looked at her sister. "I've never heard of that."

"It's similar to horseshoes," Louise said. "Opponents toss heavy metal rings called quoits at a pin. The ring that lands closest to or over the pin receives the highest number of points."

"Where did you learn about this?" Alice asked.

Louise only shook her head. "I can't believe you have never heard of quoits. The national championship is played in Pottstown, Pennsylvania, just outside of Philadelphia."

"Quoits," Jane said thoughtfully. "And you think I could master it?"

"Perhaps not master it," said Louise truthfully, "but if you learn to play and practice, I should think you stand a good chance of winning a game against another amateur. The problem is, I don't know of any place to go to play just for fun. Most of the people I've heard of who play do so because they want to enter competitions." She snapped her fingers. "Oh wait. Viola has a friend who competes in quoits tournaments regularly. Why don't you ask her to introduce you to him?"

"I think I will." Jane picked up her fork and began to eat with more vigor. "Thank you, Louise."

"You're most welcome," her eldest sister said. "Now let me tell you about the interesting thing that happened at the library today."

∽◌∾

The following morning, Alice made a beeline for the laundry as soon as she had dressed. "Good morning, tortoise," she said as she peeked in at it. "How are you feeling?" She was gratified to see that the animal had moved during the night and now had its head and legs exposed. At the moment, it was parked on its heat pad, which resembled a large, flat black pan turned upside down. A cord was attached to one end and Alice had duct-taped it against the floor and wall right up to the outlet so that M.P. did not accidentally unplug it. Above the heat pad, she had suspended the heat lamp Dane had lent her. It was fitted with a special infrared light bulb, which he told her would provide plenty of warmth without fully illuminating the room at night.

The tortoise did not move until Alice walked into its field of vision. Then, seeing her vigorous movement, it hissed and withdrew its head and legs into its shell so fast that it made a loud thud as the shell hit the pad.

"I'm sorry, my friend." Alice knelt and examined the animal. "I'm going to leave you alone today so you can adjust to your temporary home."

Reentering the kitchen, she saw that Jane had arrived and was buzzing around with breakfast preparations.

"What are you making this morning?" Alice asked her. She had no idea where Jane came up with the many recipes she regularly tried, but since so very few of them tasted anything less than stellar, Alice wasn't one to object.

"Oatmeal-apple pancakes," Jane replied. "With sides of bacon and wedges of orange."

"Yum," Alice said.

"By the way," Jane said as she sliced some apples into a bowl, "I invited Aunt Ethel and Lloyd to breakfast. She called last evening and wanted to know if she could see the tortoise."

"And I bet she hinted around at a breakfast invitation until you gave in," Alice said, laughing.

"You've got it," Jane said. "I always start feeling guilty when she talks about how difficult it is to eat alone, and how she hates to cook for just one."

"But she and Lloyd make two," Alice pointed out.

"True, but she didn't mention him until after I'd already invited her. Then she just happened to say that Lloyd was also eager to see the tortoise."

"Right." Alice rolled her eyes. "Somehow I can't see Lloyd bonding with our tortoise."

"Aunt Ethel and Lloyd are walking this way," Louise announced, entering the kitchen from the hallway.

"Good morning," Alice said tranquilly. "Jane invited

them to join us for breakfast." She rose and walked toward the back door. "I'll let them in and introduce them to M.P."

"Hello," she called to her aunt and her companion as she saw them approaching. "You've picked a good day to visit. Jane is making oatmeal-apple pancakes, and they smell divine."

"Everything Jane makes smells divine," boomed Lloyd. His face was a bit red from the exertion of the short walk from Ethel's house next door. A fan of bow ties, Lloyd wore a beautiful navy paisley bow tie with a navy pinstriped suit and a pale yellow shirt. "I can't wait to taste them. But first, I want to see this giant turtle."

"Come on in," Alice invited. "She's in the laundry room."

"In the laundry room?" Ethel sounded taken aback. "Is that sanitary? I thought turtles carried diseases."

"They can," Alice admitted. "But she's only temporary, and we plan to be extremely careful to ensure that there is no chance of contamination while she is here. Actually, you could help me find her owners."

"Me? How?" Ethel accepted Lloyd's courteous offer of a hand as she walked up the steps. She was dressed more casually than her gentleman friend, in a green velour track suit. With her bright red hair and green clothing, she reminded Alice of Christmas.

"You see a lot of people in the course of your day," Alice said tactfully, not mentioning that local gossip was Ethel's lifeblood. "Perhaps you could mention the tortoise to folks as you get around town. The sooner we find her family, the better."

"I'd be happy to," Ethel said graciously.

"And I'll do the same," Lloyd said as he stepped inside and Alice led the way to M.P. "Well, I'll be! That thing is huge," he blurted as he got his first look at the tortoise. He edged toward the door, shepherding Ethel ahead of him. "Is it dangerous?"

Alice shook her head, smiling. "No. In fact, she has barely moved since we found her. She seems quite content to bask beneath her heat lamp this morning."

"It *looks* dangerous," Lloyd said dubiously.

Ethel stopped in the doorway, forcing Lloyd to quit pushing her along. "When Louise told me you girls found a big tortoise, I was picturing something the size of a dinner plate. Do you mean to tell me someone actually had this as a pet?"

Alice nodded. "That's what both the vet and the wildlife expert think. Sometimes people abandon them when they grow too big to care for, but I'm hoping this one is only lost." She made a wry face. "This animal really needs a much larger space. I looked them up online and people who rescue them recommend that they be kept on several acres of land. It seems they like to roam."

"Better not let Jane get a good look at that thing. She's liable to start hunting up recipes for turtle soup," Lloyd said, a twinkle in his eyes. "You know, I had turtle soup once," he went on in a thoughtful tone. "It was delicious. I wonder—"

"Lloyd!" Ethel could see that Alice was not amused by her friend's attempt at humor. "This is someone's pet. You wouldn't eat a dog, would you?" When he shook his head vigorously, she went on. "Then no more talk about harming this turtle."

"Tortoise," Alice said faintly. "She's actually a tortoise. They live in the desert and need very little water."

"Come on," Ethel said to Lloyd. "You wanted to see it and now you have. And you've offended Alice as well. Come into the kitchen and be quiet until Jane feeds you, or she might just decide not to."

"Sorry, Alice," Lloyd said, sounding genuinely contrite. "I was just joking, you know."

"It's all right," Alice said. "But any help you can give me in finding her owners is very welcome. This is one guest I won't mind getting rid of."

Louise returned from serving breakfast to their inn

guest, and Jane called out that breakfast was ready for the kitchen group a few moments later. After a flurry of hand washing, the three Howard sisters and their guests sat down at the table. Lloyd had just finished offering grace when someone knocked on the door that led to the dining room.

"I'll get it." Jane hopped up. When she opened the door, Eva stood on the other side. Dressed in a forest-green sweater set and a plaid skirt with the same green running through it, she reminded Jane even more strongly of an elf. Jane could almost see a small, jaunty cap on her head.

"Good morning," Eva said in a sprightly tone. Then, seeing the people seated at the table, she said, "Oh, I'm so sorry. I didn't mean to interrupt your meal."

Jane smiled. "It's all right. Is there something you need?"

Eva nodded. "My water."

"I forgot." Jane hurried to the refrigerator and pulled out the bottle. "Here you go. Tomorrow, I'll be sure to remember it."

"Thank you so much."

"You're welcome."

"I really appreciate your offer, Jane. Have a lovely day."

"You too."

To Alice's ears, Jane's response lacked some warmth, but Eva did not appear to notice.

After their guest had left, Jane returned to her seat.

"What water?" asked Louise.

"I volunteered to chill a bottle of water for her to take with her each day." Jane's expression was neutral, but Alice suspected she would have had more to say if they had not been dining with guests.

There was an awkward silence for a moment, as if Eva's appearance had disrupted the pleasant flow of the conversation.

"You look very professional today, Lloyd," Louise finally said. "Not that you don't always, but I really do like that navy suit, and the tie is a gorgeous fabric."

"It is, isn't it," Lloyd said. "Thank you, Louise. I thought I'd better put on my best duds this morning. At noon, I have a mayors meeting in Potterston."

"A mayors meeting?" Jane asked curiously.

Lloyd nodded. "All the mayors of the towns in the county get together for lunch once every quarter. We discuss all sorts of civic issues. It's really very helpful."

"I imagine it is," Alice said. "If I were a mayor, I know that I'd enjoy having lunch with all the other mayors."

Ethel set down her fork. "If you were a mayor, your town would have all kinds of regulations about animals. 'Brake for all turtles,'" she said with a smile.

"There would be birdbaths on every corner," added Louise.

Alice only smiled. "I can think of worse regulations to enact. God put all these animals on earth and gave us dominion over them, not domination, as some people seem to believe. We are merely stewards of this earth."

"Oh boy," Jane said. "You did it now, Aunt Ethel. Alice is on a roll."

∽

Louise needed stamps. The sisters routinely sent thank-you-come-see-us-again cards to guests who had stayed with them throughout the year, and she had realized the day before that they were nearly out of stamps in their little office area.

Shortly after breakfast was finished, she dressed in a cardigan and matching shell in the palest of blue over a navy twill skirt and matching flats that were among her most comfortable. She picked up her purse and her keys and went out to her old car. It was still in excellent condition. She so rarely drove any distance that she had not accumulated a large number of miles on the odometer. As she slid behind the steering wheel, her memory winged backward to the day that she and her husband Eliot had bought the car. He would be surprised if he knew she still was driving the old boat after all these years.

Then again, perhaps not. Eliot had been well-acquainted with her strong streak of practicality. She simply could not see the necessity of buying a new car when the one she drove worked just fine.

When Louise turned the key, the engine started as smoothly as it always had. It only took her a few minutes to drive from the inn to the post office, located at the far side of town.

When she finished with her errand, she returned to the car, but before she could slide into her seat again, a voice hailed her. She turned around to see Rev. Kenneth Thompson striding toward her with a smile on his face.

"Good morning, Kenneth," she said as he drew near.

"Good morning, Louise." Rev. Thompson had taken over the pastorate of Grace Chapel after her father's passing. He was tall and dark-haired, a man whose sober demeanor gave him an air of authority when he spoke of God's Word. In addition, he could be charming and charismatic. Upon his arrival, several women in the congregation had been inspired to brush up their baking skills and to volunteer for church activities. Fortunately for the pastor, the Howard sisters were inclined to respect his privacy, and they had become good friends with the new minister.

This morning, he wore charcoal-colored trousers with a cable-knit pullover in a beautiful powder blue. The collar of his button-down shirt beneath the sweater carried the small gold cross that he affixed to nearly every outfit.

"You're looking spiffy," Louise said as they met on the sidewalk.

"I might say the same of you," he returned courteously. "What brings you out on this fine autumn day?"

She held up the coil of stamps she had purchased moments earlier. "We ran out of stamps." She held the little roll of stamps higher. "I've gotten spoiled by the ones with adhesive backing. The thought of licking a stamp holds no appeal for me anymore."

Kenneth shuddered. "Nor for me. Say, what's this I hear about a Civil War battle being fought in Acorn Hill? I realize I'm relatively new to the area, but I can't believe I've never heard of it before."

Louise groaned. "Who told you? Aunt Ethel, I bet. I asked her not to—"

"It wasn't Ethel," he said soothingly. "It was Nia Komonos."

"Oh. Nia?"

"Yes. I suppose, to be accurate, she said that there was a *possibility* that a battle had been fought here, although she considered it unlikely. But everyone in the Coffee Shop earlier was excited by the notion."

"Good grief!" Louise was dismayed. "Did she explain what actually occurred?"

"She said something about a library patron who had brought in a letter from the era that mentioned a skirmish."

"Not a skirmish. A *fracas*," Louise told him. "The very fact that the letter never mentions fighting of any sort makes me think it refers to something else altogether."

"They're still talking about it at the Coffee Shop," Rev. Thompson said. "Perhaps you had better stop in there and set the record straight."

"Perhaps I should." Louise determined to put the incident out of her mind for the moment and stood chatting with the minister in the autumn sunshine. After concluding their conversation, the two parted. As Louise got into her car, she decided that her friend was right. A visit to the Coffee Shop might be in order. Fortunately, there was a space almost directly in front of the little restaurant. Even better, it was the last space in a line of four with a no-parking zone behind it. Louise was able to glide smoothly into it without having to maneuver the big vehicle into a not-so-big slot.

Chapter ✦ Five

When she entered the Coffee Shop a few moments later, she heard her name called immediately.

"Louise!" The speaker was Pauline Sherman, a member of Grace Chapel. The mother of two daughters, Pauline was a pretty brunette.

She was seated in one of the red booths with Loueda Ullman. Loueda and her husband had moved to Acorn Hill after his retirement, and Loueda had joined the Grace Chapel choir right away. She was normally so quiet and reserved that she was easy to overlook.

It seemed an odd pairing until Louise remembered that Ethel had recruited Pauline and Loueda to help with a committee to evaluate charitable work at Grace Chapel. In her capacity as Committees Director, Louise's aunt was in her element. Asking Loueda to work with the more outgoing, gentle and friendly Pauline was an excellent idea.

"Hello," Louise said as she crossed the room to stop beside their booth.

"Good morning," Pauline said. "Would you like to join us?"

"Thank you," said Louise. She slid into the booth beside Loueda. "Good morning," she said to the quieter woman. "It's nice to see you somewhere other than at choir rehearsal."

Loueda smiled. "It was good of Ethel to ask me to help with this committee idea. I'm not sure how I can be of much assistance, but I'm willing to try."

"You'll be fine," Pauline said gaily. "If I can manage this, anyone can." She was wearing a soft apricot-colored sweater that brought out the roses in her cheeks, and she looked closer to her preteen daughters' ages than she did a thirty-something homemaker.

Hope Collins, the waitress, sailed by just then with a tray full of eggs and pancakes. "I'll be there in a sec," she called out as she passed them.

"No rush," Louise told her. "I would like some hot tea whenever you have time." She had a soft spot for Hope, who had known the sisters' father and had enjoyed the stories he told. Hope had a penchant for changing the color of her short dark hair, which normally held a lovely luster. Today, it was graced with startling streaks of a distinctly deep purple shade. Louise didn't know whether a comment was expected or not, but since she wasn't sure exactly what to say, she decided that keeping silent was the better course of action.

"No pie?" Hope said with a smile.

"No pie," Louise confirmed. "I have more willpower than Alice." Her younger sibling freely admitted to her weakness for the extraordinary pies that June Carter, the owner of the Coffee Shop, made daily.

Hope laughed as she went along to deliver the breakfasts on her tray.

"I made a first draft listing the causes to which the congregation has made donations," Pauline said. She showed Louise a piece of notebook paper. "Do you think I should have Ethel check over this?"

"I don't think it's necessary," Louise said, "but if it would make you feel better, go ahead."

"Maybe we could just go over it with you," Loueda suggested diffidently.

"I'd be happy to look at it," Louise said. "In fact, if you need additional help with your project, just let me know."

"That would be lovely." Pauline scribbled a note and then passed her list to Louise, who looked over the entries for a few moments. "This seems fine," she assured the other two.

"I'm back." Hope plunked down a mug, a basket of assorted teabags and a small pot of hot water in front of Louise. "Have you heard about the Civil War battle everyone's discussing this morning?"

"Civil War battle?" Louise straightened.

"First, Nia Komonos mentioned it, and then Herb Hoffstritt came in here yesterday with some family papers from Civil War times, and one of them indicated that there was a battle right here in Acorn Hill." Hope's expression was awed. "Can you imagine?"

Louise sighed. "No. I can't. I saw that correspondence yesterday at the library, and nowhere does it mention anything about a battle."

"But it's right in the letter," Hope said.

"The writer used the words *fracas* and *dustup*, as I recall," Louise said. "Neither one of those is synonymous with *battle*."

"And both of those words bring to mind a smaller altercation," added Loueda.

Louise turned and stared at her in surprise. It might have been the first time she ever had heard Loueda offer any unsolicited opinion. "You're exactly right," she said.

"Well," said Hope, grinning, "don't tell Duane." She gestured across the room to the counter, where Duane Van Dinkle had one hip hitched onto a stool as he blew on a cup of steaming coffee.

Duane was the local exterminator and general remover-of-all-things-unpleasant. He was dressed in blue-striped coveralls with his name embroidered on the pocket.

"What does Duane have to do with this?" Pauline asked, her smooth brow wrinkling.

"He's an amateur metal-detector," Hope explained. "He's always scouring the fields around here for artifacts made of metal. He's decided to go through all the grassy areas around downtown here to see if he can find any bullets or fragments that might tell us where the battle occurred."

"Good heavens," Louise said. "This has gotten totally out of hand."

"Oh, don't be such a fuddy-duddy, Louise." A new voice chimed in, and Louise turned to see Florence Simpson craning her neck over the back of the booth behind them. Across the table from her was her husband Ronald, who met Louise's gaze with an apologetic smile and a spreading of his hands, as if to offer sympathy regarding his wife's interruption.

"I beg your pardon?" It was Louise's coolest, frostiest tone, but it appeared to have no effect on the eavesdropping Florence.

"There might be something to this battle theory," Florence said authoritatively. As always, Florence was turned out impeccably, her dark hair coiffed and her makeup carefully applied. Her stout figure was encased in a gun-metal gray pantsuit with an ivory shell, and the outfit was complemented by a necklace and earrings of gleaming black pearls. "I seem to recall my grandfather's saying something about Acorn Hill and the Civil War, although I cannot remember his exact words. I'll have to go home and look back through the old family records."

Florence's family had been prominent in the area for three generations, a fact she was fond of bringing up as frequently as possible.

"Wouldn't your grandfather have been a bit young to have fought in the Civil War?" Hope asked, winking at Louise.

"Of course," Florence said impatiently. "He was born in 1864, though, and as he was the youngest of fifteen children, three of his older brothers fought for the Union."

"It seems to me you would have heard something about it if a battle ever had been fought around here," Louise said.

Florence shrugged. "As I said, I'll have to go home and begin searching." She turned back around.

Louise sat in silence for a moment.

"A battle," Pauline said finally. "If it's true, it's an important piece of local history."

"That's a big 'if,'" Loueda said. "I think Louise has a point. If it ever happened, surely local historians would have some record of it."

"You never know," Hope said. "Things have a way of getting lost as time passes." She glanced around the room. "Yikes! I'd better get hopping. I see some new folks who need service. See you later." And off she went, having effectively stirred up the waters.

∽

On Thursday morning, Jane was on the second floor cleaning the bathroom attached to Eva Quigley's room when she heard Alice calling.

"I'm in the Garden Room," she called back.

A moment later, a shadow darkened the doorway of the bathroom. "Hello," Alice said.

"Hi. Where did you disappear to after breakfast?"

"I didn't exactly disappear," Alice said, "but I did go down to the library and do a little more research on the tortoise. I feel more confident that she is doing as well in a strange environment as we can expect."

"I noticed she is beginning to move around during the night," Jane said, going back to wiping down the shower stall. "When I went to bed, she was in the far corner by the washing machine, and this morning she was basking beneath the light on her heating pad." She laughed. "I can almost hear her saying, 'Ah-h-h-h,' as she warms up."

Alice chuckled too as she arranged fresh towels on the

towel bars and dumped the others in a clothes basket Jane had set on the floor. "I bought some bok choy on the way home from my last shift. That was one of the things I was told she might like. But since she was fed yesterday, I won't offer her food again for a day or two. Dane Rush said they are eating machines and will keep stuffing themselves if anything's put in front of them. And I don't want her to get fat."

"How can you tell if a tortoise is fat?" The question made Alice smile, but Jane was genuinely puzzled. "It's not like you can see its belly bulging."

"No, but it's easy to tell because it starts getting too fat to fit into its shell. It gets fatty deposits around its legs and it literally can't retract them. Dane warned me about that, and I saw some pictures when I was looking up the information."

Jane shook her head. "I suppose I never thought about things like snakes and turtles getting fat."

Alice glanced around the room, peering into the bath. "Ms. Quigley must be neat. This place looks almost like it does without any guests staying in it."

Jane nodded. "Neat, tidy, apparently flawless. Except that she's got such a strong competitive streak that she's not fun to play games with."

"Are you still thinking about that?" Now it was Alice's turn to shake her head. "Gracious, Jane, don't you think it's time to let go of your anger?"

"I have," Jane insisted. "That doesn't mean I have to stop thinking about it. I'd just like to find one thing that I'm better at than Eva is."

"What about that game Louise mentioned? What was it called? Koi?"

"No, that's a fish. You mean quoits." Jane grinned. "I have to confess, I already called Viola and she set me up with the friend whom Louise mentioned this morning. I have an appointment to visit him on Saturday."

Alice's eyes widened. "You're really serious about this."

"I am," Jane confirmed stoutly. "Viola recommended a

book that has been quite interesting, and I also started looking for information on the Internet. It's hard to believe that I've never heard of it before. Quoits games came with English settlers when they arrived in America in the 1600s, and they have been played, with various rules and levels of popularity, ever since. Horseshoes has been more familiar to most Americans since World War II, though."

"Is it like horseshoes?"

"It's similar in that you pitch an item at a peg or stake, but there are some important differences. First, there is the shape. Quoits look like doughnuts. Traditional American quoits are smaller than horseshoes, but much heavier. The ones for regulation play are cast in foundries and are made of metals like iron, steel, brass and bronze, although in some other places people play with rubber ones. And they are pitched a shorter distance than horseshoes, into clay pits. I'm sure there is much more, but that's all my brain could soak up in one sitting."

"That's a considerable amount," Alice assured her. "So if you're doing all this research on your own, why are you going to visit Viola's friend who's the expert?"

"I want him to teach me how to throw them," Jane said smugly. "And then I'll challenge Eva to a game."

"Jane! That's . . . sort of cheating, isn't it? Luring her into a competition in which you have practiced and she hasn't?"

"No more so than challenging an ordinary person like me to Scrabble, when you know you're a walking dictionary," Jane said. "She could have warned me, you know."

"Yes, but—"

"It's just a game," Jane said, feeling a bit defensive. *Didn't anyone understand how it had felt to be made to look like such a fool?*

"I suppose," Alice said, although it was clear she wasn't convinced.

Just then, the telephone rang. "Where is Louise?" Jane asked. "Will she get that?"

"I'm not sure. I'd better check." Alice turned to dash out of the room as the telephone rang again, but just then, they heard Louise picking up the receiver downstairs at the desk.

"Grace Chapel Inn, this is Louise speaking."

There was a moment of silence, and then Louise said, "Hello, Carlene. How are you? . . . That's good . . . Yes, I'm fine . . . You *what?*"

"Uh-oh," said Jane under her breath. She and Alice both knew that tone of voice did not bode well for a pleasant end to the conversation.

"No," Louise said in a definite tone. "I do not wish to give you a quote. Anything I say in this conversation is off the record . . . No, he did not say anything about an actual battle. He showed us the letter, which I'm sure he would be happy to share with you. It mentioned an episode labeled a 'fracas' in one sentence and a 'dustup' in a second reference. That does not a battle make. There very well may be an interesting incident in Acorn Hill's history, but I am not at all convinced that it has anything to do with warfare, other than the fact that some of the participants were Confederate soldiers."

There was another short silence. Then Louise said, "Thank you for calling, Carlene," in a patently false tone that let Carlene know Louise felt little gratitude. "I strongly urge you to contact Mr. Hoffstritt and get a copy of that letter. Good-bye."

Alice looked at Jane, her eyebrows raised. "Remind me not to mention the Civil War or a battle to Louise for, oh, say, the next six months."

Jane choked back laughter. "Perhaps Carlene is the one I had better remind, don't you think?"

Jane woke up full of anticipation the following morning. She hummed the whole way through the half-hour drive to Merriville, where Buck Dabney, the man to whom Viola had referred her, lived.

The Dabneys' home was a restored farmhouse down a long lane. Sheep and goats grazed in pastures along the lane, and Jane could see a field of pumpkins on a nearby hill, fat and round and almost ready for autumn festivities.

Jane parked her small car at one side of a gravel turnaround. As she walked along a brick path toward the front door, she admired a garden of herbs and flowers that fronted a split-rail fence parallel to the walkway. Although it was autumn, many of the plants had not been cut back. Some, she saw, were hardy things that could withstand winter, while others had faded and dried but retained interesting shapes that would show nicely throughout the winter, especially when decorated with a covering of snow.

She recognized perennial geraniums, scabiosa, thyme, rosemary and euphorbia. A line of coral bells similar to the ones she had planted at the inn still held their dried bloom stalks high above the plants. Bushes of viburnum and evergreen hollies sported brilliant berries. A burning bush, so named for the flaming red hues of its fall foliage, shone brightly among the foundation's shrubs near the house. *Holly*, she thought. *Wonderful for winter color. We should think about adding a bush or two.*

As she approached the front door, it was flung open, and a large man with a bushy brown mustache boomed, "You must be Jane. I'm Buck." He stuck out a huge hand, and when she placed hers in it, he shook her hand so vigorously she felt the effect clear up to her shoulder. "Come on in."

"Thank you for taking the time to see me," Jane said. "Viola told me that you farm, and I know fall can be a busy time."

"It's always a busy time on a farm," he told her. "Even in the winter, my wife has a million indoor projects that need to be taken care of, but I set them aside until it gets too cold to do much outdoor work. I'm never too busy to talk quoits, though. Viola said you want to learn everything about the game."

Jane laughed. "Something like that."

He grinned and winked. "Well, that might take more time than we have, but I think I can give you enough information to keep you busy for a while. The first thing you should know is that there are a million different ways to play quoits, depending on the person you talk to. The first documented instances of similar games can be found at the Greek games about two centuries before the birth of Christ. The Romans spread them across Europe during their conquests, and they showed up in Britain sometime in the second century."

Jane was stunned. "I had no idea! I can't believe I haven't heard of quoits before."

"Most people haven't. The United States Quoiting Association was founded in 2003, and it is working to promote the game throughout the country."

"So how did you get involved?"

"My dad played. He taught me, and eventually I discovered the USQA. I play on the USQA Tour every year. There are several tournaments held in Pennsylvania."

Jane was fascinated. "So this really is an organized sport."

"Oh yes indeed." Buck indicated that she should follow him. "I built my own quoit court at the back of the house. The best way to learn about the game probably is to try it."

That met Jane's needs perfectly, so she said, "Thank you. I would enjoy that." She followed Buck on a slow walk through his home, noticing the many antiques and folk art items that decorated the interior. They suited the house well. "How old is your house?" she asked. "It's lovely."

"It was built in 1797," he told her. "My family has owned this land for more than two hundred years now. I was born in this house, just like many of my ancestors. My son, though, was born in a hospital." His eyes twinkled. "Progress trumps the past, I suppose." As they walked through a dining room with a long trestle table, he waved at a fireplace against the outer wall. An iron kettle hung near the hearth. "We don't use that much anymore, but when I was a kid, fireplaces provided much of the heat for the house."

"So you modernized it?"

"Well, my folks put in plumbing and running water and electricity a long time ago. We added a few amenities, like heat and air-conditioning and a modern kitchen, as unobtrusively as possible."

Jane continued to nod approvingly as they walked through a small pantry into the kitchen. The floor was an uneven dark brick that surely must have been the original floor.

"This was a separate kitchen off the original structure," Buck told her. "People often kept the kitchen separate so that if there was a fire—which was frequent—it wouldn't spread to the main house. My parents added the little room in between and used it as a mudroom. When my wife and I remodeled the kitchen, we had the cupboards and counters put in so it could be used as a service and storage area. I added a laundry-slash-mudroom at the back."

Jane thought the kitchen was charming, retaining the ambience of its age and historical context while offering a user all the modern conveniences.

He led her through the final small room about which he had spoken. Although clearly newer than the kitchen, it faithfully followed the style and design of the original structure, right down to weathered-looking bricks on the floor. Jane saw a patio outside, which contained a glass-topped circular table with an umbrella and four chairs. In the verdant yard beyond the patio were two box frames set into the ground.

"Here is the quoit court," Buck said, ushering her into the backyard. "Each pit is a yard square. They are twenty-one feet apart from pin to pin." He walked over to the table. "This is a quoit."

Jane reached for the object he handed her. It resembled

a saucer, slightly concave on one side, with a hole in the center. But when Buck released the quoit, she nearly dropped it.

"Wow!" she gasped. "I wasn't expecting it to be so heavy." She chuckled at herself as she got a better grip on the heavy metal ring. "I knew they were made of metal, but I didn't realize how much. I could get muscles in a hurry if I tossed one of these around regularly."

"You sure would." Buck took the quoit from her. "Here's what you do." He walked to one of the pits and faced the other. The toss he used looked, to Jane's untutored eye, much like a horseshoe pitch. The quoit sailed through the air flat and clanked against the pin in the center of the pit. "There," Buck said. He picked up another one. "Want to give it a try?"

"I'd love to." This time Jane was prepared for the weight of the quoit. She gripped it as she had seen Buck do, then exclaimed, "Oh dear, I believe this one is damaged." She held up the quoit to display the small chunk that marred the circular edge.

Buck chuckled. "No, they're all like that. The notch helps to spin the quoit properly." He fitted his into his right hand as if he were holding a Frisbee, sliding the tip of his index finger into the notch. "This is how you want to hold it." He assumed a stance and then pointed down at his feet. "Put one foot in front of the other. Whichever seems natural is fine. It doesn't matter. Then you want to bend your knees and center most of your weight over your forward foot."

Jane did her best to copy his stance and follow his directions. "Then I just toss it?"

"Pitch it," he corrected. "It's almost like rolling a bowling ball, except that the release changes because of the way you're holding it." He demonstrated again, and Jane heard the dull thunk of the quoit's weight as it landed in the soft clay inside the box.

She tried to copy Buck's motion. Planting her feet, she cocked her right arm back with the quoit held firmly in the grip he had shown her. Then she swung her arm forward and released.

Her quoit flew wildly through the air, wobbling from side to side like a spaceship piloted by a drunken alien. It landed far short of the pit, wrong side up.

Buck grinned. "Not bad for your first pitch."

"Not good, either," Jane said, scowling. "May I try again?"

He laughed. "Sure. It kinda grabs you, doesn't it?"

Jane nodded. "It does."

She pitched quoit after quoit under Buck's direction. While she practiced, he explained the strategy of the game to her. It differed significantly from horseshoes because a good player could alter the trajectory of his throw so that the quoit would land with the leading edge spearing down into the clay. This could block an opponent's pitch, as could a quoit that landed vertically directly in front of the pin. An opponent then would have to waste pitches trying to move that quoit before the pin was accessible again.

The minute adjustments required in the stance, the hold and the pitch in order to effect such strategic changes would take a long time to develop, Jane could see. Still, she suspected that she could best Eva if ever she had a chance to play quoits with her.

"I can see how a person could get hooked." She walked across the grass to the opposite pit and picked up the quoit she had thrown. "So how do I get it to stick in the dirt on its edge the way you described?"

Buck smiled broadly. "Jane, you *are* hooked on quoits."

Chapter 🐢 Six

Alice was dusting the parlor when Jane returned from her trip to the quoits expert on Saturday afternoon. "Hello," she called when she heard her sister enter through the kitchen door. "How was your visit, Jane?"

Jane appeared in the doorway, paused for a moment with a wide grin on her face, and then dropped down onto one of the three sturdy Victorian chairs with her legs stretched out before her. "It was really interesting. I can see how players could become determined to win competitions."

"I want to hear about it, but first, I need to tell you that we got some walk-in guests this afternoon."

"Oh? How many is some?"

"Two. A father and son, traveling across the country on bicycles. They started in Oregon."

"Wow!" Jane said. "That's neat. How long are they staying?"

"Two nights. Just enough to get rested up to finish the last few days. Now, tell me about the quoits."

"Sheesh! Where do I start?" Jane shook her head slowly. "My brain is swimming in new information."

"Is it like horseshoes?" Alice unwittingly asked a question upon which Jane could impart all her newfound knowledge. While Jane spoke, Alice continued to dust, carefully lifting pieces of a collection of Roseville pottery from one of the curio cabinets, gently wiping their surfaces. She took special care in cleaning her favorite pieces, the delicate green with the pinecone motif.

"Not exactly," Jane said. "You do pitch the quoit at a pin in a pit, but the similarity is superficial. Quoits is much more complex than horseshoes." And she proceeded to regale Alice with all that she had learned.

Alice sank down onto one of the antique chairs, absently running a finger over the pretty tapestry upholstery done in shades of green, which echoed the green in the dainty violet-strewn wallpaper. She listened patiently as Jane talked on.

Finally, when her younger sister showed signs of slowing down, Alice said, "So you're planning to practice at quoits and then invite unsuspecting Eva to play?"

Jane shook her head. "I might, except that there's no place to go to play just for fun, as far as I can tell. The only way to play quoits casually is to put in a quoits pit or hang out with someone who has one."

"I guess that would be a problem." Alice glanced at her watch. "I need to finish this dusting and change out of these grubby jeans. Some of the ANGELs are coming over to see M.P."

"Have you heard from anyone who might know who that critter belongs to?" Jane stood and moved toward the door.

"No." Alice began to dust again. "But the information is probably just getting out to all the vets, so perhaps in a few days, someone will call."

"I hope so." Jane's voice floated back to Alice as she started toward the stairs. "I'm going to change clothes too, and then I'll start working on dinner."

Alice quickly completed her work and then went upstairs where she donned a clean pair of denim pants and a neat white blouse. She was just rolling up the sleeves when the doorbell rang.

"I'll get it," she called over the banister as she descended the stairs.

Reaching the front door, Alice pulled it open.

"Hi, Miss Howard!" The speaker was Pauline Sherman's elder daughter Tiffany. Behind her were at least a half dozen other preteen and early teenage girls, members of the small group Alice had founded. One of their primary objectives was to complete anonymous good works, both individually and as a group. Often at their weekly meetings on Wednesdays, each girl wrote down a good deed she had done anonymously that week and placed it in a basket. Alice then read each good deed out loud, although no mention ever was made of the particular ANGEL who had completed it.

Alice had found the exercise a surprisingly effective way to help the girls remember to act as Christians throughout their week. It pleased her to think that because of their efforts, the world was a slightly better place. It pleased her even more to know that through her ANGELs ministry, she was helping to instill a strong sense of doing for others in these young women.

"Hello, girls," she said, stepping back. "Come on in. I know you're eager to meet my guest."

A couple of giggles greeted her statement as the girls trooped inside. Everyone began to shed jackets and Alice noticed that Kesa Waters, one of the youngest members of the ANGELs, had a small boy by the hand. "Hello, Kesa. Who's this?"

Kesa smiled as she helped the child take off his coat. "This is my cousin Blaine Waters, Miss Howard. Blaine, this is Miss Howard, who leads my group. I'm watching him for my aunt this afternoon," she said in an aside.

"Hello, Blaine," Alice said.

"Hi," the little boy said. He looked to be about kindergarten age, with light brown hair side-parted and neatly combed. Blaine wore a pair of belted tan pants and a long-sleeve polo shirt neatly tucked in. Alice tried to recall the last time she had seen a little boy wearing a belt other than when he was dressed up for church. Nothing came to mind.

Then the child moved. In three seconds, he darted toward the registration desk. "What's this?" he asked in a high voice as he reached up over the edge of the counter and pulled over a small brass box that contained several fountain pens.

Brianna Sherman grabbed for the box and caught it before it hit the floor. The other ANGELs scrambled for the spilled pens, and Sissy Matthews snagged Blaine by a loop at the back of his pants as he began to rush off. "Whoa!" she said firmly.

Alice had to smile. Sissy's ten-year-old brother Charles had been an extremely active young child, and Sissy clearly knew the capabilities of one small boy on a tear.

"Blaine!" Kesa looked as if she were near tears. "You come here and hold my hand. You are not going to run through Miss Howard's house like some little brat."

"I'm not a brat," the boy said mutinously.

"Kesa didn't say you were." Alice thought it prudent to step in while the girls replaced the pens and the box. She offered Blaine her hand. "Are you ready to come and meet our tortoise?"

"Yeah!" Blaine took her offered hand. "Let's go."

The ANGELs followed Alice and her young friend back to the hallway and into the kitchen, where Jane was getting something from the refrigerator.

"Well, hello," said Jane. "I see we need some cookies for this crew."

"Yes, cookies!" said Blaine.

"That would be lovely, Ms. Howard," said Lisa Mazur. "Thank you."

"Our tortoise is out here," she told the group. "She probably won't be very exciting. She still is settling in, and she doesn't move around much at all." She led the children onto the porch. "We call her M.P.," Alice explained, "because we found the initials M.P. on the bottom of her shell."

"How do you know it's a girl?" asked Ashley Moore.

Alice hesitated. "The wildlife expert told me." That was unquestionably the safest explanation she could give. She opened the door to the laundry room. "Now try not to stomp on the floor," she cautioned, "and be fairly quiet. She's resting on her heat pad right now."

The girls filed into the room behind Alice in hushed silence. Alice had a firm grip on little Blaine's hand. "You're doing a wonderful job of being quiet," she told him in a stage whisper.

Blaine's eyes were the size of half-dollars. "That's a big turtle," he whispered back.

Alice nodded, smiling down at him.

The tortoise was basking beneath the heat lamp on her warm pad. Her head was out and her eyes were closed and she looked as relaxed as Alice had seen her. Then, as if she sensed the scrutiny, she opened her eyes and turned her head to stare directly at the little group.

"Wow!" said Sarah Roberts. "She's extremely cool."

"She's extremely scary," said Jenny Snyder nervously, taking a step back.

"She won't hurt you," Alice assured the group. "First of all, you can outrun her." The girls giggled. "And second, she isn't aggressive. I picked her up and put her in my car when I took her to visit a wildlife specialist."

"I bet she was heavy," remarked Kate Waller.

Alice nodded. "She weighs thirty-seven pounds."

"I feel bad for her," Sissy announced. "She probably is all confused about where she is."

"We're hoping to find her family soon," Alice explained.

Kesa goggled. "You mean that's someone's pet?" She stared at the tortoise, clearly surprised by the idea.

"I'd take her," Sissy said.

"I wanna ride it." Blaine tugged at Alice's hand.

"Oh no," Alice said to him. "You're much too big to ride her. It would be very uncomfortable for her."

Blaine's lower lip protruded. "I wanna ride it," he repeated.

Kesa stepped forward and took his hand again. "No," she said to Blaine. "But if you're good, I'll take you into the kitchen for a cookie."

Blaine appeared to consider this for a moment before he nodded. He took his cousin's hand. "Okay."

Then, to Alice's astonishment, the tortoise, obviously feeling more at home, moved. It was the first time Alice had seen her walk inside the inn. M.P. slowly pushed herself off the heat pad, and her shell made a scraping sound as she moved onto the level floor.

"Yikes," said Kesa. "What does she want?"

Alice wasn't sure. "She's probably just curious."

"Probably?" Jenny backed up a step, pulling Linda Farr and Ashley with her.

M.P. trundled closer.

Sarah, who was in the front row of girls, squatted down. "Hello," she said. "Aren't you beautiful!"

M.P. stopped, staring at Sarah.

Sarah slowly reached forward. "May I pet you?" she asked. She had to lean forward to stretch her arm far enough to get her hand on the massive shell. M.P. watched her, but only flinched a little when the girl's arm came closer. Then, without warning, Sarah fell forward onto her knees.

M.P. instantly withdrew her head into her shell with a loud hiss that sounded like steam escaping, as her front legs overlapped to make an impenetrable barrier in front of her head. Everyone jumped and a couple more of the girls stepped back.

Sarah leaped to her feet. "Blaine, I am going to clobber you!" she announced.

Kesa had a death grip on the little boy's hand, but Alice could see that he had been close enough to nudge Sarah in the back so that she lost her balance. He had a devilish smile on his face. "You say you're sorry to Sarah," Kesa said fiercely to him.

Blaine continued to grin. "Nuh-uh."

"Blaine . . ."

"Kesa, why don't you and all the girls go into the kitchen for those cookies Ms. Howard promised you. I'll keep Blaine with me."

Kesa looked relieved. "All right."

Alice took the child's hand as all the girls streamed into the kitchen. She heard Jane cautioning them all to wash their hands as the door shut behind them.

Blaine looked up at her, clearly concerned. "I wanna go get cookies too."

Alice feigned surprise. "Oh, I'm sorry, Blaine, but people who do unkind things, especially people who refuse to apologize for being unkind, don't get cookies here at Grace Chapel Inn." She watched as the little boy's eyes filled with tears and his lower lip began to quiver. She felt like the worst sort of ogre, but she knew it was important to show the child that there were consequences to his misbehavior. Half the tears, she suspected, were designed to change her mind.

She was even surer a moment later when she caught him glancing slyly up at her out of the corner of his eye, and her wavering resolve firmed.

He tried to tug his hand from hers.

Gently but firmly, she held on.

Blaine howled louder.

Alice studiously ignored the crying. M.P., who had slowly begun to peer out of her shell again, began laboriously turning around to head back to her heat source, apparently not wanting to be any closer to the screaming child.

Suddenly, Blaine stopped howling as abruptly as he had started. "I'm s-sorry," he said to Alice, gulping as his breathing hitched.

"I am not the one to whom you need to apologize," Alice said quietly. "Would you like to go into the kitchen and talk to Sarah?"

He nodded, hiccupping a little.

Alice released his hand, patting his shoulder. "All right. After you say you're sorry to Sarah, I bet Ms. Howard can find a cookie for you."

"O-okay." Chastened, the child preceded her into the kitchen, where he quickly crossed to Sarah. "I'm sorry I pushed you," he told her.

Alice knew the name Sarah meant princess in Hebrew, and Sarah was indeed as gracious as a princess as she accepted the little boy's apology. "Thank you, Blaine." She led him to the sink and helped him to wash his hands. Then she picked up the platter of cookies that Jane had set in the middle of the table and extended it to him. "Would you like a cookie?"

He sniffed and nodded, knuckling a final tear from his eye. Very carefully, he looked over the mouth-watering selection and chose just one. His cousin helped him onto a chair, and Jane set a glass of milk in front of him. "There you go," she said.

Kesa smiled at Alice over the top of the little head. "Thank you," she mouthed, nodding as if to approve of Alice's actions.

"Miss Howard!"

Alice whirled toward the sound of Jenny Snyder's voice. Jenny was pointing toward the laundry.

Alice had forgotten to close the door behind her. While everyone had been attending to the minidrama in the kitchen, the tortoise apparently had wanted to see what was going on. M.P. was planted solidly in the doorway with what Alice only could think of as an inquisitive look on her face, her head cocked slightly to one side.

"Oh no, you don't!" Jane said. "Alice, get your friend before she comes into this kitchen."

Hastily, Alice crossed the floor. "Sorry, girl," she told the tortoise. Placing her hands at the front of the tortoise's domed shell, she gently slid M.P. back just far enough to close the door. "Jane's room is off-limits to you."

⚯

The Howard sisters attended services at Grace Chapel the following morning.

There was a crisp autumn chill in the air as they walked along Chapel Road toward the little church. "What a lovely morning," Jane said appreciatively, taking a deep breath. She was wearing a navy blue pantsuit with a dashing scarf of wool and ribbon woven in hues of navy, deep purple and lightest lavender. The ends fluttered as she walked.

Louise smiled at her youngest sister. "Indeed. I love autumn."

Louise and Alice each wore a skirt. Louise had paired her gray pinstriped skirt with a light blue cashmere twinset and the pearls that she customarily wore at her neck, while Alice had donned a brown skirt with a white blouse and a practical brown sweater-vest with appliquéd autumn leaves on it.

"I love all the seasons." Alice waved her arms expansively. "We're so lucky. We live in a beautiful area of the country."

"I imagine there are people everywhere who think that their little corner of the country is the loveliest," Louise said with a smile.

"Good morning, Aunt Ethel," Jane called as they reached the church. Their father's younger sister was just about to enter the church, but she paused, waved and waited for her nieces.

"Good morning, girls," Ethel said. "Have you had any luck finding the owner of that turtle, Alice?"

"No." Alice shook her head. "I'm hoping someone calls about her this week." There was no use reminding Ethel that M.P. was a tortoise rather than a turtle.

"Aunt Ethel," Louise said, "I was planning a trip to the store for Jane tomorrow morning. Would you like me to pick you up, so you can get your groceries?"

Ethel beamed at Louise. "Why yes, dear. I would appreciate that a great deal." She shook her head sadly. "When I never bothered to learn to drive, it didn't occur to me that Bob might not be there to chauffeur me someday." Ethel's husband Bob Buckley had passed away ten years before.

"Hello, Howards. And Ethel." Hope Collins came toward them with a wide smile. "Have you still got that turtle, Alice?"

Alice sighed to herself and simply said, "Yes. I don't suppose you've heard of anyone who is missing a giant tortoise?"

Hope laughed. "No, but if I do, I'll know where to send him." She turned to Louise. "Duane's been out with that metal detector every day this week, but he hasn't found a single thing. At least, not a thing relating to a Civil War battle. He did find seven buttons, a couple of coins, soda bottle tops, and a wedding ring someone either lost or dumped near Fairy Pond years ago. It was buried in the mud."

"Gracious sakes. You'd better tell Carlene about the last one," Ethel suggested. "Maybe if she prints that in the paper, someone will come forward and claim it."

"How can you lose a wedding ring on a walking path?" Alice wondered out loud. "I can see dropping it down a drain or something, but—"

"Maybe it wasn't lost," Jane suggested mischievously.

"Maybe some angry wife threw it at a no-account husband who failed to catch it."

"Or didn't want to," Louise commented. "Although I think it's more likely that it simply slipped off someone's finger."

"Yes, but not nearly as interesting," Hope said.

"I'm not surprised that Duane has not found any army artifacts," Louise commented. "I still am not convinced that the letter Mr. Hoffstritt found refers to a battle."

"Even if it doesn't," Jane pointed out, "it still sounds as though troops may have passed through the area, at least. If they set up an encampment nearby, there probably is something to be found."

The five women entered the church together as they finished their conversation. Alice barely made it through the door before Penny Holwell walked up and said, "Hello, Alice. I hear you found a giant turtle. Any idea where it came from?"

That was the theme of Alice's morning. If she answered questions about the tortoise once, she answered them a dozen times. It might have been more appropriate to get a tape recorder and simply keep rewinding and replaying it, she thought.

Lord, give me patience, she prayed silently, not entirely in jest. And then her prayer grew more serious. *And please help me to find the tortoise's owner. I don't feel right giving her to a wildlife center unless I know for sure that someone isn't missing her.*

Chapter 🐢 Seven

As she had promised, Louise took Ethel along to get groceries Monday morning.

When Louise knocked on the carriage house door, Ethel came out immediately. She wore taupe pants with a tweed jacket and matching loafers. Over her head was a large chiffon scarf that covered her brilliant red hair and tied beneath her chin. When she pulled large sunglasses out of her handbag and perched them atop her nose, Louise was amused to realize that Ethel momentarily reminded her of Jackie Kennedy.

"Good morning, dear." Ethel said as they headed to Louise's Cadillac. "I do appreciate this so much."

"Why are you wearing a scarf?" Louise asked.

"I have an appointment at the Clip 'n' Curl this afternoon, so I didn't do my hair this morning," Ethel explained. "Florence offered to pick me up later since she is going in for her color then. My red needs a touch-up, and Betty was able to fit me in. Isn't that convenient?"

"It is," agreed Louise.

They drove to the grocery store, where Louise picked up the items on the list Jane had given her and Ethel shopped for her own foodstuffs. In less than an hour, they were finished and on their way home again.

Then Ethel said, "Oh, Louise, would you mind stopping at Lloyd's office for a moment? I'd like to know his response to the suggestion of a special memorial ceremony."

"All right." Louise obligingly swung the wheel and began turning onto Hill Street. "Special ceremony for what?"

"For the Civil War battle," Ethel said as if it were a well-known event.

"For the . . . !" Louise was speechless. "Who on earth suggested that?" she demanded when she finally rallied her thoughts and could speak coherently.

"I don't believe I know," Ethel said serenely, apparently unconcerned about the repercussions of planning something to commemorate an event that may never have happened at all. "Lloyd just mentioned it last evening when we had dinner together."

Good heavens! Louise hardly could wait to speak to Lloyd.

Lloyd's office was in Town Hall, which fronted Berry Lane. As Louise turned into the driveway and proceeded to park in the Town Hall lot, she told herself to calm down. After all, Lloyd generally was known for his common sense. She carefully avoided thinking about some of the more interesting predicaments he and her aunt had gotten themselves into over the years. Lloyd was the mayor. He would never countenance something like a ceremony unless he was convinced there really was a historic event.

Was he convinced?

Louise got out of the car and rounded the front to meet Ethel. It was yet another comfortably pleasant day, much like the day before, and distinctly warmer than the previous week. She wanted to pursue the topic of the ceremony with Ethel, but she sensed her aunt had been truthful when she said she didn't know anything more.

She motioned to Ethel to precede her up the path that led around to the front door, and moments later they were walking into the cool foyer and heading past the Visitors Center. Ethel moved on toward the office but Louise hesitated. She blinked as her eyes adjusted to the light before she followed her aunt.

"Hello, Ethel," Lloyd's secretary Bella said.

"Hello, dear. Is Lloyd available? I won't keep him, I promise. Louise and I have a quick question for him."

"Well, hello, Louise. It's nice to see you." Bella Paoli was one of the sweetest people in Acorn Hill. Louise occasionally thought that Bella might marry again someday although she had not been known to date after her husband's passing. Just a bit older than Jane, Bella kept herself slim and blond and looked much younger than her age.

"It's nice to see you too, Bella." Louise smiled with genuine pleasure. Bella had that effect on people.

"Let me see if Lloyd has time to talk." Bella stood and vanished into the inner office. A moment later, she reappeared and beckoned. "Come in, ladies."

"Well, well, well. My day has gotten immeasurably brighter." Lloyd beamed as he rose and came around his desk to greet Ethel and Louise. Today he wore a silk bow tie in light gray with a black polka-dot pattern, and a charcoal pinstriped suit. His jacket buttons strained where they were fastened over his generous girth. Louise thought he looked every inch the mayoral type.

His green eyes sparkled with warmth as he took Ethel's hand and led her to one of the two leather chairs positioned in front of his desk. "What a lovely scarf," he said to Ethel. "It really brings out the blue in your eyes."

"This old thing? I've had it for years," Ethel said, but Louise was tickled to note that her aunt blushed.

Courteously, Lloyd offered the other seat to Louise.

Once both women were settled into the sturdy chairs

with their brass nail trim, Lloyd rested a hip against his desk and crossed his arms, giving them his full attention. "To what do I owe this pleasure?"

Ethel beamed at him. "Louise took me to the grocery store this morning. I asked her to stop here because she and I were discussing the likelihood of a battle in the area, and I realized you and I never finished our conversation last night. Have you decided how to handle all this talk of a ceremony to commemorate the event?"

"If there was one," put in Louise. She was feeling calmer now that she was sitting in Lloyd's office. She was sure he would be the voice of reason.

"Oh, I guess we did get sidetracked," he said. "Florence Simpson was here earlier. I've decided to ask her to chair a committee to explore the best ways to highlight a historical event in our community."

"You have?"

"What?"

Ethel and Louise spoke at the same time.

Ethel, no doubt, would be piqued that Lloyd asked Florence to help before he approached Ethel. It was logical, since Ethel already was quite busy with her responsibilities at Grace Chapel. But Louise knew Ethel would not see it that way.

Louise herself was dismayed for other reasons. "But Lloyd," she said, "advertising anything about a Civil War battle will bring tourists by the busload to town. Whatever happened to, 'Acorn Hill has a life of its own away from the outside world, and that's the way we like it'?" Lloyd was known for both the phrase and the sentiment.

"Oh, I don't believe a small celebration will attract too much attention," Lloyd said genially. "Florence mentioned something about a reenactment, which might be going a bit far, but it's only fair to let her look into it."

"A reenactment?" cried Louise. "Of what? We don't even know what may have occurred."

"Yet," Ethel said. "I'm sure it's just a matter of time until we learn more about whatever Herb Hoffstritt's ancestor alluded to in that letter."

"I was thinking," said Lloyd, rubbing his hands together, "that we could tie it into our Fourth of July celebration. The band shell in the park always looks great draped in red, white and blue bunting, doesn't it?" His sharp green eyes grew uncharacteristically dreamy.

"Oh, it does." Ethel clapped her hands together. "I volunteer to head up a decorating committee."

"Thank you, Ethel." Lloyd uncrossed his arms and hurried around his desk. Grabbing a notepad, he scribbled something on a piece of paper and stuck it in a file lying atop his desk. "I'll put that on hold for now, and once Florence reports back, we can make more plans."

Louise dropped her head and rested her forehead against her thumb and forefinger. *Good heavens, this is a nightmare!* She felt as if she were invisible. Were her concerns really that far off the mark? Ethel had read the same letter she had, as had Nia and Herb Hoffstritt. Was she, Louise, the only one reluctant to leap to the conclusion that Acorn Hill had seen some sort of action during the Civil War?

Dropping her hand, she folded her arms and sat in silence while Lloyd and Ethel chattered away about possible decorating ideas for "the commemorative ceremony." If she had to do every ounce of research herself, she was going to get to the truth behind the incident to which the letter referred.

∞

Jane still was thinking about quoits as she chopped chicken into small pieces to mix into a chicken salad for lunch.

Louise had indicated that she would be back from the store before lunch, and Alice had not worked today, so all three of them would be eating together.

Wendell strolled into the kitchen, his belly swinging from side to side.

"Well, hello." Jane laughed as he wound around her ankles. "You aren't fooling me, you sneaky thing. You're not here because you adore me. You smelled chicken."

Alice, unloading the dishwasher, laughed. "It could be both, you know. He adores you, *and* he smells chicken."

Jane chuckled. "Right."

They heard Louise's footsteps coming up the back steps a few moments later, then the porch door opened and closed. When Louise entered the kitchen, Jane could tell instantly that something had not gone right during her morning.

"Hello," her eldest sister said wearily, setting down her large purse and two bags of groceries, and dropping into a chair.

"Welcome back," Alice said. "What's the matter?"

"She took Aunt Ethel to the store," Jane reminded Alice. "I'm sure there's a story in there somewhere."

Louise grimaced. "The visit to the grocery store went fine," she reported. "But on the way home, we stopped at Lloyd's office because Ethel wanted to check with him about a memorial ceremony to commemorate the battle that everyone is suddenly sure happened here during the Civil War."

Alice smiled. "Good old Lloyd," she murmured. "I bet he squelched that idea."

"But that's just it," Louise said. "He didn't. In fact, he already has appointed Florence to head a committee to come up with ideas for a celebration. And Ethel volunteered to handle decorating. Lloyd has it in his head that something could be planned to mesh with the Fourth of July festivities."

Alice's eyes grew round. "You're kidding."

"I wish I were," Louise said darkly. "People in this town seem to be living in fantasyland all of a sudden."

"Lloyd usually is so sensible," Jane said. "I'm surprised he isn't being more cautious."

"No one was more surprised than I," Louise told her. "I even quoted his own words to him. You know, that saying he has about Acorn Hill's having a life of its own?"

"And that's the way we like it," Alice and Jane said in unison. Jane pumped her fist in the air, and they both laughed.

But Jane sobered quickly when she saw that Louise barely summoned a halfhearted smile. "I'd be glad to help you research this if you want to pursue it," she said to Louise. "I'm sure Nia could point us in the right direction. I know the library has a collection of local historical documents. Maybe there's something in one of them that has been overlooked."

"Nia," said Louise, frowning, "has helped to spread this ridiculous notion all over town."

"I'm sure she didn't mean any harm," Alice opined. "It's just that people hear what they want to hear, and what they apparently want is to have some Civil War fame rub off on Acorn Hill."

"We'll go to the library this week," Jane promised Louise. "If there's any information there about this incident, whatever it really was, we'll find it."

"Thank you, Jane," Louise said. "I appreciate that."

In the moment of silence that followed, the sisters heard a sudden loud *thump* followed by a thud and a sound like steam escaping from the brakes of a train.

"What was that?" Louise said, rising.

Alice already was on her feet. "It's the tortoise," she said, hurrying toward the laundry room.

The door was ajar, and as Alice pushed it wider, she was surprised and alarmed to see Wendell in the room, facing the tortoise. M.P. had retreated into her shell.

Louise and Jane came up behind Alice and peered over her shoulders.

"Could Wendell hurt that thing?" Jane asked.

"I don't know," Alice said. "I doubt it. Her skin is quite tough. Not to mention covered with those little spiky protrusions."

As the sisters watched, Wendell crouched in front of the tortoise, his tail twitching. He reached out one white-stockinged paw and patted the tortoise's shell experimentally. Then he rose and walked all the way around her, inspecting her from every angle.

Meanwhile, the tortoise slowly began to peer from beneath her shell. Her front legs relaxed and returned to the ground, and her head came out. Wendell returned to face her. He sank into a crouch right before her and watched with rapt attention as she emerged from her shell. Finally, he could not stand it any longer, and he reached out and batted her on the head.

M.P. made the loud hissing noise again as her head jerked backward, but she did not retreat into her shell. Moments later, she was eyeing the cat again.

"I think they're playing," said Jane in a hushed tone as the two animals repeated the sequence.

Alice shook her head. "I think *Wendell* is playing," she countered. "The tortoise isn't nearly so thrilled. She is just trying to be sure she knows how serious this strange creature is about trying to harm her."

"I don't believe Wendell intends any harm," Louise offered. "He's just curious."

"I agree," Alice said. "But the tortoise doesn't know that."

Soon, however, it became apparent that the tortoise had figured out that Wendell wasn't much of a threat. She lumbered over to her heat pad, completely ignoring the way he paced along beside her. Once she had clambered onto the pad and settled down contentedly, she did not even react when Wendell continued to bat at her shell.

Finally, Alice picked up the cat. Snuggling him to her, she walked back into the kitchen. "Sorry, fella," she said. "Playtime is over."

Alice and Louise retrieved the groceries and put them away while Jane completed lunch preparations and Louise set the table. Soon the three sisters were seated.

"I'll offer grace," Jane volunteered. "Dear Heavenly Father, bless this food and make us mindful of the many blessings You shower on us, and remind us to reach out to those who are struggling to make ends meet, to feed their families, to keep their jobs. In Your name we pray. Amen."

"Amen," echoed her sisters.

As they dug into the tasty chicken salad and the plate of fresh vegetables Jane had placed on the table, Louise said, "So, Jane, Alice tells me you had a very interesting visit with Viola's friend."

Jane nodded. "Yes. Mr. Dabney is quite enthusiastic. He even gave me a few lessons on how to pitch quoits."

"Indeed." Louise cocked her head. "And are you planning to introduce our Ms. Quigley to the game?"

Jane shrugged. "I don't think so. Even if I wanted to, there isn't really a place for amateurs in the world of quoits."

Two hours later, Jane still was thinking about quoits. Too bad there wasn't anywhere to play unless one went to the trouble and expense of building quoits pits in one's own backyard.

For an instant, she actually considered it. If she put in quoits pits, she could offer it to inn guests as one more experience unique to their bed-and-breakfast. Then she came to her senses. Not only would it require an enormous amount of work to install them properly, they would require lots of maintenance. She thought of Buck's carefully mown lawn, the boxes full of clay that had to be just the proper consistency and the myriad rules and specifications for playing the game. She barely had time to keep the landscaping around the inn presentable and still produce gourmet fare for their guests, much less run a training facility for would-be quoits players.

She went to the computer and did a search for quoits tournaments in Pennsylvania. The United States Quoiting Association, the organization Buck had mentioned, had several tournaments listed. It would be interesting to see one, even if her admittedly flimsy scheme to involve an unsuspecting Eva in a quoits game had fizzled. Glancing at the dates, she saw that there was one coming up in Pottstown a week from the coming Saturday.

She picked up the telephone receiver and dialed Buck Dabney's number, which she had written on a slip of paper still tacked to her small bulletin board.

"Hello?" It was a deep, masculine voice.

"Hello. This is Jane Howard. May I speak to Buck, please?"

"Hey, Jane. This is Buck. You have more quoits questions for me?" He chuckled. "I told you it grabs you."

"You did," Jane admitted. "I've been thinking about it. I see there's a tournament coming up in Pottstown."

"Yeah. National tournament," he told her. "A big deal. There will be teams from all over coming to compete. If you want to see some good quoiting, you should go."

"Maybe I will," she said. "Could you give me directions?"

"Sure. I'll e-mail them to you. You know," Buck said, "you could play if you wanted to."

"I could? But you only just showed me how to pitch a quoit, and I don't begin to know all the rules. I'd have to practice for months, I think, to get good enough to compete."

"Usually that's true. Most people who play get interested because they know someone in their community who has a pit set up. They don't enter tournaments until they have been playing for a while and have gotten the hang of it."

"There you go."

"You're lucky, though," Buck went on, "because at the national championship, they have an on-the-spot beginners class and competition."

"Really?" Jane was utterly delighted.

"Right."

Jane felt her excitement rise. "I'm going to do it."

When she had thanked Buck and set the handset back on its cradle, Jane walked to the kitchen. She had been asked by a member of the Daughters of the American Revolution to submit a recipe for a cookbook featuring Acorn Hill residents' recipes, and she needed to decide on an offering, and e-mail it to the committee chairperson today.

She took down her bulging recipe file. There was a recipe for almond mint brownies that she loved, although she did not make them often. Pulling out a chair, she seated herself at the table and began thumbing through her recipes. Oh, here was that recipe for chicken divan that she had gotten from her first real friend in San Francisco, where she had gone to study art after high school. She had not even begun to consider a career as a chef then, but in all the years since, she had never found a chicken divan recipe as tasty as that one.

And here was the key lime cheesecake recipe that had become one of her signature desserts at the Blue Fish Grille, the last restaurant where she had worked before coming back to Acorn Hill. Perhaps, she thought, unfolding the double-sized recipe card, she should submit this one instead.

An odd little thumping sound penetrated her absorption, and she glanced around absently. Her gaze sharpened as she saw that, once again, the laundry door had been left ajar. This time, Jane could see the tortoise framed in the doorway, looking for all the world as if she intended to stroll right into the kitchen.

"Whoa!" Jane said, rising. "You don't belong in my kitchen." She started across the kitchen, intending to gently move the tortoise backward with her foot and close the door. But at close range, she could swear the expression on the animal's face looked almost hopeful.

"What's the matter?" Jane asked. "Are you lonely? Or maybe hungry?" She changed direction and went to the refrigerator, pulling out an apple. With a few deft chops of one of her large knives, she split the apple into four sections. Jane picked one up and walked to the door. She glanced around to be sure there were no witnesses, then knelt and offered a piece of apple to the tortoise. "Would you like this?"

She had seen Alice offer M.P. apple slices, although Alice usually set her food on a large rubber mat on the floor. M.P. eyed the apple, then looked at Jane again. Jane held the section of fruit closer.

Slowly, the tortoise's head emerged. Her neck was surprisingly long as she stretched forward. Then her beak opened wide and her head surged forward far enough to take a healthy chomp of apple.

Jane stifled a gasp. Although she didn't think the animal used her mouth for anything other than eating, Jane suspected that her beak was strong enough to inflict harm. Hastily, she set the remaining section of the apple on the floor. M.P. chewed slowly and deliberately, then reached down, angling her head to get a good grip on the remaining apple with her beak. In very short order, the rest of the slice was gone.

Jane rose. "I'll tell you what," she said. "I'll give you more apple, but you have to eat in your room, not in my kitchen." She turned back to the counter and picked up another piece of apple, then carried it into the laundry room and set it on the floor.

When she turned, M.P. already had turned and was moving toward her with what Jane considered quite a bit of speed for a tortoise. Jane chuckled. "Guess you like apple." She considered the animal. "You're smarter than you look, do you know that?" Chuckling again, she returned to the kitchen, firmly closing the door to the laundry room behind her.

Chapter 🐢 Eight

A lice planned for her ANGELs to make autumn greeting cards at their next meeting on Wednesday evening, so on Tuesday afternoon, she went downtown for construction paper, glitter glue pens and stickers. The cards would be sent to members of the church and community who were ailing.

It was a beautiful, moderately warm autumn day. Much warmer, in fact, than the day they had found M.P. Alice decided to walk into town. Wearing a light jacket over her jeans and T-shirt, she made short work of the walk to Fred's Hardware, where she located a package of construction paper as well as some strips of seasonal stickers in the section where the children's toys were stocked.

Approaching the counter, she said, "Good afternoon, Fred. It's a beautiful day outside."

"I know." The sandy-haired store owner grimaced. "I had a few jobs to do this morning, so I was out for a while, but I've been stuck in here all afternoon." He smiled. "Fortunately, you are just one of a steady stream of visitors to stop in, so I haven't minded all that much."

Alice smiled. Fred Humbert was one of her favorite people in town. He was unfailingly cheerful and friendly to everyone who crossed his path. "How's Vera? I haven't spoken to her in a few days. I need to call her and get back to a regular walking schedule. It seems as if the past week or so has been unusually busy."

"And you've got a turtle to take care of." Fred's eyes twinkled. "I wonder where in tarnation that thing came from."

"I can't imagine." Alice shook her head. "I feel so bad for whoever owns her. I'd be worried sick if my pet wandered away."

"Somebody's bound to turn up to take it soon," Fred assured her. "It's not every day you lose a turtle that big. Lloyd said it was bigger than the magazine basket in his office." He shook his head. "That must be one big animal."

"It is."

"Say, Alice, have you heard what people are saying about the Acorn Hill Battle?" Fred leaned on the counter.

Alice rolled her eyes. "No. I've been trying not to get drawn into that argument. Louise is positive that no such battle ever occurred, but she seems to be one lone voice getting lost in a crowd that's all excited about putting Acorn Hill on the Civil War map."

"Sounds as if she might be right about wanting to confirm the battle," Fred remarked. "Herb Hoffstritt was in this morning and showed me the text of that letter. It doesn't say one word about any battle."

"You saw the letter?"

"Yep." Fred nodded. "And I agree with Louise. The words *fracas* and *dustup* don't necessarily mean there was fighting here."

"Louise will be so relieved to hear that," Alice said. "I think she's felt like the smallest Who in Whoville, trying to get people to listen to her."

Fred scratched his chin. "Well, I can't guarantee they'll listen to me either, but until somebody proves to me that there was an honest-to-goodness battle between the Army of the Potomac and Jeff Davis' boys, I'm sticking to my theory."

After bidding Fred good-bye, Alice walked over to Sylvia's Buttons. While Sylvia Songer specialized in fabric craft items, she did stock glitter glue pens, largely because Alice and the ANGELs went through a couple of packs during every change of season when they made their cards.

On the way into the shop, Alice stopped to admire the scene Sylvia had created in her front window. It was a pumpkin patch, with a small section of wooden fence intertwined with grapevine. Several sizes of fabric-stuffed pumpkins in various shades of rust and orange were scattered artistically around. Looking closer, Alice saw that the pumpkins actually were oversize pincushions that had a number of pockets on their sides for items like small scissors, tape measures, fabric-marking pencils and safety pins. A heart-shaped leaf atop each was designed to hold needles. It was an extremely clever idea. Alice nearly was sorry she didn't sew.

"Hello, Alice, it's lovely to see you." Sylvia darted out from behind her worktable to greet her with a quick hug. "It's been ages, hasn't it? I was just telling Jane that very thing the other day." Jane and Sylvia, close in age, had formed a special friendship since Jane's return to Acorn Hill. They both were creative and loved to experiment with many kinds of crafts, a bond that had drawn them together initially and only had grown stronger over time.

"It's good to see you too." Alice grinned. "You do realize you have a crochet hook in your hair, right?"

"Oh bother." Sylvia groaned as she reached up and removed the article from her strawberry-blonde hair. She wore a denim skirt and blouse, and over it she had layered an apron in a bright candy-corn fabric with nearly a dozen pockets that Alice could see. "Thanks. I was wondering where I had laid that." She gestured down at herself. "I'm trying something new. I made this apron especially for my tools, so that I wouldn't always need to be hunting for them." She made a face. "Unfortunately, I can't seem to remember to put things in the pockets, so I wind up hunting for them anyway."

Alice laughed. "And I see your pins are still attached to your blouse." Sylvia nearly always had straight pins stuck in the front of whatever shirt or sweater she happened to be wearing. In addition, she occasionally stuck them into a small pincushion that she wore attached to her wrist.

"I bet you're here for glitter glue pens," said Sylvia, leading the way to a wall rack and taking down the items in question.

"I am." Alice smiled. "Someday I'm going to come in here and purchase something else just to see you do a double take."

As she paid for the pens, she said, "I suppose you've heard the speculation floating around about the battle that may or may not have taken place here."

"I have." Sylvia's eyes glowed with interest. "Isn't that just amazing? How could something that important get lost from our town's history?"

"Perhaps it didn't," Alice said. "The letter doesn't exactly mention anything about a battle."

"Well, you know how it is," Sylvia said confidently. "Back then, folks often understated important events."

Alice gave up. She didn't know any such thing. She just might have to join Louise and Jane on that research trip to the library.

∞

Jane took down the curtains in the living room that same afternoon so that she could send them out for dry cleaning. She was just beginning the task when their guest, Eva Quigley, returned from her day's work.

"Hello, Jane," Eva called enthusiastically as she spotted

Jane perched on a ladder carefully removing a valance. The material's subdued gold and creamy white stripes echoed the fabric of the throw pillows that graced the sofa.

"Hello, Eva." Jane knew from several days' experience that she did not need to ask Eva any questions about how her day had gone. Eva was more than happy to describe every detail of her workday, apparently under the impression that Jane found it riveting.

"Cleaning?" Eva didn't wait for an answer. "I think some aspects of running an inn would be enjoyable—interacting with the guests, for example—but I feel my time would be wasted on the more menial aspects of the operation."

Jane rolled her eyes, but since she was turned away from Eva, the expression went unnoticed. "I've found that it's possible to be thinking of one thing while doing something else," she said, trying not to sound defensive. "I come up with some of my best ideas while I'm cleaning."

"What about cooking?" Eva wanted to know.

Jane shook her head. "Generally, I need to pay attention to what I'm doing when I'm creating a meal." She emphasized the fact that her work was far more than a rote activity. "If I want a dish to turn out beautifully and if I want to give it a stellar presentation, I often need to time or count things. I can't be daydreaming."

"That makes sense," Eva conceded. "See? I'm too poor a cook to realize that. Your meals truly are an art form, Jane."

Slightly mollified, Jane turned and smiled at her. "Thank you."

"Would you like to play another game of Scrabble this week?" Eva asked.

Jane was taken aback. Did Eva really not realize how demoralizing and insulting her behavior had been during their last game? "Um, I don't believe I'll have time," Jane demurred. Then, the imp of inspiration she had been trying to ignore decided to speak up. "I did want to extend an invitation to you, though," she said.

Eva's eyebrows rose in interest and she smiled. "Yes?"

"I will be attending a quoits tournament a week from this coming Saturday," she explained. "It's the national championship and it's held in Pottstown, which is about an hour from here. I have never gone, and I thought perhaps you might enjoy it as well."

"Quoits?" Eva's forehead wrinkled. "I've never heard of it. What is it?"

"Really? It could make a valuable Scrabble entry," Jane said airily. "It's just a game, something like horseshoes. It's played more widely here in southeastern Pennsylvania than anywhere else."

"I would love to go along." Eva beamed. "It sounds interesting. Thank you for the invitation, Jane."

Jane smiled. "You're welcome."

"I'm going to go and change out of these clothes," Eva said. "And then, if you're sure I can't tempt you into a game, I'm going to take a walk."

"I'm sure," said Jane. "I need to start supper shortly. But thank you for the offer."

As Eva turned and drifted toward the stairs, Alice came into the living room. She gave Jane a surprisingly stern look, and then she spoke in a low tone. "Jane Howard, are you planning to hoodwink our guest into competing with you at quoits?"

Jane flushed. "Of course not, Alice." Then she felt compelled to add, "I would never hoodwink anyone. I simply invited her to attend the tournament with me. I think she would enjoy it."

"And you're not going to play?"

Jane felt her cheeks burn even hotter. "I'm not sure. Buck did mention that there's an opportunity for amateurs to try their hand at pitching quoits. But it would be difficult for Eva to do that, given that she's never even seen the game before."

Alice tapped her foot. "Why do I think I've just been given the runaround?"

Jane grinned. She had no intention of asking Eva to play a quoits match. Having seen the woman's competitive streak, Jane suspected that as soon as Eva realized the game had a winner and a loser, *she* would suggest it herself. "Oh, come on, Alice. Don't lecture me. It's just in fun. In fact, you're welcome to join us if you like."

Alice considered. "Perhaps. I'll have to check my work schedule and see what's going on around here before I commit."

"I figure I'll have time to serve breakfast before we have to leave," Jane said, "So it shouldn't interfere too much with our normal routine. I may have to ask Louise to make up the rooms, but I can prepare a casserole for dinner that she can heat up if I don't get home in time to start it."

Alice nodded. "That's a good idea." She started out of the room, then stopped and turned back. "Jane, M.P. appeared to have bits of apple crusted around her beak this afternoon, as if someone had been feeding her between meals. You wouldn't know anything about that, would you?"

Jane blushed again, for an entirely different reason. "She looked hungry," she explained. "I only gave her part of one apple."

"You're such a softie," Alice told her younger sister.

"I'm a softie?" Jane looked amazed. "May I remind you that I'm not the one who took in a giant tortoise in the first place."

Alice still was chuckling. "I thought you didn't like her."

"I like her," Jane protested. "I realized she has a lot of personality after I spent a little time around her. But that doesn't mean I'm any less worried about transferring some kind of turtle bacteria to food surfaces around here."

☯

Alice called Vera Humbert, and Vera agreed that they needed to get back to the thrice-weekly walks that they had gotten away from recently. Vera taught fifth grade at Acorn Hill Elementary and normally would be busy on a Wednesday morning, but she had parents' conferences that evening, and was taking comp time in the morning as a result. So the two friends met for an invigorating hour of exercise during which they covered many of the major thoroughfares in their little town.

Afterward, they decided to stop at the Coffee Shop for a cup of tea before heading to their respective homes.

As Alice pulled open the door, she caught sight of the daily menu that always was posted in the front window. "Oh no," she groaned. "Cherry pie is the special dessert of the day."

"That's bad?" Vera grinned. She knew that of all the delicious pies June Carter made, Alice's absolute favorite was the cherry pie.

"That's bad," Alice confirmed. "I realized the other day that my pants are getting just a tad tight in the waist. Time to stay away from cherry pie."

"The walking should help now that we intend to get back into a regular schedule," Vera pointed out.

Alice nodded. "That's what I am hoping. But eating pie is guaranteed to make it more difficult to take off pounds."

"True." Vera made a face. "I guess I'd better skip the pie today too. I wouldn't feel right eating it in front of you."

"Oh, don't let me stop you." Instantly, Alice was distressed that she might have spoiled a pleasurable experience for Vera.

But her friend laughed, her blue eyes twinkling. "Oh, Alice, I was teasing you." She patted her generous hips. "I had no intention of eating a piece of pie this morning. If you hadn't called me yesterday, I had intended to call you this morning."

"Are you sure?"

"Positive." Vera pushed her gently into the Coffee Shop. "Let's get a cup of tea and catch up on all the latest gossip. It's not as good as pie, but it's comforting."

Alice laughed as she went ahead of Vera into the homey restaurant. It was a busy time of the morning and all of the silver-trimmed red booths were occupied, but the two women found a table for two by the window. As they slid into their chairs, Hope Collins came by.

"Hi, Alice. Hi, Vera. You gals having pie and something hot to drink?" The waitress paused, though she had her hands full of breakfast platters for another table.

"Scratch the pie and just make it tea for both of us," Vera told her.

"Dieting again?" Hope asked with a grin. "Good luck. I'll be back with that tea in a sec."

As Hope turned away, someone called out to them. "Hello, ladies." The speaker was Henry Ley, the associate pastor at Grace Chapel. He came to stand beside their table, smiling broadly.

"Hello, Henry. Would you like to join us?" Alice invited.

"Th-thank you for the offer," he said, "but I must be on my w-w-way. I have several home visitations to make this morning."

"Is anyone ill?" Vera asked.

Henry shook his head. "No. I'm visiting the usual 'suspects.'" He chuckled at his own wit. "Hey, have you two heard about the r-reenactment?"

"Reenactment?" The women spoke the word in unison.

"Of the battle," Henry said. "R-r-ronald Simpson told

Hope that part of the commemorative ceremony they're planning will be a reenactment of the Battle of Acorn Hill." His eyes gleamed behind the lenses of his glasses. "I'm hoping to be able to participate."

Alice cleared her throat. "What, exactly, will you be reenacting?"

Henry shrugged. "I didn't hear that part. Hope might know. She waited on R-ronald and Florence earlier." He glanced at his watch. "Well, I must be off. You two have a lovely day."

After Henry's departure, Alice and Vera were silent for several moments. Finally, Vera said, "I hadn't heard that they confirmed the fighting of any battle."

"As far as I know, no one has," Alice told her

Vera's eyebrows shot up. "How do you reenact something that might never have happened?"

Alice shrugged and shook her head. "I have no earthly idea. But here comes Hope with the tea. Let's ask her."

"Hope," said Vera as the waitress brought their tea, cream and sugar, "can you tell us what Florence and Ronald were talking about earlier this morning? Henry says they're planning a reenactment of some sort."

Hope nodded. "Oh yes. Florence is checking with the historical society to see how we might find a quantity of Union and Confederate troop uniforms."

Alice was flabbergasted. "Based on what evidence?"

Hope leaned forward. "Well, Florence keeps talking about her ancestor who fought in the Battle of Acorn Hill, but just between us, I don't think she has a clue what went on," she added. "I've seen a copy of that letter Mr. Hoffstritt brought by the library, and it doesn't say word one about any battle."

Alice nodded. "That's exactly what Louise has been saying."

"And Fred agrees," Vera put in.

One of Ethel's closest sidekicks, Clara Horn, came stumping over to their table. She apparently had been listening in, because she announced, "Lloyd told me this morning that he wants to be a Union officer."

"I'm going to be a Johnny Reb," proclaimed Sherman Marlowe, an auctioneer from the community. "My great-granddaddy fought with a regiment out of Virginia."

"But Sherman, that would mean you support secession," said Oscar Billings. Oscar and his wife Nanette were members of the Grace Chapel congregation.

"I don't, and wouldn't have supported slavery." Sherman normally was the gentlest and kindest of souls, but he sounded distinctly put out.

"Well, I think it would be just plain wrong to be a Confederate," Oscar decreed. "Give me Union blue any day."

At that, a stranger at the counter turned and glowered at Oscar.

Hank Young, a recent college grad who seemed to know everything there was to know about computers, swiveled his chair around from the table behind Vera's seat. "We should create a Web site about the battle."

"Why?" asked Hope. "I don't think anyone in this town really wants to encourage too much tourism, and that is what we would get if we became a historic battlefield site. Look at Gettysburg and Antietam."

Alice glanced at Vera, who rolled her eyes and inclined her head toward the door. Alice nodded, and as one, the two women rose.

"Excuse us," Vera said. "We have some things we need to get done. You all have a wonderful day."

"Yes, do," Alice added, placing money on the table to cover the drinks and a tip for Hope.

A chorus of good-byes followed them as they hastily exited the restaurant. They stopped for a moment on the sidewalk. Alice stared silently at Vera, her hand to her mouth.

"A Web site?" Vera said.

"Like Gettysburg?" Alice added incredulously. "I seem to recall Gettysburg's being a well-documented battle that lasted *three days.*"

"Unlike the fictional Battle of Acorn Hill, which appears to be well-documented only in the minds of some of its starry-eyed residents." Vera clapped a hand over her mouth, as Alice had done earlier. Her face was red and she snorted with laughter. "I thought that Oscar and Sherman might get into a scuffle right there in the Coffee Shop." She broke into fresh hilarity.

"Let's go our separate ways. Their feelings might be hurt if they see us laughing," Alice urged.

Vera nodded in agreement and waved as she crossed the street to the hardware store.

Halfway down Chapel Road, heading for the inn, Alice succumbed to an irresistible urge to giggle. *Just wait until Louise hears this.*

Chapter 🐢 Nine

L ate in the afternoon, Jane walked into the laundry room, loaded down with a basket of sheets and towels. A couple on a second honeymoon would be arriving tomorrow, and she had put their room in spotless condition.

Holding the basket on one hip, she opened the washer and adjusted the dials. Once the load had begun to wash, she took a step backward and froze as she felt something large directly behind her heel. Whirling, she saw that Alice's tortoise had followed her across the room.

"You scared me to death, M.P.," she informed her. Then she decided it was a bad sign that she was beginning to address it by name. "You're a reptile," she told the attentive creature. "I am not getting attached to you."

Sidestepping, she marched around the tortoise and took the ironing board down from its hook on the wall. She needed to touch up a cotton blouse she wanted to wear later. As she dialed the iron to the proper temperature, she moved one foot a slight bit backward and felt a solid thunk as her heel struck the tortoise's shell again.

Exasperated, Jane turned around and knelt. "Stop following me," she said.

The tortoise had become accustomed to her movements,

apparently, because it seemed quite at ease with her. It stared up at her with what she was sure was another hopeful expression. For a long moment, the two took each other's measure.

Finally, Jane sighed and rose. "All right, you win." She headed for the kitchen, where she opened the refrigerator and pulled a small carrot from the hydrator. After rinsing it under the tap, she returned to the laundry, muttering to herself. "How ridiculous am I, losing a staring contest with a tortoise?"

She knelt again and offered the carrot to M.P. "Here. Will this make you happy?" Gently she placed the vegetable on the floor and watched as the animal craned her neck and took an impressive bite. Jane's heart softened as she realized how dependent the poor thing was on the kindness of strangers. "Enjoy your carrot," she told M.P. "And this time, I'm coming back to wipe your face so Alice doesn't scold me for feeding you between meals."

She returned to the kitchen, shutting the door to the laundry room, while the iron heated to the temperature she wanted. For dinner, she planned to serve pulled pork in gravy over fresh buns. She had placed the pork in the slow cooker early that morning, and as she removed the lid and stirred it, she inhaled appreciatively. She had done a great job, if she might say so herself.

Setting the spoon in a rest that lay beside the slow cooker on the butcher block countertop, she went to the refrigerator. She and Louise had made applesauce one day recently while Alice was working, and although most of it had been frozen in preparation for winter, Jane had reserved enough for a meal or two. Pink and very lightly seasoned, it made an excellent companion to the pork as did fresh lemon-garlic broccoli spears.

She turned from the counter and once again came face to face with Alice's lumbering reptile.

In her kitchen!

"Alice," she called, uncaring that her voice sounded a bit more strident than usual. "Come get your friend."

The sound of feet rushing through the hallway was followed quickly by Alice's banging through the hall door. "What's wrong?" she asked breathlessly.

Jane merely pointed. As Jane moved across the black-and-white checkerboard tile floor, the tortoise slowly turned and hauled its bulk in her direction.

Alice's eyebrows rose. "Why did you let her in the kitchen if you didn't want her here?"

"I didn't let her in," Jane said indignantly while she rinsed spinach for a salad. "She followed me. The catch on that door is not working properly and I suppose when she bumped at it, it opened."

"It's really quite flattering that she's seeking you out," Alice remarked with a twinkle in her eye. "Must be all those treats you're feeding her."

"Past tense," Jane said succinctly, drying her damp hands on a red dish towel. "No more treats from me." She looked down at the tortoise and waved a wooden spoon for emphasis. "And that's a promise."

M.P. just stared up at Jane as if she was certain another treat was forthcoming.

Alice snickered as she stepped over and gripped each side of the tortoise's shell. "Come on, my friend. Time to go back to your room. You're not welcome here."

Jane followed as Alice lifted the tortoise and carried it back to the laundry room. "Seriously, Alice, I know I asked for that by feeding her, but we simply cannot have her wandering into the kitchen. We could get in real trouble if the Board of Health found out we have a giant reptile wandering around the inn."

Alice set down the tortoise and returned to the kitchen with Jane close by. She vanished into the pantry for a moment, although Jane could hear her voice as she said, "Let me get out a screwdriver. I'm pretty sure I can fix that door. Then we shouldn't have any more escape issues."

"As long as we *all* remember to close the door," Jane said.

"Close what door?" Louise entered the kitchen from the hall.

Jane briefly explained the incident to Louise while Alice knelt in front of the door and used the screwdriver to adjust the catch hardware.

"I think that should help," Alice said, testing the door several times and hearing the satisfying click as it caught and held.

"Thank you," said Jane with relief. She stirred the pork one more time. "I believe this is ready. Let's eat."

Louise washed her hands at the sink while Alice headed to the hallway powder room to do the same. Then the sisters took their seats at the maple-topped table. Jane had set it with everyday dishware on cheerful paprika-colored placemats that matched the paint on the cabinets.

Alice drew her napkin into her lap. She led the sisters in a short grace. "Dear Heavenly Father, we thank You for the beauty of this day and for the bounty You have provided. Provide food, also, for those who have none, and let us be ever-mindful of their needs. Amen."

After the prayer, Jane picked up the basket of biscuits and handed it to Louise, who was seated at her left. Alice then began passing the serving dishes around the table.

"You will never believe what happened to Vera and me this morning," Alice began. She was eager to tell her sisters about the scene in the Coffee Shop. "What a trip—"

"Oh, don't tell me one of you fell," Louise said, somewhat alarmed. "Diana Zale's grandmother tripped on her own front walk last week. She broke her nose and blackened both her eyes." Diana was one of Louise's best piano students.

"No," said Alice. "We—"

"And Aunt Ethel told me that Irina Stonehouse fell right outside her door a month ago and knocked out two teeth." The Stonehouses were residents of the Three Seasons Retirement Home on the outskirts of Acorn Hill. "Poor Irwin doesn't handle blood very well, and when he saw her face, he passed out and banged his head. They called an ambulance and took both of them to the hospital. I believe they were treated and released."

"That's terrible," Jane said. "Sounds like they're lucky they weren't hurt worse. I hear so many stories about folks breaking hips, collarbones—"

"No one fell, for goodness sake!" Alice broke in. "We stopped at the Coffee Shop and nearly got caught in the middle of an argument over who was going to portray Union and Confederate soldiers in the reenactment." She raised her hands and made quote gestures as she said the last word.

Louise froze. "The *what*? Oh this is terrible! I never thought Florence would mention that ridiculous idea publicly until we had traced the source of the story."

"You must be kidding." Jane said to Alice. She leaned forward. "Tell us everything."

Alice recounted her adventure as best she could, trying hard to recall all the details of the bizarre conversation she and Vera had witnessed.

Jane was laughing by the time Alice finished. "I can't believe people are talking about making Acorn Hill a historic site like Gettysburg."

"*I* can't believe Lloyd isn't putting a stop to this," Louise said indignantly. Clearly, there was nothing funny about it in her eyes. "He's usually so . . . so sane."

Jane chuckled. "Yes, but you know how he is about genealogy and historical issues. I can see him getting a little offtrack about something like this."

"A little?" Louise said in a huffy tone. "Practically everyone in town seems willing to invent an entire historical incident. That's more than a little offtrack."

"Fred and Vera think it's out of control too," Alice volunteered, recalling her separate conversations recently with each of the Humberts. "But Sylvia seemed willing to believe it really might have happened."

"We need to get to the library," Louise said, "and begin going through everything we can find from the Civil War era. What are your schedules like tomorrow?"

∞

Alice had to work on Thursday, but Jane had agreed to go with Louise to the library to try to find any information about the old Hoffstritt letter's contents. So after Jane gave Eva her bottle of water for the day and they had cleaned up the remnants of breakfast, the two sisters walked to Acorn Avenue and on to the public library.

"So explain to me what we are looking for and how you plan to attack this search," Jane asked her elder sister as they walked along.

Louise sighed. "I wish I knew. I suppose I shall ask Nia to direct us to the best sources, and then we'll begin looking for any materials or records from the time period in question. The other thing we should look for is a record of any commemorative events to see if there's some mention of anything pertaining to the Civil War."

"Oh, that's a good idea," Jane said. "Those often highlight our local history."

At the library, they found that Nia had run to the bank to make a deposit, and Malinda, the assistant librarian, was on duty at the circulation desk.

"Hello, Mrs. Smith and Ms. Howard." She smiled as they came through the door.

"Hello, Malinda," said both Louise and Jane.

"Are you looking for a good read today?" asked the young librarian.

"I wish I were," Louise said. "But no, today we would like to do some historical research."

"The section for history is right that way." She gestured toward an aisle behind the desk. There is a copier in that area, and you can make duplicates of things that interest you."

"Thank you."

Louise turned away but Jane stopped. "You must have heard the recent rumors about a Civil War battle that happened in or near Acorn Hill," Jane said. "We're trying to find materials that either support or disprove that the event occurred."

"I've heard." The young woman nodded, her eyes dancing. "My mother thinks it's the silliest thing she's ever been told."

"As do we," Louise assured her.

"I'm sorry, but I'm not aware of any information that would clarify it." She raised her hands helplessly. "Well, either way, I hope you find something. It would be nice to know for sure." Malinda turned back to her desk computer as Louise and Jane walked through the fiction area toward the back of the library.

As they reached their destination, Louise stopped so suddenly that Jane nearly plowed into her.

"What's wrong?" Jane asked.

Louise heaved a sigh. "This is going to be like looking for the proverbial needle in a haystack. In short, impossible."

"Nothing's impossible," Jane said stoutly.

"But I don't even know where to start," Louise said, looking around at the shelves, no doubt imagining the plethora of printed information they would have to go through.

"Where's a search engine when you need one?" Jane asked lightly, making her sister smile just a bit. "This won't be so bad, Louise. There are two of us. Let's start systematically looking through the books and files to see which ones might contain information of interest to us."

Louise perked up, looking more like her normally calm, efficient self. "You're right, Jane. I'm sorry I got discouraged."

"I'll forgive you this time, Louie." Jane grinned and winked, and Louise returned a nod to acknowledge the pet name that her sister had used. They had brought along a small satchel with yellow legal pads and pens, and Louise unpacked two of each and laid them out on the table.

Jane shucked off her jacket and hung it over the back of a chair, and Louise did the same. "I'll start at this end," Jane said, indicating the bookshelves. It looks like there are a lot of census and military enlistment records here. I don't know if those would be helpful or not."

"Probably not," Louise said, "except possibly to tell us which Acorn Hill residents fought in the war. Do they give birth and death dates, and have they recorded where the death occurred?"

Jane took an oversize tome to the table and gently turned some of the pages. "No," she reported. "The military ones only have dates of enlistment and discharge and the circumstances—oh, look, here's one that was dishonorably discharged. I wonder what he did."

"We need *less* to research, not more," Louise joked as Jane replaced the large book in its spot. "I'll start over here."

"What's over here?" Jane asked as she perused the shelves to see what came next after the records.

"These all are books written by local people. Local being defined as from Acorn Hill, from the towns around us, from the county and even from the state. Here's one on the surveying of the Mason-Dixon Line."

"Wait, didn't they finish that in 1760 something?" Jane asked. "Is the book that old?"

"Seventeen sixty-seven," Louise answered. "But the book itself wasn't written until 1915."

"Is there anything written in the 1860s?" Jane wanted to know.

"I don't know. I'm not quite sure how they're shelved. It could be by category, by historical date, or by author."

"If the information we need is arranged according to the Dewey Decimal System," Jane said, "it's probably catalogued in the 900s, but I don't know exactly where."

Louise turned around to stare at Jane. "Now *that's* trivia. Where on earth did you learn that?"

Jane shrugged. "I had to write a paper on it years ago when I was in school. I guess it stuck because I find it useful when I visit the library."

Louise chuckled. "There aren't many people who know anything more about the Dewey Decimal System than its name and that it's used to catalog books."

"That's me. One in a million." Jane laughed aloud.

Silence fell in the library as the sisters concentrated on their initial survey. As the clock drew closer and closer to noon and the work became wearisome, Louise said, "I don't know about you, but my stomach is telling me it's time for a lunch break."

"Sounds good," Jane said. "Anything in particular you would like? I made chicken-corn soup yesterday, and I have some of those biscuits left over from supper last night."

"Sounds delicious. Any more applesauce?" Louise asked hopefully.

Jane laughed. "There is. I'm beginning to think we should have made more than we did."

The two sisters walked back to the inn and quickly assembled their lunch. Jane opened the door to the laundry room, saying to Louise, "I feel guilty leaving that tortoise in here alone all day. I'm just going to say hello so she knows we're back."

Louise began to chuckle as she took her seat. "Do you realize what you just said? You're greeting a tortoise."

Jane looked sheepish. "If you tell Alice, I swear I won't lift another finger to help you."

"Tell Alice what?" Louise assumed an exaggerated innocent expression, making Jane laugh aloud.

Jane stuck her head into the laundry room. "She looks content," she reported. "She's lying on that heat pad with the light shining down on her." She paused. "Do reptiles sweat? I'd be roasting with all that warmth aimed at me."

"You're warm-blooded, which I believe changes the equation a bit," Louise reminded her dryly. "And I have no idea whether or not reptiles perspire. That piece of trivia has, thankfully, never crossed my path."

Wendell chose that moment to stroll into the kitchen. He made a beeline for the door to the laundry room, then sat in front of it. With a loud meow, he turned and looked at them over his shoulder.

Louise's eyebrows rose. "What does he want?"

Jane shrugged. "I don't know. I wasn't here for treat time, so perhaps that's it." She went to the pantry door and turned the knob, leaving the door ajar. "Here you go, boy." She had taught him to fetch his treat packets himself and usually, if the door to the pantry was open, he was quick to demonstrate his trick.

Wendell glanced at the door, then ignored it, sitting with his face tilted up at the laundry doorknob.

"I can't believe he's not hungry," Jane said in disbelief. "He's *always* hungry."

Wendell meowed again. Then he raised one paw and scratched at the door.

Jane turned and eyed Wendell before she walked back to the door and opened it. "Snoop. You just want to see if that tortoise is still in your territory."

The moment the door opened, Wendell slid through the entrance. His tail was held almost straight upright and its black tip waved this way and that, reminding Jane of a submarine's periscope. As Jane watched, he trotted right over to M.P. and rubbed himself against the side of her shell. The tortoise hissed and withdrew a little, but she quickly came back out of her shell as she recognized the creature beside her.

Jane was astonished. "He likes her," she reported to Louise. She grew even more amazed as she watched Wendell turn in several circles and then lower himself into a satisfied curl right at her side. "You have to see this," Jane called to Louise in a stage-whisper. "Come here."

Louise set aside her napkin and rose. Going to Jane's side, she looked into the laundry room and did a double take. "That's unbelievable."

"I know. I'm going to get a camera, or Alice will never believe us." Jane hurried away, remembering that there was a small digital camera on a shelf behind the reception desk.

Louise leaned against the doorjamb and regarded the two animals. "Aren't you the surprising one?" she murmured to Wendell. The cat merely regarded her through sleepy eyes. He was purring so loudly Louise could hear him clearly even from a distance. "Do you just like the heat or is it the company you're keeping?"

Jane returned and snapped several photos. "I can't shut the door and trap him there," she said with a troubled frown. "But I can't leave the door open or we might have a tortoise greeting our guests."

Louise smiled. "Why don't we try laying a folding chair across the doorway?" she suggested. "We could set something behind it to anchor it so Little Miss Curiosity couldn't push it out of the way."

"Do you think she would do that?" Jane asked. Clearly, the idea had not occurred to her.

"I think she *could* do that," Louise said. "Whether or not she would, she certainly is capable of moving a single chair, I'd think."

Jane hurried to the pantry and returned with one of the four folding chairs kept in there. The two sisters propped the chair on its side against the door. The space between the seat and the chair back was not large enough for the tortoise to get through, although Wendell would have no trouble if he wasn't averse to jumping over it. Jane found two boxes full of old magazines in the basement that kept the chair in place very nicely.

"There," she said. "Now those two can bond all they like, and Wendell can still get back into the house when he wants."

Chapter 🐢 Ten

Over lunch, Louise and Jane decided to work until three-thirty that afternoon. Louise had students coming for piano lessons beginning at 4:00 PM and Jane needed to start working on dinner. So after a hurried meal, they returned to the library about one o'clock.

This time, Nia was at the desk.

Nia wore a jacket and matching skirt in a soft shade of gray, and her long dark hair was braided and wound tightly at the back of her head. She smiled when she heard what they were doing. "I called the historical society in Potterston," she told the sisters, "I have great confidence in the people there, but the next day they called to say they could find no record of any kind of battle."

"Oh no," groaned Jane. "That puts the ball back in our court."

Louise nodded. "I'm afraid so." She inclined her head toward the rear of the library. "We need to get back to work."

"Have a good time," Nia called after them in a cheerful voice.

"A good time?" Louise muttered under her breath. "Is she trying to be funny?"

"No," Jane said. "I'm sure that Nia thinks of research as fun."

They reached their spot, and Jane took off her jacket once again, draping it over a chair as before. Louise did the same with the sweater she wore, and both women figuratively rolled up their sleeves and went back to their methodical search.

Half an hour later, a youthful voice piped up behind them, "Hello. Would you like some help?"

"We'd love some." Jane's voice was muffled because she had been leaning into a lower cabinet drawer. Leaning back, she sat on her heels and blew hair out of her eyes.

"I'm off this afternoon, and I'd be happy to help," the assistant librarian said.

Louise clasped her hands together. "Oh, Malinda, that's a generous offer. Are you sure you want to spend your free time cooped up in here with two ladies twice your age?"

"Or more," added Jane cheekily, grinning at Louise.

"Or more," Louise agreed, taking no offense at Jane's wry jest.

"I think it will be interesting," Malinda said. "I've been meaning to become better acquainted with this section, and you have given me the perfect excuse. Tell me what you want me to do."

Louise eagerly took Malinda through their search before leaving her at a set of bookshelves. She barely had gotten back to work when another voice called out softly.

"Need an extra pair of hands?" Rev. Thompson asked.

"Hi, Kenneth. How did you know we were here?" Jane asked.

"Nia might have mentioned it," he replied, his hazel eyes twinkling. "I'm taking a brain break from writing this week's sermon. The distraction will be good for me."

"A brain break?"

"Yes. When the sermon isn't going well, my brain starts moving in circles and I feel as if I'm just sitting there spinning my wheels. So God and I had a little discussion, and He suggested I take a break."

"All right," said Louise. "Let's have your brain do something different." And she promptly put him to work as well.

∞

Alice got home shortly after four that afternoon. She went into the kitchen through the back door and stopped, studying the odd barricade at the entrance to the laundry.

"Hi. We've got her corralled," Jane called.

Alice looked at the tortoise, which appeared to be asleep under her lamp. She smiled at the cozy scene, then removed her jacket, and hung it on one of the hooks near the back door.

Jane was at the counter, vigorously stirring something in a bowl. Alice could smell onion and garlic, and indeed, Jane's eyes were watering as if she had recently chopped onion.

"How was work?" Jane asked.

Alice smiled. "Fine. I worked in obstetrics today, so I got to cuddle a few babies." She pointed toward Jane's barrier. "I take it that is a tortoise escape preventative?"

Jane nodded. "You take correctly, and it seems to be working."

"It's nice of you to be concerned about her getting lonely," Alice said.

Jane looked startled. Then she stopped stirring and laughed. "I admit I did feel a little bad when she was confined out there all alone, but that's not why I did it. Wendell seems to have taken a shine to her. Either that or he just likes the warmth from the light and the pad. I don't know which."

Alice chuckled. "I understand now. Wendell can walk right in and out, but our adventurous reptilian friend won't fit through there."

"Exactly."

"Excellent idea, Jane. I wish I had been here to see them bonding."

"I did take a picture," Jane admitted. "So you'll get to see it. Louise and I were quite surprised."

Mention of their elder sister made Alice ask, "Is Louise giving lessons now?"

Jane nodded. "Until five-thirty. So we can eat supper shortly after that. Say, five-forty-five?"

"Works for me. I'll be ready for a meal by then."

"Do you need a snack? After all, you did work all day."

"I'll just have one of these pears. That will hold me off." Alice walked to a fruit basket in the corner of the counter. "Did the new guests arrive?" she asked as she selected her pear.

Jane shook her head as she scraped the mix in her bowl into a pot gently simmering atop the stove. "No, but I expect them any minute. And Eva is back from work, but only for a bit. I believe she's dining in Potterston with some friends this evening."

"Did she get her water this morning?" Alice asked with a sly smile.

"Of course," Jane said, sticking her tongue out at her sister. "I am the soul of professionalism. If I say I'll do something for a guest, I will do it."

"Are you still planning to take her to that tournament next weekend?"

"Yes, but I haven't asked her to play." Jane wanted to make that clear. "I'm not even going to mention competing to her."

"Promise?"

"I promise," said Jane. "Am I allowed to discuss it if she brings it up?

Alice rolled her eyes. "So that's the plan. You're going to manipulate her into—"

"Are you going to come along with us?" Jane interrupted.

"I don't believe so," Alice declined. "I was asked to work the day shift the Saturday after this coming one."

"Too bad. I think you would have enjoyed it."

"I'm sure I would have." Alice headed for the door to the hall. "I need to get out of these scrubs and clean up." She chuckled. "I smell like baby oil, but I don't even care. It was worth it to be able to snuggle those babies."

∞

The incoming guests were late. They still had not showed up when Jane put supper on the table at a quarter to six. Finally, shortly before seven, the couple who held the reservation arrived.

Alice had gone upstairs to gather a load of her own laundry, and Louise was playing the piano. She had left the doors to the parlor open, so that the haunting strains of a melancholy piece floated through the hallway. She stopped when she heard the voices in the hall.

Jane was on her way to the front desk, but she stopped and said, "Gracious, Louise, that was beautiful, but it sounded so sad. What was it?"

"It's 'Sonata in F sharp minor,' by Jan Ladislav Dussek, and you are absolutely right about the sadness. It was a tribute to Prince Louis Ferdinand of Prussia, a personal friend of the composer, who was killed in battle."

"Well, I feel for both men, but unless you want our guests to end up in tears, maybe you should try some ragtime instead, Louie."

Louise smiled as she walked to the desk with Jane. "You can be certain that I will take that under consideration, dear." Then she called out in a welcoming tone, "Hello, folks. Are you the Krupkes?"

"We are, indeed," the man replied. He had a thick accent that sounded Eastern European to Louise. He offered a hand. "My name is Anton and this is my wife, Yelena." The woman also extended her hand.

"Thank you for holding our room. I apologize for our

late arrival." She was as tiny and petite as her husband was tall and broad. The size difference was so great as to be almost amusing.

Jane shook hands with each of them, introducing herself, as did Louise.

"Welcome to Grace Chapel Inn," Jane said. She slipped behind the desk and consulted the book. "We're going to put you in the Garden Room, which I believe you'll find very comfortable."

"Oh, I'm sure it will be lovely if it's as well cared for as the rest of this magnificent place," Yelena said. Her English also carried a trace of an accent but far less than her husband's.

Jane efficiently went through the information she shared with all new guests and confirmed Mr. Krupke's credit card. Last, she handed them a list of all the local eateries in Acorn Hill and the surrounding towns. Some time before, she had found that she was repeating the same information regarding meals to so many guests that this was the easier thing to do.

Then Louise stepped forward. "I will be happy to show you to your room." She took the key that Jane handed her and marched toward the stairs, guests in tow.

When Louise returned a few moments later, Jane said, "Very impressive, the way you remembered their names without any sneak peeks at the reservation book. How did you do that?"

Louise began to laugh. "It's a music geek thing. In the musical *West Side Story*, there's a character featured in a song. His name is Officer Krupke." She sang a few bars from the song.

This time when she laughed, Jane laughed with her.

∽

Another group of guests, a family with two children, was expected on Friday afternoon. The Osbournes arrived promptly at three and were shown to the two bedrooms that shared a connecting bath across the back of the house, the Sunrise Room and the Symphony Room. The mother told Jane that they were from Rhode Island and were in the area for the funeral of her husband's father. The two children looked as if they might be young teens, and their faces were drawn and unhappy. Jane suspected that this loss of their grandfather might be their first experience with losing someone they loved, and she wished that they could be spared the pain.

There were few smiles among the little group, and Jane felt terrible for them as she escorted them to their room. Surely there was something she could do to lighten their heavy hearts and take their minds off their grief, if only for a short while.

Then inspiration struck, and she extended an invitation for tea.

"Oh," said Mrs. Osbourne, "that's very kind of you but we're on a tight budget and—"

"This will be our treat," Jane replied. "Everyone needs a little TLC sometimes."

The woman's eyes welled with tears. "So true."

"Thank you," said her husband. "You're very kind."

"You must come too," Jane informed the children. "I have something you'll enjoy seeing." She addressed the parents again. "Why don't you meet me in the dining room as soon as you are settled in?"

Jane headed down to the kitchen and just had finished heating water and setting homemade cookies on a plate when Alice came in. Quickly, she told Alice about the Osbournes and her invitation.

Alice smiled and wrapped her arm around Jane's shoulders for a brief hug. "That's a thoughtful thing to do," she said.

"I was hoping," Jane said tentatively, "that I could show M.P. to the kids. Would you mind?"

"Of course not," Alice said. She grinned. "I suspect if you move that barricade in front of the laundry room and open the dining room door, M.P. would introduce herself."

"I think not," Jane said, but she was chuckling as she arranged a tea tray and carried it into the dining room.

The Osbourne family entered moments later. "What a lovely house this is," Mrs. Osbourne said. "Is this a retirement venture?"

"Not exactly," Jane shook her head. "This was our family home. After our father passed away, we thought it would be fitting to open a bed-and-breakfast. And I have to say it has lived up to our expectations. We meet all manner of interesting people."

While the children attacked the cookie plate with gusto, Jane entertained their parents with stories of some of their more unusual guest experiences. When everyone had partaken of the fare, she turned to the boy and girl. "We have a very unusual guest right now. I think you would enjoy meeting her." She rose and beckoned to all. "Follow me."

The entire family trailed behind Jane as she led them through the kitchen. Mrs. Osbourne smiled when she saw the barricade at the entrance to the laundry room. "A puppy?" she guessed.

Jane shook her head. "Oh no, nothing that commonplace." She grinned as she moved the barrier aside. "Ladies and gentlemen," she said with a flourish, "Meet M.P., the African spurred tortoise."

The children surged forward with shining eyes.

"Cool!" the boy pronounced. "That's one major turtle."

"Better not let my sister Alice hear you calling her a turtle." Jane had said that to at least a half-dozen people, she was sure. She laughed and began explaining the events that had transpired in the past two weeks, including the reason for the animal's odd name.

Jane was delighted when M.P. put on what was, for her,

quite a show for the Osbourne children. She crawled off her heat pad and trundled over to examine them when they sat on the floor. Alisha, the daughter, was wearing a red sweater and to Jane's surprise, M.P. tried to crawl right into Alisha's lap.

Jane was pulling the tortoise backward a few feet when Alice paused in the doorway.

"Tortoise-wrestling, Jane?" Alice inquired, winking at the visitors.

"Your tortoise seems to love Alisha," Jane panted. "This is my sister, Alice Howard," she told the Osbournes. "Alice, our guests, the Osbourne family."

Alice greeted the family and then turned to Alisha. "I'm sure you're quite lovable, dear," she said, chuckling, "but I suspect the reason she's so interested in you is that sweater. I've been doing some research on sulcatas and apparently they are attracted by the color red."

"She sees in color?" Mrs. Osbourne asked. "Gracious. I just assumed she was like a dog. You know, black-and-white vision."

"How do we know that's true?" her husband asked. "I always wondered who researched that. It's not as if the dogs themselves are going to tell us they can't see in color."

Everyone laughed at that.

Alice went to the kitchen and returned with a cabbage leaf so that the family could watch M.P. eat. "If there's anything she won't eat, we haven't found it yet," she explained as she laid pieces of the cabbage leaf in various spots around the laundry room.

"Why are you spreading them around?" asked Alisha.

Alice shrugged. "She needs all the exercise she can get," she explained. "In the wild, she would have to forage for her food, so spreading her food around the room is our way of making her forage."

"Yes," Jane added. "I've been trying to keep this floor extra clean because she will eat lint from the dryer, scraps of newspaper and anything else that gets dropped and overlooked. The other day I caught her about to taste a sock that I had dropped out of a laundry basket."

Mr. Osbourne shook his head. He and his wife had crouched down along with their children to observe the tortoise. "I can't imagine keeping one of these as a pet."

"Well," said Alice, "to be fair, they start out very small. She probably was only about the size of a tennis ball when she was sold initially. And it's rather shameful to note how pet store salespeople manage *not* to explain how big an animal will get as an adult. Even those cute little water turtles they used to sell when I was a child can grow to the size of a catcher's mitt."

"Which isn't going to fit in a tiny bowl with a plastic palm tree," Jane added, shaking her head.

Mrs. Osbourne gasped. "A *catcher's mitt*? See, James," she said, turning to her son. "I told you it wasn't a good idea when you tried to buy one of those. Where on earth would we have put it when it grew up?"

The boy's face grew scarlet. "I just wanted to save it," he said defensively. "It looked unhappy in that teeny little container."

"It was a noble thought," his father assured him. "But I'm glad we didn't buy it."

"While we were on vacation a few months ago," Mrs. Osbourne explained, "James saw someone selling tiny, red-eared slider turtles, and he was convinced we should buy one. I knew who would wind up taking care of it, though," she said with a knowing expression.

"Yes. Funny how that works." Alice smiled as she looked back at Mr. Osbourne.

"Will M.P. live very long?" Alisha asked.

"A wildlife expert told me that these tortoises can live eighty years," Alice said.

All four of the Osbournes looked surprised.

"That's *old*," said the boy.

Mrs. Osbourne rose from the floor. "Thank you," she said warmly to Jane and Alice, looking much more relaxed than she had half an hour earlier. "This was exactly what we needed."

Chapter 🐢 Eleven

Jane! Just the person I wanted to see," said Eva Quigley when she came in the door after dinner. "I can't wait for next weekend. I looked up quoits online and have been learning all kinds of fascinating things."

Jane was behind the counter using her computer to compare prices on some new curtains she was looking at for her room. "Oh?" she asked politely. "What have you found out?"

"It's different from horseshoes," Eva said. "The object of horseshoes is simply to get a 'ringer,' while the object of quoits is twofold. First, you want to try to pitch your quoit closer to the hob than anyone else. Second, you also want to play strategically, to try to block your opponent."

"Sounds fascinating," Jane commented, carefully not looking at Eva.

"Oh, it is," Eva continued. "The scoring sounds complicated. Players earn points for getting their quoit closest to the hob, for touching it or leaning against it, for getting a ringer and for getting more ringers on top of one ringer. If it touches the wooden box in any way or lands outside the box, it gets no points and has to be moved away from the pit. When a quoit lands upside down and—"

"Heavens!" Jane interrupted. "You have been studying. It would take me weeks to memorize all that."

"I have a near-perfect photographic memory," Eva said matter-of-factly. "If I read it once, I remember it. It's just one of my gifts, I suppose."

"An excellent one to have." And Jane was beginning to understand why a game like Scrabble had fit so well with Eva's strengths. She had been considering telling Eva about the quoits class for beginners with its subsequent competition, but now . . . now she was afraid that any advantage she had dredged up had evaporated in the face of Eva's enthusiastic pursuit of knowledge. "I bet you would be good at the game."

"No. I'm much better at 'thinking games' than 'doing games.'" For the first time since Jane had met her, Eva's cheerful façade slipped.

So Eva did not want to try to beat Jane at quoits. It was an unexpected stumbling block. Still, Jane could not imagine Eva's competitive spirit just sitting back and letting the parade go by. Jane felt sure that when they got to that tournament, Eva would decide to play. But if Eva were to try the game, Jane reassured herself, she lacked the practical pitching experience. Knowledge wasn't everything; Eva was beatable.

∞

By Saturday morning, Louise felt quite discouraged. Despite the help that Rev. Thompson, Malinda and Jane had provided, not one among them had come close to finding even a hint of information about any Acorn Hill battle during the Civil War.

She had her hair trimmed at the Clip 'n' Curl that morning, after which she stopped by the Coffee Shop for a cup of coffee. In truth, Louise was eager to hear the latest rumors swirling around about the unsung Battle of Acorn Hill.

She barely had gotten through the door when she was

hailed by June Carter. "Hey, Louise, what's the latest on this battle business?" June smiled at her. "And would you like a piece of key lime pie? I just made it this morning."

Louise groaned. "Oh, I shouldn't . . . but I will, along with a cup of coffee." She took a seat in a booth, placing her purse on the wide seat beside her. June soon came to the table with her coffee and pie. After setting it in front of Louise, June sat also. The shop was not busy, and Hope seemed to have a good handle on all the customers' needs.

"The latest on this silly battle talk . . ." Louise mused. "There really isn't much to tell. Jane and I, along with some additional help, scoured the library's historical resources, but we never found a single mention of any fighting. Not," she added dryly, "that a simple fact like that would stop all the talk of a reenactment."

June chuckled. "I know. I heard a couple of folks in here this morning dispensing advice on where to go to get the most authentic-looking Civil War costumes."

Louise rolled her eyes.

"But I also heard something more interesting." June sat forward. "Do you know Earl Padgett?"

Louise frowned thoughtfully. "The name doesn't ring a bell. Should I know him?"

June shrugged. "He's Francie Litmore's grandfather. He grew up in Acorn Hill but moved away for many years. After his wife passed away two years or so ago, Francie brought Earl to live with her."

"Francie Litmore? Is she the dispatcher at the police station? The one with the curly red hair?"

June nodded, smiling. "That hair is unforgettable, isn't it? All three of her kids have hair just like that too."

"Gracious." Louise shook her head. "There must be no way to miss them. That's for sure."

"Quite right." June glanced up as a patron came into the

shop, but when Hope hurried over to greet him, June turned her attention back to her conversation with Louise. "Francie brings Earl in here once or twice a week to eat so that he can talk to a couple of the buddies he's had from years ago.

Louise nodded, wondering where June was going with this. "So this Earl said something interesting?"

June smiled. "I thought so. Florence was here, and she didn't find it nearly as palatable."

Louise leaned forward. "Spill the beans, June."

June leaned forward too. "Earl perked up pretty fast when he heard all the talk about the battle that might have happened here. Only thing is, he said it was a bunch of baloney. He said he was 'dead certain' there hadn't been any Civil War battle here—but then he couldn't say why he was so certain."

"What do you mean?"

June's eyes held compassion. "I wonder if he isn't in the early stages of dementia. Some days he's pretty good, other days he really isn't quite right, if you know what I mean. I could tell he was frustrated that he couldn't recall the information he needed. When he's good, though, he's sharp as a tack. He'll remember that stuff eventually. Just wait and see."

"I do hope so," Louise said. "That would resolve a lot of problems, wouldn't it?"

Louise and June had a pleasant conversation while Louise savored the delicious key lime pie. Afterward, Louise rushed back to the inn. She intended to call Earl Padgett to see if his memory had come up with anything more about the Civil War era in Acorn Hill.

She hurried into the house and divested herself of her pocketbook and sweater. Then she made a beeline for the reservation desk, where the sisters kept a local telephone book.

Flipping through the tissue-thin pages, she came to the *P*'s and began to run her finger down the page. There was no listing for "Padgett," but she hadn't really expected there to be. Flipping back, she found one entry for "Litmore."

Picking up the telephone receiver, she carefully pushed the buttons for the unfamiliar number.

She heard the telephone ring once, then a second, third and fourth time. She was just about to give up when she heard a woman's voice say, "Hello?" in a harried tone.

"Mrs. Litmore?"

"This is she. Who is this?"

"My name is Louise Smith. I—"

"Oh my goodness! Mrs. Smith. Have your ears been burning? I was just saying to my husband last night that I was going to call you about piano lessons for my daughter Letitia."

"Oh." Louise was taken aback. "How old is your daughter?"

"She'll soon be eight. She wants to learn to play in a big way, and I've been putting her off for two years now, thinking it was just a phase and she would change her mind. Do you have any space available for a new student?"

Louise thought for a moment. "Could you bring her on Tuesdays at seven for a thirty-minute lesson? That's really the only time I have open right now."

"Tuesdays at seven would work. Oh thank you! Thank you! Letitia will be so thrilled."

Louise efficiently mentioned her fees, her absentee policy and the annual recital in which she insisted all her students participate. "I look forward to meeting her next Tuesday, then." And she meant it. Louise taught a great many students who only studied piano because their parents insisted on it. It always was a pleasure when a child genuinely wanted to play. Even if Letitia didn't have any particular gift for the keyboard, a willingness and desire to play would make their lessons much more enjoyable.

"Terrific!" There was a pause. "Oh, I'm sorry. I should have asked why you were calling, Mrs. Smith."

"Oh my stars! I almost forgot." Louise shook her head at herself. "I was hoping to speak to Mr. Padgett. Is that possible?"

"Grandpa?" Curiosity laced Francie's tone. "Sure. He's right here watching one of his programs on TV. Are you acquainted with him?"

"No, but I am hoping he can help with some information I'm seeking. I understand he grew up in Acorn Hill."

"He did, but I'm not sure he'll be much help." Francie's voice was troubled. "Gramps is getting . . . a little forgetful, Mrs. Smith. I'll let you talk to him, but I'll warn you that he gets agitated when he can't remember things."

"Oh." Louise had no wish to upset the old man. "If you don't think it's a good idea, I won't bother him."

"I wouldn't say it's not a good idea," Francie said hastily. "Let me get him to the phone. I can always calm him down again, if necessary. Truly, Mrs. Smith, there's no harm in talking to him."

"Thank you," Louise said. She heard Francie loudly talking to the old man, telling him there was a lady on the telephone who wanted to talk to him about the old days.

There was a scuffling sound and then some labored breathing. Finally, an old man's querulous voice said, "Hello?" Quite loudly.

"Hello, Mr. Padgett." Louise pitched her own voice at high volume. "My name is Louise Smith. My maiden name is Howard, and my father was Daniel Howard, who used to be the pastor of Grace Chapel."

"Daniel Howard, you say? I grew up here in Acorn Hill, y'know. I knew Daniel Howard. He was a couple of years older'n me. Nice boy. Grew up to be a fine man."

"Thank you," Louise said.

"Gone now, isn't he?" Mr. Padgett said. "I read it in the paper. My wife's gone now too, y'know. Just didn't wake up one morning. Miss the old girl somethin' terrible sometimes."

"I'm sure you do," Louise said, her throat suddenly aching. The naked longing in the man's voice made her think of her own beloved husband Eliot. Although her life was full and productive and extremely happy most of the time, occasionally she was overwhelmed by the memories of her married life and so lonely for the one man in the world who had understood her better than anyone else did. Even her sisters or her daughter Cynthia, as precious to her as they were, could not fill the void Eliot had left.

"Just so you know," the old man went on. "I ain't huntin' for a new woman."

Louise could hear Francie's scandalized, "*Grandpa!*" in the background. The old man's comment made her chuckle and lifted her spirits again. "I understand," she said. "I only want to ask you some questions, Mr. Padgett."

"Questions 'bout what?"

"When you were young and growing up here, do you ever remember anyone talking about the Civil War? Did you have ancestors, perhaps, who fought in it?"

The old man was silent for a moment. "The Civil War," he mumbled. "Was just talkin' about that in the Coffee Shop the other day. Some durned fool was trying to tell me there'd been a battle right here in Acorn Hill."

Florence's face flashed through Louise's mind, and she immediately banished the association between *Florence* and *fool*, thinking *Forgive me, Lord, for my unkind thoughts.* "So you don't believe there was one, sir?"

"Nope," he said immediately. "Don't believe it for a minute," he advised her. "There was somethin' . . . somethin' . . . aw, durn my memory. I remember someone talkin' about somethin' . . . You just give me time, girlie, and it'll come to me."

"I would appreciate it, Mr. Padgett, if you would contact me if you remember anything specific," Louise said, trying hard to mask her disappointment.

"I surely will," he said. "I know there was some kinda trouble. I seem to recall my own mother talkin' about her father mentioning it. My great-granddaddy fought for the Union, you know."

"I did not know that," Louise said. Her spirits rebounded once again. This was the first time she had spoken to anyone who had a direct link to the era, other than Herb Hoffstritt, who had discovered the letter that had started all the commotion. "I bet you heard some interesting stories from him when you were small."

"Aw, I never met him," Earl Padgett said. "He was dead and gone before I was born. My granddaddy was fourteen years old when his daddy died. Mostly I know about him from what my granddaddy said and from the letters."

"Your grandfather kept letters that his father wrote while he was a soldier?"

"Yup." The old man did not seem to notice how momentous Louise found this news.

"Do you still have the letters, Mr. Padgett?" Her heartbeat quickened.

Silence. "I got lots of letters," Earl said. "All stashed away in boxes somewhere, I guess."

"Lots of letters from your great-grandfather?"

"And from my wife," he said proudly. "I served in the Pacific Theater, you know."

Louise did not know. And she was pretty sure Mr. Padgett had forgotten the original topic of conversation.

"Mr. Padgett," she said, "I am very interested in finding your great-grandfather's letters from his Civil War service.

There might be something in there that tells us about whatever happened in Acorn Hill during that time."

"Nothin' happened in Acorn Hill," he said. "I already told you that." Louise could hear him say, "Here, take this," in a distant tone, and then Francie came back on the line. "Hello? Mrs. Smith?"

"Call me Louise," Louise said absently. "Is Mr. Padgett finished speaking with me?"

Francie chuckled. "I think so. He just headed off to his room. He'll watch a little TV and fall asleep until lunchtime. Did he give you any information for whatever you're hunting?"

"I'm trying to find documentation that proves whether or not there was any fighting around here during the Civil War," Louise said. "I imagine you've heard by now that people are saying there was a battle here."

Francie sighed. "I have. Seems like we'd know it if there had been."

"I agree. Your grandfather indicated that he recalls letters that were written by his great-grandfather while he was enlisted. He believes he has these letters packed away somewhere, if I understood him correctly."

"Oh, he's probably right," Francie said. "When I brought him back to Acorn Hill, we got a bunch of his things out of storage. There are at least three old trunks filled with family stuff. I think there's even a Civil War uniform worn by my great-great-grandfather. Would you like me to look for the letters you mentioned?"

Louise was astonished by the offer. "That would be wonderful. I would be happy to come and help you sort through things."

"Thank you," Francie said. "Tell you what. I'll take a look when I have a minute, and we can talk about it more when I bring Letitia for her lesson on Tuesday. Oh, I can't wait to tell her she's starting piano."

Louise laughed. "I hope she'll be as excited as you are."

"Oh, she will be," Francie predicted.

"Thank you for all your help," Louise said.

"No problem at all. See you Tuesday."

"Yes, I'll see you on Tuesday," Louise replied.

∽

Jane was in the garden digging up iris roots and separating them when Alice turned her small blue car into the driveway after a trip to the post office. Jane waved as Alice drove back to the parking lot.

Alice parked in her usual spot and climbed out of the car, walking behind the inn to where her sister was working. Jane had laid out the new, smaller clumps of iris roots. Index cards lay at intervals on the tarp. Picking up one card, Alice realized it displayed the name, height, color and whether the plant bloomed early, medium or later in the iris season, which typically fell in May.

"Goodness," Alice said, smiling. "You do like to be organized, don't you?"

Jane sat back on her heels and looked up at her sister. The organized gardener wore faded green overalls with equally faded green sneakers and a bright purple-and-green striped shirt. Although the day was cool, she had her sleeves pulled up and her jacket lay discarded on the ground near the tarp that she was using to haul the leaves back to the compost area. "Well, they have to be planted properly," she said a bit defensively, "or we'll have short irises blooming behind tall ones, and beds of too many early ones that have spent their blooms, leaving little color the rest of the season. And you wouldn't want me to put a Copper Classic beside a Happenstance, would you?"

"Heaven forbid! A Copper . . . what?"

"Orange. Beside pink. It would look hideous," Jane said.

"Oh. Right." Alice hid a smile from Jane at the same time that Louise came hurrying out of the house.

"Guess what?" Louise called as she drew near.

"What?" Jane paused in her work and wiped the back of one hand across her forehead. "Whew, it's warm out here."

"Only if you're working," said Alice. "What's got you so excited?" she said to Louise.

"I talked to an old man from town today who believes he may have letters written by his great-grandfather during his Civil War service."

Jane's eyes widened. "Oh, my goodness. Do you think you might find out something about this battle business?"

"I hope so. Mr. Padgett, the gentleman in question, had a vague memory of some occurrence, but he couldn't pinpoint it. His granddaughter is going to try to find the letters."

"That would be quite a discovery." Jane glanced at her watch. "It's time for lunch and I am starving. Let's go in. I'll finish this after we eat."

"I'll be glad to help you," Alice said.

"I'm not very hungry. I had a piece of key lime pie at the Coffee Shop a little while ago," Louise confessed.

"Oh, June's key lime is fantastic," Alice said, a dreamy look coming over her face. "I still like her cherry the best, though. I don't know what she does with those sour cherries, but the flavor just explodes on my tongue." She shook her head in appreciation.

Jane laughed. "Aunt Ethel and Lloyd brought me a bushel of apples this morning and I was thinking about making apple pie. But I'm a little intimidated now. Maybe I'd better make something else."

Alice and Louise both laughed as the three of them walked toward the back door.

"Oh, Jane, your apple pie will be fabulous, I'm sure," Louise said.

"But you could always make more applesauce," Alice added. "I adore your applesauce. Not," she added hastily, "that your apple pie would be anything less than stupendous."

Jane grinned as she opened the side door of the inn and moved inside. "Good save, Alice." Then she stopped suddenly.

"What on earth . . . ?" Louise began.

"Jane, what's wrong?" Alice asked simultaneously.

All Jane could do was point, her mouth a grim line. Her elder sisters followed the direction of her pointing finger.

Someone, perhaps Lloyd, had set the bushel of apples inside the laundry room, and the tortoise had discovered them. The floor around the basket was littered with juicy bits of apple and core and seed. The sisters caught M.P. in the act of swiping yet another apple. The tortoise had managed to drag herself up far enough to get her shell to rest on one of the basket slats. She was precariously balanced on her hind feet, her front ones braced against the side of the basket.

As the sisters watched, her head darted forward and her sharp beak impaled an apple. Clamping her jaws shut, M.P. heaved herself backward, dragging the apple to the floor with her. She appeared oblivious to the three outraged women watching her antics.

"Oh, Jane, I am so sorry," Alice said. She rushed forward and snatched up the apple basket, setting it atop the washing machine. "I had no idea tortoises could climb like that."

"Who knew?" murmured Louise.

"It's my own fault," Jane said, shaking her head. "I saw Lloyd set it there. I never gave a second thought to our grabby little guest."

"She seems to like apples quite a bit," Louise said lamely. "How many do you think she ate?"

Alice looked into the basket. "If this was full—"

"It was," Jane said.

"Then she probably ate two or three. There still are lots left," Alice said in an overly cheery tone, glancing at Jane's expression.

Jane walked across the floor to the tortoise, which was munching happily on its latest snack. "You little traitor," she said. "Just wait until the next time you come begging me for a treat."

Chapter 🐢 Twelve

The three Howard sisters and Ethel walked to church together on Sunday morning. There was a light rain falling, making the sky gray and the leaves sodden, but everyone's mood seemed cheerful. They had umbrellas—black for Ethel and Louise, dark blue for Alice and for Jane, a brilliant green one with fuchsia flowers scattered around the edges. It matched the fuchsia raincoat she had donned. Louise felt like smiling just looking at her.

The night before, while Jane had used the remaining apples to make a cobbler for dinner, Louise had told her sisters about her lead on finding information about the Civil War battle. The cobbler turned out so well that each of them had seconds, which pleased Jane.

Now, Alice was glad it was the beginning of a new week. She had a feeling that the next few days would bring contact with the owners of the tortoise.

Ethel, Jane and Alice took seats in their usual pew after greeting friends, while Louise went to the organ. A few minutes later, the prelude began. The first hymn reflected the season. "Come, Ye Thankful People, Come" was one of Louise's personal favorites. Written by Henry Alford in 1844, its verses expressed one's struggle to grow into being worthy of God and one's desire to fully enter into the eternal home.

As she played the end of the final verse, Louise was relaxed and smiling. Her inner glow lasted throughout the early part of the worship and through the reading of the Word. Then Rev. Thompson began his sermon.

To her surprise, he had based some of his homily on his experiences searching through the reference material in the library the previous week, explaining that the search for specific references had given him reason to meditate upon the early disciples' need to see Christ perform His miracles in order to believe. He made haste to assure the congregation that there was no comparison between his own research and God's miracles, and that certainly, in the case of historical research, it was imperative to find and cite specific sources. A ripple of laughter floated through the congregation at that.

Were they laughing at *her?* Louise did not think it was unusual to want to see proof of a historical event. She felt self-conscious and mildly perturbed through the offertory and the final hymn, "Now Thank We All Our God."

She wished she could leave as soon as the service ended. But of course she had to play the postlude. When she finished the last notes, she slid out from behind the organ and headed for the door.

"Louise! Wait!" She turned and saw June Carter coming toward her. "Did you have any luck speaking with Earl Padgett?"

Louise gave June an abbreviated version of her telephone call. "So I'm hoping Francie is able to find those letters that he mentioned. There has to be a reason he reacts negatively when people start talking about a battle here, even if he can't bring it to mind right now."

"I agree," June said.

"Hello, ladies." Lloyd, who had been seated on the far side of Ethel, came toward Louise and June. "Are you two planning to sign up to help with the reenactment?"

June rolled her eyes, although Lloyd did not see her.

"Sign up?" Louise shook her head. "Not until I find out one way or the other what really might have happened here during the Civil War."

Lloyd shook his head. "Oh, come on. Just think how exciting it will be. The people of Acorn Hill need a historical experience to call their own," he said grandly.

"But, Lloyd—" Louise began.

"Louise, are you ready to go?" Alice stood beside her, eyes a little more intense than usual.

"Ah, I suppose so." Louise stifled a gasp as Alice took her arm and maneuvered her toward the door. "What are you doing?" she whispered to her sister.

Alice smiled. "Rescuing you. There is no point in getting into an argument with Lloyd. If there was no battle, you'll know it soon enough and be able to lay proof in front of him. Until then, you might as well let him have his illusions."

Louise nodded. "I suppose you're right." She sighed. "I still don't understand why he has been so quick to embrace this nonsense. Lloyd is usually conscious of doing the right thing for this town. But this time, he's setting up Acorn Hill for ridicule."

"I agree." Alice relaxed her hold on Louise's arm. "I don't understand it, either. But I do know that church is the wrong place to be trying to talk him into seeing things your way."

Louise sighed. "You're right, I know. I am just so frustrated with this whole silly mess."

"Hello, ladies." As they walked down the path from the church, Dick Moore greeted them. "Interesting sermon today, didn't you think?"

"Very," Alice said serenely. "It really made me consider my attitude toward faith."

"Me too," Dick said. "Sadly, I'm afraid I may be one of those people who expect miracles to prove that my faith in my faith isn't misplaced. If that makes any sense." He grinned boyishly. Then he waved at someone behind them.

"Hurry up, Ashley. We're going to your grandmother's house for lunch, remember?"

Ashley Moore, one of the ANGELs, went racing past. "Bye, Miss Howard," she said as she slid into the backseat behind the car door Dick held open.

"Have a good day," he said to Alice and Louise.

"You know," said Louise, slipping her arm companionably through Alice's as they began to stroll toward the inn, "I was feeling rather paranoid in there right after the sermon."

"Paranoid?"

"Yes," Louise confessed. "I thought perhaps people were laughing at my expense when Kenneth was comparing the quest for local history confirmation to the early Christians' need to see evidence of Christ's miraculous feats."

"Oh, Louise, no," Alice said. "I chuckled when he said that, and I certainly wasn't making fun of you. If anything, I think all of us were laughing at ourselves, thinking of times when we put God on the spot, so to speak."

Louise smiled. "I wondered if that might be the case just now when Dick spoke." She smiled. "So I suppose I shall have to apologize to God for arrogantly assuming people were thinking more about me than about Him."

Alice chuckled. "You'll be in good company. I think we all do that occasionally."

⌒⌒

Jane served chocolate-chip pancakes along with an egg casserole and a cranberry-orange fruit dish for breakfast Monday morning. As she had begun to do daily, she brought Eva Quigley's chilled water bottle to her table after the food had been served.

"Oh, thank you, Jane," Eva trilled. "I cannot tell you how much I have appreciated your thoughtfulness."

"You're most welcome," Jane said, meaning it. In the face of the woman's obvious sincerity, part of Jane felt small and unkind for her recent pettiness regarding Eva's Scrabble win. After all, it was just a game.

"Oh, I nearly forgot," Eva said. "I looked up that quoits tournament online. You know, the one we're attending this Saturday? Anyhow, I found something you'll be excited to hear."

Jane raised her eyebrows. "What's that?"

"There's a competition for beginners. They offer a class and actually give people the opportunity to practice pitching quoits. Then you can sign up either singly or on teams to compete in a novice match. Isn't that exciting? I think we should do it!"

"You do?"

"Well, of course. It's not really my thing, but I know you enjoy games. It could be fun."

Jane pretended to think about it. "Sounds interesting. I suppose I'm up for that," she said diffidently. "What time do we need to be there to sign up?"

Her mind was awhirl with thoughts while she finished cleaning up the kitchen and putting away the breakfast dishes. Granted, Eva said she was not good at physical games, but could Jane trust her? She had not been exactly forthcoming about her Scrabble prowess.

Coming to a sudden decision, Jane went to the phone and dialed Buck Dabney's number. When Buck's pleasant baritone came on the line, Jane didn't give herself time to reconsider.

"Hello, Buck. This is Jane Howard. I've been thinking about quoits ever since I first visited you, and I was wondering if you'd have time to give me another lesson."

Buck laughed. "I knew it. Didn't I tell you how people get hooked on this game? I'd be delighted to give you another lesson, Jane."

"Wonderful," she said enthusiastically. "Would this week work? Is there a time that particularly suits you?"

The two agreed on Wednesday afternoon at one. Jane hung up the telephone with a distinct sense of relief. She just could not face being beaten by Eva again after the way the woman had crowed. This time, Jane intended to be prepared.

She felt a good deal more cheerful as she sat down at the table with several of her favorite recipe books. She decided that she had not been giving Alice and Louise her best efforts at dinner lately, and she wanted to find some different recipes to try.

She picked up a *Southern Living* from two decades ago and flipped through its pages. Her fingers hesitated at a recipe for cream of squash soup.

That would be wonderful. She had grown some squash of her own this year, and she was sure that she would have enough.

She glanced over the recipe. Onion, garlic, fresh parsley, white pepper—it was a straightforward recipe that she suspected her sisters would love, and she could pair it with the buttermilk biscuits that made everyone's mouth water.

She jotted notes on a yellow legal pad she had set down for that purpose and moved on to a different book. This one was a compilation of recipes from the Grace Chapel congregation in the midsixties. A recipe for venison paprika caught her eye. *Hmm.* Deer season was just weeks away, and it was a good bet someone might offer her venison again this year.

A broccoli and beef pasta recipe also got her attention. She still was making notes when Alice entered the kitchen. She was carrying a basketful of her work uniforms. Jane knew she often washed them separately, adding a judicious amount of bleach that presumably scared away any stray hospital germs.

"Are you looking for recipes?" she asked as she noticed the cookbooks scattered around Jane.

"Yes. I found several that I think you'll enjoy."

Alice's eyes sparkled. "I'd love to see them. Let me get these started." She turned and walked to the door of the laundry room, where Jane's makeshift barrier still kept the tortoise out of the kitchen while allowing Wendell his customary freedom.

Then Alice stopped and said in a whisper, "Jane. Come here and look at this."

Jane rose and went to the laundry room door, where Alice stood with her laundry basket. Alice nodded toward the far end of the room, indicating that Jane should look that way.

The tortoise's heat pad and lamp were set up there, but M.P. was not on the pad. Instead, Wendell lay sprawled on his back, legs wide and floppy, right in the middle of the heat pad with the lamp blazing down on him.

Jane began to giggle. "He looks like he's sunbathing."

Alice chuckled too. "You're right. And look at the tortoise."

Jane's gaze traveled around the room. At first she did not see the reptile, but finally her gaze lit on a laundry basket that had been set in front of the washer. A white sheet trailed liberally over the edge. Beneath the part that draped to the floor was a suspiciously tortoise-shaped bulge.

"She's hiding!" Jane exclaimed.

"I suppose that makes her feel more secure," Alice suggested.

"It's pretty cute." Jane turned and headed for the hallway. "I'm going to get the camera. I want a photo of each of them."

Alice stepped over the barrier, hauling her laundry basket with her. "Good idea. This is definitely something we want to remember."

∽∾

"Louise, this is Nia calling."

"Good morning, Nia," Louise said. It was Tuesday and

she had been sorting through a box of her old sheet music when the telephone had rung. "How are you?"

"I'm great." Nia's voice was as sunny as always. "Do you have time to come down and chat with me today?"

"I could come in this afternoon. What are we chatting about?"

Nia cleared her throat. "I have been doing some online research on Civil War battles to see if I can find any reference to troops or action near Acorn Hill. I'd like to talk with you about it and hear what you found last week when you and Jane were researching here."

"Gladly." Louise checked her watch. "I'll be down after I have some lunch. Around one-thirty?"

"Great! See you then."

Louise put away her box of music after using an index card to mark the spot where she had stopped. She washed her hands and went to the kitchen, where she found Jane watching a chef on television. Every few minutes, while keeping one eye on the TV, Jane would frantically scribble something on a recipe card she had in front of her.

"Do you want a sandwich?" Louise whispered and pantomimed eating in order to ask Jane the question.

Jane nodded, whispering back. "That would be great."

Respecting her sister's concentration, Louise went to the refrigerator and pulled out some ham slices that Jane had cut it into tissue-thin slices. She found two Kaiser rolls, the top halves of which she slathered in mayonnaise and mustard. After washing a few lettuce leaves, she added those. On the bottom section of the rolls, she layered several ham slices and thinly sliced Swiss cheese. Cucumber slices atop the meat and cheese completed her preparations, and she put the top and bottom halves of the rolls together. The result was a satisfyingly thick, tasty-looking sandwich.

Removing two plates and two glasses from the cupboard,

Louise set the sandwiches on the plates and filled the glasses with some zesty cider Alice had purchased at a farmer's market in Potterston after work one day.

"That looks delicious," Jane said as Louise set the food in front of her. "Thanks."

"You're very welcome," Louise replied. She rarely cooked anymore because Jane was so skilled and seemed to enjoy cooking, but it bothered her to think that Jane might feel obligated to make all their meals, so she tried to pitch in when she could.

Jane clicked off the television with a remote control and sat back. "That was an interesting recipe for blueberry-and-nectarine tarts," she told Louise, tapping the recipe card.

"Unconventional," Louise said. "But it looked delicious, I must say. I never would have thought to combine those two fruits."

Jane smiled. "I'm not sure I would have, either, but I'm eager to try it now." She unfolded a napkin and laid it in her lap as Louise had just done. "Shall I offer grace?"

When Louise nodded, Jane said a simple blessing, then picked up her sandwich and took a bite. "Mmmm," she said.

"It really hits the spot, doesn't it?" Louise agreed.

Jane nodded. "And if you haven't tasted that cider yet, you're in for a treat. It's fabulous."

"I love cider," Louise said. "It's one of my favorite things about autumn. Then she recalled the phone call of a few minutes earlier. "Oh, guess what? Nia called. She has done some online research, trying to find any mention of Civil War action in this area."

"Did she find anything?" Jane's eyes widened with interest. Since she had helped with the research, she felt invested in finding the answer to the battle question.

Louise shook her head. "She didn't say. I'm going to meet with her after lunch."

Chapter 🐢 Thirteen

I'm dying to know what you found last week," Nia told Louise when she arrived at the library. Malinda was also there, efficiently checking books in and out and overseeing the people on the free computers the library offered the community. Nia took Louise into her office, where they would not disturb the library's patrons.

"I wish I had an exciting answer for you," Louise told her, "but even with four of us going through records and papers, we didn't find anything that would shed light on that letter's references."

"Maybe that's the answer," Nia said, chewing her lower lip. "Maybe there simply is nothing to find."

"Maybe," Louise said. "Although that letter of Herb Hoffstritt's certainly makes it sound as if something happened. Something involving Confederate troops."

"Exactly," Nia agreed.

"How about you?" Louise asked. "You said you've been doing research online. What did you find?"

"First of all, I decided to try a different approach," Nia told her. She pulled a manila folder toward her and opened it, looking down at some notes printed from a computer. "Instead of looking for information on Acorn Hill, I tried to figure out whether the Army of the Potomac or the Army of Northern Virginia had any troops in this area at that time."

"What a good idea." Louise leaned forward. "What did you learn?"

Nia pushed a black-and-white map toward Louise. "According to everything I have read, Hanover, which is about an hour-and-a-half west of here, was the site of some action right before the Battle of Gettysburg. Jeb Stuart's cavalry ran into Union troops there on June thirtieth of 1863. After the Battle of Gettysburg, which occurred on July first, second and third, General George Meade directed his Union troops to follow Lee's forces back into Maryland. They traveled through Emmitsburg and over the mountains at Fairfield, heading down to Frederick and beyond. Eventually, they crossed the Potomac at Williamsport, Maryland, and moved back into Virginia. By the beginning of October, Lee's troops were concentrated near the Rapidan River."

"So the Confederate armies were out of Pennsylvania by October?"

"Mostly. And there is nothing to indicate that any of them came into Acorn Hill. The closest real action, other than the Hanover skirmish I mentioned, happened when the Confederates marched through Chambersburg on their way to Gettysburg in June. Most of the troops came that way. I suppose there could have been some that traveled by way of these eastern roads and passed through this area."

Louise nodded. Chambersburg lay two hours west of Acorn Hill. She had been to an extraordinary Christmas production of *A Christmas Carol* at a theater in the downtown historic district once and knew a bit of the town's history. "Is 1863 the year that Chambersburg was burned down? It was the only Northern town to be torched by the Confederacy, as I recall."

Nia shook her head. "No, Chambersburg wasn't burned

until a year later, at the end of July 1864. Confederate troops occupied the town two times before that, though."

"But in 1863, Lee didn't stick around after Gettysburg, you said."

"That's right. By late August, the main Rebel forces were in Virginia. There would not have been many Confederate troops still lingering in Pennsylvania right after that. The forces that burned the town the following year were led by General Jubal Early."

Louise's brain began to ache from sorting out all this information. "So whatever the incident was that is referred to in Herb Hoffstritt's letter, it probably occurred sometime in July or August of 1863 as Confederate forces were retreating, which does help narrow the focus."

"I think so. Postal delivery was slower in those days, and mail could take quite some time to catch up with the addressee when an army was on the move. Mr. Hoffstritt's letter is dated October second, so he could easily be replying to one that was written to him in July or August but didn't catch up with him until weeks after that."

"An excellent point," Louise concurred.

I believe I can narrow it down a bit more," Nia went on. "I'm pretty sure it must have happened in late July or early August, because Mr. Hoffstritt's ancestor was a member of a regiment that is listed as having participated in a raid into Maryland on August tenth. If the raid he refers to is *that* raid, then the 'recent fracas' probably happened shortly before."

"And that would line up with your theory about the letter's delivery time." Louise was enormously impressed. "You've done a great job, Nia."

Nia blushed, casting her gaze down modestly. "It's the least I could do. I feel . . . guilty, I suppose is the correct word, for getting this entire community into such a flap." Her fingers intertwined, clenched together where they lay atop the table.

"Oh, Nia." Louise reached out and covered the younger woman's hand with her own. "There is no need to feel bad. Mr. Hoffstritt shared his letter with other people too, remember? It would have gotten out either way." She waited until Nia raised her gaze to Louise's face. "Besides, who could have predicted the circus this has become? Planning a reenactment for something that is pure conjecture isn't the most rational of approaches." Louise withdrew her hand after patting Nia's once.

Nia smiled a little, and the smile grew wider. "You have a point." Her brow wrinkled. "Mayor Tynan sure has leaped on this. I didn't expect that of him."

Louise knew exactly what the librarian was trying to say without being rude. "I didn't, either. I keep thinking there has to be a reason for him to be insisting on pushing this whole battle idea."

"Well, reason or no reason, I am determined to find out exactly what that letter refers to." Nia stood and rolled her shoulders. "I'm going to continue researching as best I can."

"Great idea." Louise stood also. "I'm going to talk to Earl Padgett's granddaughter. Oh, I didn't tell you about that." Quickly, Louise summarized her not-so-satisfactory conversation with Earl and explained that Francie was hoping to help.

Nia's eyes were wide. "Personal letters or a diary from the period would be amazing. Especially if they helped to determine what went on."

Louise nodded. Then another idea occurred to her. "You know, Carlene called me when this all first happened. There was a brief mention of it in last week's *Acorn Nutshell*, but perhaps she would do a follow-up article asking local families to check their attics for ancestors' correspondence. There has to be someone in this town who can shed light on what really happened a century and a half ago."

"That's an outstanding idea." Nia pointed toward the

reception desk at the front. "You're welcome to use my telephone if you like."

Five minutes later, Louise reported back to Nia. "Carlene says she'll be glad to do it but that tomorrow's edition is already laid out and quite full. So next Wednesday will be the best we can do."

Nia looked momentarily disappointed. Then her normal good humor asserted itself and she shrugged. "Who knows? Perhaps by next week, we'll have this little mystery solved."

∽

Louise gave her first piano lesson to her new student shortly after supper.

Francie Litmore's daughter Letitia had hair as wildly curly and red as her mother's. It wasn't a jarring red, but a beautiful deep shade with hints of copper. Louise thought it was just about the prettiest head of hair she had ever seen, flowing down Lettie's back with a ribbon to tie it back from her face.

Lettie and Francie had arrived a few minutes early for the lesson, but Louise had another student right before them, so she had no opportunity to exchange more than a brief greeting with Francie.

The lesson went extraordinarily well, Louise felt. The little girl wanted to play, as her mother had stated. Not all children were quite as enthusiastic as parents sometimes led Louise to believe, so it was a relief to see the child's face light up when she played her first simple tune.

Louise always invited her students' parents to stay while she gave lessons. Since each lesson lasted only a half an hour —except for her older advanced students, whose lessons were an hour long—parents often sat in the living room with a book or needlework.

Louise enjoyed her lesson with Letitia, but she was so eager to talk to Francie that she caught herself being a shameless clock-watcher. After the second time she checked her watch within five minutes, Louise firmly admonished herself to stop thinking about anything other than the lesson. Letitia deserved her undivided attention.

Her mental dressing-down must have worked; the next time she glanced at her watch, the lesson had run over by nearly ten minutes. Thankfully, there was no other student scheduled for a lesson after Lettie's.

"All right," she told the little redhead. "We are finished for today. You did very well with your first lesson." She smiled at the little girl as she wrote comments in the small notebook she provided for each child's assignments. "I'm writing down the things we went over and I want you to practice them every day."

"Okay!" Letitia took the notebook and her three new lesson books and went racing out of the parlor. "Thank you, Mrs. Smith," she called.

"You're welcome." Louise followed at a slightly slower pace.

Francie rose to meet them as they entered the living room, and smiled as she received a hug from her daughter.

"Mommy, I *love* piano lessons!" Letitia hardly could contain her delight.

Francie smiled at Louise over her child's head as she handed her a check for the lesson and the new books and said, "Thank you."

Louise smiled back. "Oh, to have all my students so delightfully enthusiastic and interested."

Francie chuckled. Then her smile faded. "I wanted to let you know I dug through our attic, and I'm afraid I didn't find a single thing that might be helpful to your search. The oldest family correspondence I could find was from World War II."

Louise struggled to mask her disappointment. "Well, thank you for trying. It was a long shot anyway."

"There's one more place I can look," Francie told her. "When Grandpa moved in, my husband stored some of his things above our garage. He doesn't think there was anything like what we want in there, but I'm going to try to check next week. I'll try to talk to Grandpa too. His memory is becoming so unpredictable. You just never know what you might get."

"Thank you for your efforts," Louise said. "Sooner or later, we'll find some way to verify this 'battle' story."

"It would be nice to know whether it's true or false," Francie said. She held out her hand and Letitia took it. The little girl still had a wide smile on her face.

"Let's go home, Mommy," she said. "I have to practice."

Louise and Francie both burst out laughing.

"That's the spirit," Louise said, running a gentle hand over the little girl's brilliant curls. "See you next week, Lettie."

∞

The next day Jane could not wait to get a quoit in her hand again.

The moment she turned the key and her engine shut down, she exited her car and hurried to Buck's door. He must have been watching for her because he opened the door as she went up the stone path to the old farmhouse.

"Hello, Jane," Buck said. "Come on in. Good to see you again."

"You too." She was grinning. "I've been thinking about pitching quoits so much I've been dreaming about them."

Buck gave a deep bark of laughter as he gestured for her to precede him through the house she had admired on her first visit. This time Buck's wife was home. After a quick introduction, Buck said, "Let's go out back and see what I can teach you."

Jane knelt and ran her fingers over the clay in one quoit

pit. "This stuff is sticky," she murmured. "Almost like modeling clay."

"Almost," Buck agreed. "It's hard to find the right texture of clay, but this is what most people like."

He handed Jane a quoit. "Remember the grip I showed you? Thumb on top, fingers curled under. Get your index finger settled in the notch. Now you don't want to toss it sideways like you would a Frisbee, even though you're sort of holding it that way," Buck counseled. "You want to tuck your wrist under as you pull your arm back and toss it gently, sort of like a horseshoe except without the end-over-end flip."

Jane tried it several times with varying success.

"Good," Buck said. "Now let's work on your stance. That will make a difference. First off is where you stand. There's an imaginary line halfway through the pit. You have to keep your feet behind that foul line. You'll get nailed for that if you're not careful."

Jane looked down at her feet. She took a step back, gauging where she was in relation to the imaginary line.

"Next thing," Buck said, "is *how* you stand. There are a lot of ways to do it. Everyone has their own individual form, but I can start you off with my general stance and you can see how it feels. Are you right- or left-footed?"

Jane thought for a moment. "I have no idea," she finally admitted.

"All right. Try this. Pull your arm back and swing it forward. Do you feel more natural moving your right or left foot forward with your arm?"

"My left," Jane said after a few tries.

"All right. Then place your left foot forward with the toe right at the foul line—remember, it's imaginary—and plant your right foot back. Now bend your knees and let your right leg bear most of the weight. Don't let yourself fall or step forward over the line, though."

He demonstrated. Jane stepped up and did her best to

imitate his form as he tossed his quoit and she followed with hers. Her quoit landed in the pit, but it was upside down. "I don't get any points for that, do I?"

"No," Buck said.

"So how do I make it stick in the ground if I want to block my opponent's?" Jane asked.

Buck grinned. "You want to know it all, don't you?"

"Oh yes," Jane said, thinking of the coming weekend's tournament. "I'll take all the pointers you're willing to hand out."

"All right."

He showed her how best to pitch a ringer, sending the quoit sailing in a low arc with its front edge slightly raised. It settled onto the hub as if guided by an invisible hand.

To "dig" another player's quoit out of position or knock it off the board, he had her try pitching her quoit harder than she normally did with the leading edge a little lower. And to play for points rather than a ringer, she needed, Buck demonstrated, to pitch with the front of the quoit slightly lower.

Jane concentrated on absorbing everything Buck told her. She tossed—no, pitched, she reminded herself—quoits until her right arm felt ready to fall off.

It was so much more difficult than it looked. She could not manage a single ringer nor could she get her quoit to stick in the ground at an angle. But at least she mastered the basic pitch and had gained a feel for how much force it took to toss the game piece the length of the quoits court.

When her arm ached and her shoulder protested one more swinging motion, Jane finally was forced to stop practicing.

"So are you going to enter that novice competition this weekend?" Buck asked.

"Yes," Jane replied. "If I can. I mean, you've given me quite an opportunity to practice here."

"I know you've only had a little bit of instruction, but I don't think these two sessions would disqualify you." His eyes twinkled. "However, you'd have to spend a whole lot more time pitching quoits before you wouldn't be considered a beginner."

"I think I'll gladly stick to the novice class," Jane said, rubbing her shoulder.

She was considerably less buoyant on her drive homeward. All she had done, she feared, was to show herself how very difficult it was to master the game. She would be happy if she had any better luck than the rankest of beginners when she played on Saturday.

It would serve you right, she told herself sternly. *You have been obsessed about winning.*

She knew that Alice was disappointed in her. She even understood why. Maybe she shouldn't be going to this tournament with Eva. The woman seemed to bring out the very worst of Jane's competitive urges.

Chapter ✦ Fourteen

While Jane was finishing her second quoits lesson, Alice and Louise were headed home after an afternoon of volunteer work at the Salvation Army in Potterston. Every year, the charitable organization set up "angel trees" at different locations during the month of November.

An angel tree was an artificial tree decorated with slips of paper on which were written the names of children whose parents did not have the means to give them Christmas gifts. The parents filled out a form listing several items their child might like to receive, and then the information was copied onto smaller slips of paper for the tree. Kindhearted community members took the slips and fulfilled the children's wishes for gifts, which later were distributed by the Salvation Army. It was a significant undertaking that required a great deal of preplanning.

The angel tree effort usually started sometime in September. In one of the earliest stages of planning, letters were mailed to families who had used the program before. Posters also were put up around the community directing people to contact the Salvation Army if they were interested in participating. The two sisters had just spent two hours placing posters at numerous locations in Potterston, as well as recruiting stores and organizations to participate.

Alice was still looking over her list. "The exercise club said they would take a three-foot tree, right?"

"Yes." Louise was driving. "And the Girl Scout leader promised to take her girls to the Salvation Army headquarters so that they could pick several wish lists off the tree."

"Oh, thank you. I nearly forgot that one."

"And at that last solicitation we did, the pastor agreed to take one of the largest trees."

"Yes, the six-footer."

Alice continued to scribble. "We accomplished a lot today, Louise."

Louise covered her mouth with one hand as she yawned. "It feels like it," she said. "I'm exhausted."

"Too exhausted for pie?" Alice asked slyly.

Louise cast her sister an amused glance. "If I said no, you'd clobber me, wouldn't you?"

Alice considered her words. "No. At least, not right now, since you're driving. But after you park, yes, probably."

Louise laughed as they entered the outskirts of Acorn Hill. "Coffee Shop, here we come!" she exclaimed.

Within five minutes, the two Howard sisters were parked and walking arm in arm into the Coffee Shop. As they entered the restaurant, Louise caught a flash of distinctive red hair. *Titian dreams red*, she thought with amusement. "There's Aunt Ethel," she said to Alice.

The older woman began to wave imperatively. "Yoo-hoo! Alice! Louise! There's room to sit over here. Please join us."

Ethel was in a booth with her longtime friend Florence Simpson. As Louise and Alice approached, their aunt stood and hugged them each. "Hello, girls. How are you today?"

"Tired," said Louise. As the sisters took seats, she explained what they had devoted their afternoon to doing.

"Oh, how nice," Florence said. "That's such a worthy endeavor. I usually try to take two or three lists each year."

Louise knew that Florence didn't really intend to sound like a braggart, so she only smiled. "That's very thoughtful of you, Florence."

"Thank you." Florence nodded regally. She wore black slacks and a black and gray striped sweater today. The outfit emphasized the gray of her eyes, although frankly, Louise thought it clashed a bit with the intense brown of her dyed hair, which looked as if it had just been colored and curled.

Alice had seated herself beside Florence, facing Ethel and Louise. As Hope came by, she ordered a piece of cherry pie. Louise chose pumpkin. "Even though the holidays aren't here yet," she said, "I can't resist a piece of pumpkin pie."

"I adore pumpkin pie," Ethel said, "but I am forgoing sweets this afternoon. Lloyd is taking me to Zachary's tonight, and I want to be sure I have room for those delicious desserts they serve." Zachary's was Acorn Hill's fanciest restaurant, a supper club owned and run by Zack and Nancy Colwin.

"Jane just took two new paintings over there," Louise told her aunt. "Zack sold the two she had done of Fairy Pond."

"Oh, I thought those were lovely," Ethel said. "What was the subject of these?"

"One was of Grace Chapel at dusk," Alice told her. "The other was rather whimsical. It was a close-up study of a silver basket containing a selection of petit fours."

"Like the ever-popular fruit studio art," Louise said, "except with a much tastier item."

All four women chuckled.

Two people heading for the door moved past their table. Slowly. One of them turned and waved. "Hi, Mrs. Smith."

Louise rose as she recognized the woman. "Hello, Francie." Then, seeing Francie's grandfather shuffling along behind her, she stepped forward and held out her hand.

"Hello, Mr. Padgett. I'm Louise Smith. We spoke on the telephone the other day. I called to ask you about your family during the Civil War."

The old man took her hand. "Well, hello there." His voice, like his handshake, quivered. "I've been giving that some thought. I know my granddaddy talked about his father fighting in the War Between the States, though."

"Thank you for thinking about it," Louise said, sandwiching his hand between hers and giving it a gentle pat.

Francie had her hand beneath her grandfather's arm in a protective gesture. She smiled at Louise. "We're going to keep looking for papers from 'way back then,' aren't we, Grandpa?"

"Darn tootin," the old man said. "Gotta set the record straight so people stop this foolishness about some battle."

"Mr. Padgett." Florence leaned forward. "I am Florence Simpson." She paused as if she expected the old fellow to recognize the name. "This community needs to embrace its heritage. I feel it's very important that we commemorate our local veterans' contribution to the Civil War. Particularly those who fought in the Battle of Acorn Hill."

"Or whatever it was," Ethel inserted. "We don't know for sure that it was an actual battle."

"We know there was some type of military altercation involving soldiers," Florence said in a strident tone.

"Just 'cause soldiers were involved doesn't mean it was fighting," Earl Padgett scoffed. "You don't know what you're talking about, girlie." He tapped his temple with his free hand while Florence's mouth opened and closed in outrage. "My granddaddy talked about something that went on here, and it wasn't fightin'. . . I just have to wait until this old noggin decides to part with the information." He cackled.

Francie smiled apologetically. "It was nice to see you." She turned to Louise, carefully avoiding addressing Florence. "See you next Tuesday. Let's go, Granddaddy."

"See you next Tuesday," Louise echoed as the pair moved off. She took her seat again, noticing the angry red flush that stained Florence's complexion.

"Fiddlesticks!" Florence said loudly to no one in particular. "Obviously, Mr. Padgett is getting senile. I can't imagine that he truly knows anything of import."

"Florence!" scolded Ethel. "Please be respectful. Mr. Padgett was a contemporary of my brother Daniel when they were children. He lived in Acorn Hill all through his childhood, and he very well may have information that would help us." Her speech ended on a conciliatory note, but when Ethel reached across the table to pat her friend's hand, Florence pulled back her own chubby hand out of reach.

"I can't believe you would champion that old man over your own friend," she sniffed.

"I'm not championing anyone," Ethel said in exasperation. "I would like to organize a memorial celebration for the event that happened here as much as you would, but Louise has a valid point. We don't know what really happened yet."

"I wonder what Lloyd will have to say about your defection from his point of view," Florence said. It was clear that she intended to be the one to rush off to tell him.

Ethel's face screwed up into a ferocious frown that nearly was as scary as Florence's forbidding expression. "I'm not dependent upon what Lloyd thinks," she snapped. "I am perfectly capable of forming my own point of view."

"Fine!" Florence said in a distinctly huffy tone, snatching her napkin from her lap and tossing it on the table.

"Fine!" Ethel sat back and crossed her arms.

The two women glared at each other for a long moment. Then, without another word, Florence rose, fumbled her enormous gray leather pocketbook onto her shoulder and stalked out.

Alice, having sensed an abrupt departure, had scrambled to her feet to get out of the way.

As fascinating as the spat had been, Louise had been equally fascinated by Alice's reaction. Her sister's gaze had bounced from one woman to the other, following the conversation as if it were a volleyball at a particularly engrossing match. Her eyebrows rose higher and higher with each acid exchange and when Florence left, she blinked her eyes as if in disbelief.

As Alice sank back into her seat, she said, "Oh dear. Do you think one of us should go after her?"

"I most certainly do not," Ethel said firmly.

Louise shook her head, trying to show Alice without words that she understood that she had been the one Alice really had been addressing. "She's too . . . passionate about her opinion right now," Louise said. "I'll wait a while."

Ethel snorted. "I'd wait forever. That woman can be so closeminded sometimes."

Louise saw Alice biting her lip, trying not to smile, and she coughed to cover her own chuckle. If that wasn't the finest example of the pot calling the kettle black she'd ever heard, she didn't know what was.

∽∾

Jane had gone out to dinner Wednesday evening with Sylvia, so Louise and Alice did not get a chance to relate the story of the spat in the Coffee Shop to her until breakfast the following morning.

It was seven forty-five, just a few minutes before the guests gathered for breakfast, and all three sisters were concluding their private family meal.

". . . And then Florence jumped up and stormed out," Alice told Jane.

"And believe us, she looked like she was about to explode," added Louise. "I wouldn't have wanted to be Ronald when she got home."

"I can't believe Aunt Ethel expressed any doubt about this battle business," Jane said, shaking her head in amazement. "I thought she had jumped on the ceremonial bandwagon with both feet."

"So did I," Alice remarked. "But apparently she has been listening to Louise crying caution a little more attentively than we realized."

"It's too bad that she and Florence are upset with each other," Louise said. "I hope Mr. Padgett's memory improves or that Francie finds something in writing. It's hard to believe one little letter has caused such strife in our community."

"This is just plain silly," Alice said in a more vehement tone than one normally heard from her.

Jane checked her watch, then got to her feet. "I need to get hopping," she said. "The table is set but I haven't put out the juice."

"I'll take care of that," Alice said. "What kind are we serving this morning?"

"Orange-cranberry," Jane said. "It's in the large Tupperware pitcher on the top shelf. And would you get that chilled dish of butter balls as well, please?"

"I'll clean up these dishes so you can work your gourmet magic," Louise volunteered. "But first I better empty the trash." So saying, she tied up the bag and prepared to carry it away.

"Thanks." Jane quickly lined a bread basket with a lacy napkin and then took cinnamon scones from the oven, carefully arranging them in the basket before wrapping the napkin over them to preserve the heat. Next she removed an egg, ham and smoked cheese casserole, and placed it on a tray.

The guests began to arrive as Jane carried the food into the room. She backed through the door just in time to see Eva enter the room and take a seat, followed immediately by the Osbourne family. Oddly, Eva's usual sunny smile was not in place. Instead, she looked quite somber, and she did not meet Jane's eyes.

Jane had just opened her mouth to ask Eva if anything was wrong when Alisha Osbourne squealed, "Oh look, Mom! M.P.'s coming to breakfast."

Jane froze. Carefully she set down the casserole she had been carrying and pivoted.

Sure enough, right behind her was the large tortoise. M.P. had crawled in a moment before, if the gently swinging door between the kitchen and dining room was any indication. The tortoise's eyes were bright, and Jane could have sworn the wretched creature had a smile on its face.

At that moment, Alice bustled into the room. She came to a halt when she saw the tableau before her, and her eyes closed in dismay. "Oh no!"

Louise rushed in right behind Alice. "Jane, it was all my fault. I forgot to replace the barricade when I came back in and . . ." Her voice trailed off as she saw the expression on Jane's face.

Without saying another word, Alice bent and hefted the tortoise between her hands. Louise held the door and in a moment she, Alice and M.P. all had vanished into the kitchen.

Jane took a deep breath, suppressing the urge to scream. "I'm so sorry," she said to their guests.

"That was some turtle," Eva stated in a wondering voice. Jane remembered that Eva had never had occasion to enter the kitchen area—she only had seen it from the hall doorway —and no one had ever mentioned the animal to any of their guests except for the Osbourne family.

"Actually," Alisha said, "it's a tortoise. An African spurred tortoise, right, Ms. Howard?"

"Right," said Jane in a stifled voice. "As I was saying, I

apologize deeply for the interruption. I can assure you that animal has been nowhere near any of our food preparations."

"That was cool," said Alisha's younger brother.

"Very." Eva nodded, a small smile lifting the corners of her mouth. "I had no idea you owned a tortoise."

"We don't. Alice found it, and we're trying to find the owners," Jane said quickly. "We hope it will be leaving soon." *Very soon.*

"Oh, good luck. Poor thing." Eva bubbled over with sympathy; she seemed to have forgotten whatever it was that had made her so distant a few moments before.

"Thank you. Now please excuse me. I hope you all enjoy your breakfast. I'll be in with a tea tray momentarily." Slowly, Jane walked back to the kitchen, letting the swinging door swoosh back and forth behind her several times before it settled in the closed position. She realized she was shaking and she took several slow, deep breaths. *In and out, in and out. Calm down, Jane,* she told herself.

Alice and Louise were both standing near the counter. Each one had a paper towel. They were wiping their hands dry after what Jane assumed was a serious scrubbing.

Before Jane could speak, Alice said, "Jane, this is all my fault for bringing a tortoise here in the first place. I know the concern it has caused you."

"Although thankfully, our current guests seem delighted rather than appalled," Louise said, holding up crossed fingers.

"That's beside the point." Jane heard the quaver in her voice and she pressed her fingers hard against her eyes. "You and I know that having a tortoise walk through the *kitchen* is a huge health violation. Period." She looked at Alice. "The tortoise has to go. By Sunday, if not sooner. That gives you time to make some other arrangement. We simply cannot keep taking these kinds of risks."

Alice nodded, genuinely sympathetic. "All right. I'm sorry," she said again humbly.

Jane heaved a sigh. "I know."

∽

At about eleven o'clock, Jane went out to the garden, which she had begun to clean up in preparation for winter. She pulled out squash and watermelon vines and took out the remains of her tomato plants.

As she worked, Eva Quigley was on her mind.

At first, Jane did the same mental sidestep each time her plans to best Eva at quoits had been brought up with her sisters. Then she actively resisted, even saying aloud, "There is no reason for me to feel guilty about this. Right? Right."

But at last, she let out a long sigh. "Might as well get a drink and think about it," she told Wendell, who had been sunning himself in the grass not far from her. As she stripped off her gardening gloves and dusted off the knees of her old trousers, Wendell rose to his feet and stretched. Then he accompanied her across the backyard to the house.

Eva. Eva, Eva, Eva. Jane knew why she couldn't get the woman out of her head. She, Jane, had not been raised to be deceptive. She had not been raised to be so competitive at games that it mattered terribly who won and who lost. She certainly had not been raised to plot a strategy to even the score, either literally or figuratively.

In the mudroom, she cast a glare at the culprit of the morning's little escapade. "Don't think I've forgotten about you," she informed M.P., shaking a stern finger at the creature. "You have to go."

M.P. did not appear to be disturbed by this threat. She crawled hopefully toward Jane, the Bringer of Treats in her little tortoise brain.

"Oh, all right," Jane said, trying to stay cross. "An apple slice. That's my final offer. Take it or leave it."

She went into the kitchen and took from the refrigerator a slice of apple out of a sealed plastic bag. She returned to the laundry room, still protected by its barricade, and tossed the apple slice toward the tortoise. "There. I just want you to know this is not a peace offering. You and I are still on opposing sides in this war."

Again, M.P. did not seem cowed. She put her tree-trunk legs into high gear when she spotted something edible in her field of vision and made a beeline for the apple. She was fascinating and full of personality, and Jane admitted to herself that she had grown somewhat fond of the appealing animal with her slow, deliberate movements and her sleepy-looking eyes. But that did not mean she was going to relent on her edict to remove the creature.

The little interlude had taken Jane's mind off of her problem, but thoughts of Eva and the quoits tourney returned as she walked away from the barricade. "Rats," she said to Wendell as she took down a glass and filled it with ice and chilled water. "I feel like a real meanie."

But she hadn't done anything wrong, had she? Learning a little bit about the game of quoits couldn't be construed as cheating. *Of course it couldn't,* she assured herself. To be really good at quoits, one would have to practice endlessly, something she surely hadn't done.

Oh? Then what do you call it when you toss an imaginary quoit the length of your bedroom a dozen times before you go to bed?

Jane scowled. "That doesn't count as real practice," she informed the cat.

It's not the action, the little angel on one shoulder reminded her. *It's the intent behind the action.*

The devil seated on the opposite shoulder crossed its arms in a pugnacious manner. *Eva deserves to be taken down a peg. She enjoyed winning way too much.*

It does no good to respond to an unkind act with another unkind act. The angel shook her head sadly.

Yes, but you'd feel so much better if you whipped her, wouldn't you?

"Yes," Jane said aloud. "I sure would. But it's the wrong thing to do." The question was, could she really bring herself to abandon her plan? It really wasn't much of a plan, anyway. Chances were that Eva would prove to be as good at quoits as Jane, so what was the harm?

When the little angel on her shoulder began to speak up again, Jane put her hands over her ears and refused to listen.

Chapter ❦ Fifteen

Alice was at the registration desk that afternoon, writing personal thank-you notes to some of their recent guests, when the telephone rang.

"Grace Chapel Inn, Alice speaking. May I help you?"

"Hello. This is Francie Litmore. May I speak to Mrs. Smith, please?"

"Certainly. Just a moment." Alice hurried to the parlor, where her sister was going over lesson plans for her piano students. "Louise," Alice said, "you have a telephone call. It's Francie Litmore."

"Thank you." Louise set down her pen and made her way to the front desk.

"Hello, Francie. This is Louise."

"Hi, it's Francie."

Louise felt a surge of hope: Francie sounded as if she was suppressing excitement. "Hello, Francie. How are you?"

"I'm fine, thank you. My grandfather would like to speak with you. Do you have a minute?"

"I certainly do."

"I'll put him on."

There was a sound of fumbling and the old man's cranky voice said, "I can hold the danged thing myself, girl. I'm old, not crippled."

Louise smiled to herself.

Then Earl said, "Hello?"

"Hello, Earl. This is Louise Smith."

"Good. I got some information for you."

"You do?" Louise was delighted. "Did you and Francie find something that might give us more knowledge of the Civil War here in Acorn Hill?"

"Sure did. It'll settle this battle nonsense once and for all." The old man cackled. Then he fell silent.

"What did you find?" Louise prompted when Earl did not speak.

"Newspaper articles," he said. "My grandmother had a whole scrapbook of newspaper articles from Acorn Hill. They name all the boys who enlisted and whenever something happened to one of 'em, they wrote that in there too."

"My gracious. That's wonderful," Louise said. *But it was not what she was seeking.*

"Yeah. An awful lotta them young fellas were killed, you know. And a lot of 'em that were taken prisoner died far from home. Some other ones came home missing body parts."

"That's so sad."

"Truly is." The old man sounded melancholy. "I been readin' through these papers, and it brings back a lot of memories. My granddaddy used to talk about the war, stories his daddy told him."

"Oh?" Louise wanted to get to the heart of the matter but she realized the old man could not be hurried.

"My great-granddaddy, he got his leg torn up by a mini-ball at Shiloh. That was in 1862, you know. He came home for nigh on a year until his leg healed up, but then he was assigned to be a guard at a Union prison called Fort Delaware the next year. They took him so's a man with two legs could join up to fight. That prison was a terrible thing."

"So your grandfather was not home in Acorn Hill during

the time period we have been discussing?" Disappointment sounded in her question. "No, but my grandmama saved all the papers for him to read when he came home."

"Really?" Louise was electrified by the statement. "Are they still available to be read?"

"Not the originals," Earl said. "But my daughter Rose, Francie's mama, she took 'em and made copies on a machine 'cuz a lot of them old papers were fallin' apart."

"You have copies of a local newspaper from 1863?" Louise could not believe her ears. There had been nothing like that in the library's collection.

"Sure do."

"Mr. Padgett, have you told Nia Komonos about this?"

"Who's Nita Ko Ko—"

"Nia Ko-mo-nos," Louise enunciated. "She is the librarian who replaced Miss—"

"Why would I want to tell her?" Earl sounded genuinely mystified.

Louise took a deep breath, reminding herself that a ninety-three-year-old man deserved clear explanations. "They have a large local history collection at the library," she told him. "Nia would love to have copies of your papers, I'm sure."

"Well, she can't have mine." Earl sounded alarmed.

"No, no," Louise soothed. "She never would take them from you. But she might be very happy if you showed them to her and allowed her to make copies of them to keep at the library. Then everyone in town would be able to read them if they liked. We could arrange to have a plaque made up stating that you donated them."

"Huh."

Louise was not sure what that single syllable meant, but she knew she had planted a seed. There was no point in pushing the old man further and possibly antagonizing him; she would let the idea percolate in his head for a while.

Then she realized she had gotten sidetracked completely from the issue she most wanted to discuss.

"So, Earl, you said you found something in your papers that would settle the argument about a Civil War battle here in town. Why don't you tell me about it?"

Silence.

"Earl?"

"I'm tired," said the old man in what did indeed sound like a weary tone. "You give me a call Saturday and ask your questions."

"But, Earl, all I need—"

"Louise?" The voice was Francie's, sounding subdued. "Sorry about that. Grandpa gets cantankerous for no good reason sometimes. He's going off to take a nap."

"That's all right." Louise swallowed her disappointment. "This surely can wait."

"Why don't you call on Saturday, as he suggested? Or better yet, come by the house. Who knows? He might even have forgotten he spoke to you today."

"Do you know what he is talking about?" Louise asked, making one last and probably futile stab at getting the information that she sought.

"I'm afraid not." Francie sounded truly apologetic. "I found this old trunk that was full of the papers he mentioned, along with family diaries and letters and all kinds of things, but he's been hiding out with it in his room." A lighter note crept into her voice. "He has this huge magnifying glass he uses to read. He lays the paper on the table and gets his nose about two inches from it, looking through the glass. I've offered to read things to him, but no, he can do it himself. Reminds me of the kids when they were toddlers."

"Indeed." Louise chuckled as her feeling of disappointment faded. She recalled Cynthia's days as a young child beginning to seek out independence. She supposed that

Earl's situation was much the same, only in reverse. Letting someone else take over his reading would be seen as a loss of independence. Not something anyone would take lightly.

But oh, her curiosity was *killing* her.

"All right," she said. "Thank you for the invitation, Francie. I'll visit him on Saturday, but I'll be sure to call you first."

When Louise hung up, Alice approached her. She had been in the living room, from where she had heard Louise on the phone.

"Mr. Padgett feeling a bit grouchy today?" she asked, smiling sympathetically.

"You could say that," Louise answered, nodding.

"He'll be ready to share his information in a day or two," Alice said, coming to her sister's side. "I see a lot of geriatric patients, and they can have sudden mood swings. But the moods don't often last long."

"I hope not," Louise said in a forlorn tone. "He said the information he uncovered will put an end to the talk of a battle."

"Maybe Saturday will be the day you get answers."

"And perhaps tomorrow or Saturday will be the day you find the owners of the tortoise," Louise said. "Did you make any calls after the reptile invasion at breakfast?"

Alice nodded, her forehead wrinkling in concern. "Dane Rush, the rehabilitation expert, has not returned from his vacation yet. Or if he has, he's not answering the phone at the wildlife center. I also called several veterinarians and animal shelters where I had left information, but no one has inquired about the tortoise or recognized it as belonging to someone they know."

"Oh dear." Louise pursed her lips. "We really have to find another place to keep it if the owners don't turn up soon."

"I know." Alice heaved a sigh. "Jane's right. An inn is not the place for M.P."

"Maybe Aunt Ethel would take her for a bit," Louise said, thinking aloud.

Alice looked at her sister as if Louise had lost her mind. "That was a joke, right?"

Louise pictured Ethel with the tortoise. "Yes," she said, blowing out a huff of laughter. "I suppose it was."

"What we need is someone with a mudroom or rec room that is not close to the kitchen," Alice said.

"One that can be closed off to prevent M.P.'s wanderlust from causing trouble," Louise added.

"It would have to be someone responsible," Alice mused. "Someone who would not allow her to overeat. Someone without small children or less tolerant pets that might harass her."

"Yes, dear Wendell certainly has proven himself to be a gentleman, hasn't he?"

Alice nodded and went on. "Someone who has enough space to let her get adequate exercise."

"And someone who makes sure she seems happy." Louise thought that she probably sounded silly, worrying about a tortoise's happiness, but the creature had crawled a slow, deliberate path into her heart as much as Alice's. And even Jane's, though she might not be in the mood to admit it at the present time.

Alice looked clearly distressed about her dilemma.

"Let's pray," said Louise impulsively. She angled herself toward Alice and took her sister's hands. "Dear Lord, we need help, and we need it now. You know when we're desperate. You know what we need long before we ever need it. Please help us to find a placement for our tortoise friend where she will be safe and happy until her family can be found."

Alice picked up the prayer when Louise fell silent. "We

thank You for leading M.P. to our home, Father, and for trusting us to care for one of Your creatures in trouble. Enable us to get M.P. back to her family or to another more appropriate home."

"Father, we pray these things in Your name, trusting Your wisdom to lead the way," Louise added. "Amen."

"Amen," echoed Alice. She opened her eyes and smiled at Louise. "Thank you. Sometimes I forget that I need to give my problems to a higher power and quit trying to solve them alone."

"You're not alone," Louise said, leaning forward and hugging Alice. "None of us is, as long as we are willing to communicate our needs to God."

On Friday morning, Alice got out of bed the moment the alarm rang. She pulled on a pair of jeans and an old T-shirt and went down the stairs to be sure the tortoise had not pulled any new tricks during the night.

Thankfully, when she reached the kitchen, all was well. "Good morning, M.P.," she said, shaking her head at herself for being so cautious.

"Good morning, Wendell," she said as the cat entered the kitchen a minute or so later.

Wendell meowed once—was that hello?—and vanished through the barricade for his morning bonding with the tortoise.

Alice checked to be sure the magazine boxes anchored the barrier securely against the door frame, then retraced her route to her bedroom, where she showered, dressed and made her bed before heading back downstairs.

Louise and Jane were both in the kitchen when she returned. The sisters exchanged morning greetings and sat down to their own breakfast, for which they typically gathered before serving their guests.

"I'm taking Aunt Ethel to the eye doctor this morning," Louise said.

"I'll help Jane with anything she needs for breakfast," Alice assured her. "I am working an evening shift today, so I don't go in until a little before three."

"What are you up to today, Jane?" Louise asked.

Jane shrugged. "Not much, other than feeding our guests and the regular chores. I need to make a large pot of chili for the youth group. They are having a prayer vigil this weekend, and I promised them a pot of my special white chili and corn bread."

"Yummy," Alice said. "I don't suppose there would be enough of that for us to sneak a little taste?"

"There might be," Jane said, smiling. "In fact, there might even be enough for us to have for supper one night this weekend."

"Heavenly," Alice said. "Thanks, Jane."

The telephone rang, interrupting the moment of camaraderie.

Jane sprang up and answered it, then held it out to Alice after a moment. "It's your wildlife guy," she said. Her face looked hopeful, and Alice prayed Dane had some good news for her about M.P.'s family.

"Hello, Dane. This is Alice," she said. "I hope you had a pleasant vacation."

"South Africa was great," Dane replied. "Actually, it was a working vacation, and now I'm in Florida."

"So what did you do in South Africa?"

"I volunteered at a wildlife preserve that rehabilitates and conserves many endangered species native to the area. I was working with a program that has had success breeding serval cats." Dane sounded utterly exhilarated.

"What's a serval?"

"A serval cat is a very rare feline species. The goal is to

reintroduce serval cats to the many areas where they had been wiped out."

"That sounds fascinating," Alice said. "I would love to be involved in something like that."

"You could go," Dane told her. "Volunteers do not need any special training, just a willingness to work and the where-withal to get to South Africa. After that, it's free room and board. Because of the distance most volunteers travel, the minimum recommended stay is three weeks."

"That's certainly something to think about," Alice said. She knew it would be difficult for her to get away from work and the inn for such an extended period, but it sounded like something she would enjoy immensely. She would, of course, have to find the "wherewithal"—translation: money for air-plane fare—to get there.

"So how is the tortoise?" Dane asked. "Have you found an owner?"

"No owner," Alice said regretfully. "The tortoise is well and doing fine. Too fine, perhaps. She has become so com-fortable here that she likes to wander. Since we have guests coming through on a regular basis, it is not an ideal situation. Is there any way you could take her soon?"

Dane sighed. "I just flew into Miami, and I'm going to be staying overnight at my sister's home here before my next flight tomorrow. I won't even get back to Potterston until Saturday evening, and I'm going to be totally jetlagged for a day or two. Tell you what, though. Call me on Sunday and I'll make some phone calls and try to find a new temporary placement if you still have her."

"Oh, thank you," Alice said. "You don't know how happy that will make my sister Jane. All of us, really. We are living in fear of the Board of Health paying a surprise visit."

Dane laughed. "I know that's not really funny, but I have this image of that big tortoise greeting your guests."

"You don't know how accurate that has been," Alice said. There was a moment of silence. "All right. We'll figure something out." Dane assured her. "I'll talk to you Sunday." "Thanks again," Alice said. "Be safe traveling home." "Thanks. Bye, Alice."

Chapter 🐢 Sixteen

Ethel walked over to the inn to meet Louise. Louise drove her to her eye appointment in Potterston, where the ophthalmologist pronounced Ethel's vision excellent, and then the two women headed back to Acorn Hill.

"Oh, Louise? Could you stop at the dry cleaner's, please? I had my black wool coat dry-cleaned and I want to pick it up before we get hit with a real cold snap."

"I'd be glad to," Louise said. "I can check to see if our things are done too." Jane had brought in a lacy tablecloth and matching lace-edged napkins a week earlier.

Louise carefully parked outside the dry-cleaning shop, and the two women walked inside. Louise was pleased to learn that the linens were finished, so she picked them up for Jane while Ethel retrieved her coat. Then they made their way outside again.

As they crossed the parking lot, Louise saw a man coming toward them in a pair of dark coveralls. When he drew near, she recognized Duane Van Dinkle, the exterminator who Hope Collins said was using a metal detector to search for Civil War-era artifacts around town.

"Hello, Duane," Ethel called.

"Hello, Mrs. Buckley. Hello, Mrs. Smith. How are you ladies today?"

"Fine, fine." Ethel answered before Louise even began to respond. "Have you found any artifacts from a Civil War battle yet?"

"No," he said. "I've found metal buttons, coins, safety pins and such, but not a thing from the nineteenth century. I'm starting to wonder if there's anything to find."

"I read that at Gettysburg, one still can find bullets at numerous locations. Even things like medical instruments, eating utensils and the rare sword surface occasionally. But that is happening less and less, especially since so many of those historic sites are protected and off-limits to tourists' metal detecting," Louise told them.

Duane frowned. "It sort of seems like we ought to be finding stuff like that around here, doesn't it? Especially since none of this area ever was identified as a battleground and probably never was checked over."

"That's true." Ethel said as if Duane's words had struck a chord of truth. "I wish we knew where this battle took place."

Louise bit her lip, knowing that she did not need to remind Ethel that there was a big, fat question mark surrounding the battle's supposed existence. Ethel was as loyal to Lloyd as she could be, but even Ethel recently had appeared to be having difficulty trying to convince herself that the episode had happened. Her current state of disharmony with Florence was proof of that.

"I've checked over just about every piece of public ground in this town in the past couple of weeks," Duane said. "Along with the occasional backyard and garden. The most exciting things I found were a wedding ring near Fairy Pond and the OC pin off Sadie Mitler's WAVES uniform from World War II."

"OC?"

"Officer's Commission, I think," Duane said. "She told

me she lost it right after she came home from North Africa after the war. She kind of laughed to think she'd had it all through the war, then came home and did laundry and lost it."

"I bet she was thrilled to get it back," Ethel said.

Duane nodded. "She sure was."

"Hope told us you'd found a wedding band. Did you ever learn whose ring you found?" That was a mystery Louise wanted to have solved.

Duane brightened. "Yes. Carlene put that little notice about it in the *Nutshell* last week. It's a funny story. Kendra Villeneuve came forward and described a ring her mother lost years ago near the pond."

"Kendra Villeneuve." Louise mused, trying to place the name. "Is she the plumber's wife?"

"That's the one," Duane said, nodding. "Turns out it was her mother's ring."

"What was so funny about that?" Ethel inquired.

Duane grinned. "I guess Kendra's parents were taking a walk around the pond one evening and had a fight. Kendra is the oldest of six girls in her family, and she says when her mother told her daddy she was expecting the sixth child, he told her it better be a boy or he was packing his suitcases. Kendra's mother didn't think that was so funny, and she threw her wedding ring at him and said she'd pack for him that night."

Louise put a hand over her mouth to hide a smile. "Gracious! Is Kendra sure she wants a reminder of that?"

"Oh, it turned out all right," Duane assured her. "Kendra's folks celebrated their fiftieth wedding anniversary last month. She said her father gave her mother a new ring after the sixth daughter was born. But this one certainly will have some sentimental value."

"Of a rather notorious sort," Ethel added, chuckling.

"It sounds," said Louise, "as if some good came of this artifact hunt after all. Even if you never find another thing, you've done a very good deed for two families."

"I'm going to keep looking," Duane told them. "But I'm starting to think this is nothing but a lot of made-up hype."

Louise shepherded Ethel back to the car after another moment chatting with Duane, and soon they were on their way back home again.

Louise stopped her car near the front of the carriage house and came around to carry her aunt's dry cleaning. She was following her aunt through the door when Ethel stopped suddenly. "Oh, Louise, I almost forgot to tell you about the meeting."

"What meeting?" Louise shifted her grip on her aunt's coat. "Could you tell me after we hang this up?"

Ethel chuckled. "Sorry. I just don't know how it slipped my mind." She started walking back to her bedroom, talking over her shoulder as she went. "Lloyd has decided to have a meeting on Monday evening for anyone interested in participating in the memorial celebration."

"What memorial celebration?" Louise knew exactly what her aunt was going to say, but she wanted to hear it anyway.

"You know Lloyd has talked about a reenactment if he ever figures out exactly what happened here," Ethel said. "He definitely has decided to combine that with our Fourth of July festivities and make it a special commemorative event to remember the battle."

"Is that so?"

Ethel sighed. "I did tell him that perhaps this was putting the cart a bit before the horse, but he is just determined not to be shown up by the other towns."

"What do you mean?" This was a new line that Louise had not heard before.

"Remember that meeting of all the local officials two weeks ago?" Ethel asked. When Louise nodded, she went on. "Lloyd said all the towns around us do special things on the Fourth to celebrate their heritage. I can't remember exactly what all he told me, but one town has an inn where George Washington spent the night. Another remembers a family of four brothers who fought in the Second World War and only two came home, both injured." She waved a hand in the air as if to brush away the rest.

"So *that's* it," Louise said under her breath.

"That's what?" Ethel might be aging but her hearing was as sharp as ever.

"That's the reason he's so dead set on finding something that we can hold up as Acorn Hill history."

"Well, yes," Ethel said. "Lloyd loves our little town, you know. I believe it really bothered him that we don't have anything of historical import to call our own."

"I thought this whole notion was odd, considering how cautious he usually is about not letting us be turned into a tourist attraction."

As she opened the door to her closet, Ethel said, "I think between the celebration possibilities and Lloyd's love of history, he's sort of sidestepped any concern about linking Acorn Hill to the Civil War."

Louise hung Ethel's coat in the closet. "There must be a way to remind him somehow."

❦

Saturday morning dawned clear and surprisingly warm. The weather forecast promised an extremely pleasant autumn day.

Jane bounced out of bed and put on a pair of jeans and a short-sleeved, long-tailed cotton shirt in dainty rose and orange stripes. She went on to French-braid her long, dark hair so that it would stay out of her way when she took her turn pitching quoits. She wished breakfast were over so that she and Eva could get on the road to the tournament.

The first thing she did when she entered the kitchen and flicked on the lights was to walk to the laundry room door and turn on the light in there.

"Good," she muttered when she saw the tortoise was basking under her heat lamp as usual. "You stay right there all morning, and we'll get along just fine."

"Pardon?" Alice said as she walked into the kitchen. She, too, wore jeans, but hers were paired with a practical dark green knit polo shirt.

Jane coughed. "I was, er, talking to the tortoise."

"I see," said Alice.

"Don't laugh," Jane warned. "I hear you talking to her all the time." She began mixing a thin batter to make apple crepes for their guests' breakfast, along with baked bananas brushed with coconut sauce. The Osbournes arrived for breakfast promptly at eight, and Alice was ready to help.

"I'll serve," she offered. "I know you really can't take your eyes off those crepes."

"Thanks." Jane grinned. "I guess I could, but the end result might not be pretty."

Alice picked up the tea tray as they heard another chair being pulled out in the dining room. "Sounds like everyone's there now. Let me offer tea, and then I'll come back for the coffee pot."

As Jane poured batter into the pan, she heard Alice greet Eva, who replied in a subdued murmur with words that Jane could not quite catch.

Alice returned to the kitchen in a few moments and picked up the coffee pot. "Eva would like to talk to you when you have time, Jane. I suggested that perhaps you could sit down for a few moments once all the breakfasts have been served."

"All right." A frown furrowed Jane's brow. What could Eva want that wouldn't wait? After all, they would be spending the entire day together.

Quickly she garnished the crepes to make an attractive presentation and took the baked bananas from the oven. Alice carried in plates of crepes until everyone had been served, and when the last additional crepes were made, Jane picked up the serving dish of baked bananas and took it in.

Eva was seated near the Osbournes, but she had left an empty chair between Alisha, who was closest, and herself, creating an instant impression of distance. It had worked. The Osbournes were laughing and chattering with each other while Eva sat still and silent in her chair.

Jane smiled at everyone. "Good morning. I hope you enjoy your breakfast."

Mrs. Osbourne already had taken a bite of her crepes. "Enjoy? Oh, what a woefully understated word. Jane, this is absolutely fantastic."

"Thank you." Jane beamed with pleasure. Her smile faded into concern as she caught sight of Eva's face. The woman looked positively despondent. Jane knew a moment of genuine concern. Had Eva had bad news from home or something equally upsetting? While Alice refilled cups and made small talk with the Osbournes, Jane slipped into a seat beside Eva, who barely had touched her food.

"Good morning. Alice said you wanted to talk to me. Are you ready for our adventure?"

"I have a confession to make, Jane," Eva said quietly.

"Uh-oh. This sounds serious." Jane tried to sound jovial. *A confession?* Jane could not imagine what it possibly could be.

"I never should have accepted your invitation." Eva's eyes swam with misery. "I didn't want to disappoint you when you were kind enough to include me, but I should have told you the truth."

Kind? Jane knew her thoughts recently had been far from kind, and she felt ashamed. "The truth about what?" Guilt shot through her when she thought of the real reason she had invited Eva. "Why on earth wouldn't you accept?"

Eva looked shockingly sad and dispirited. "Because I'm absolutely terrible at sports and physical games," she said. "I'll probably come in dead last." Her tone was so morose and her words so unexpected that Jane was momentarily speechless.

"Oh, I can't imagine that," Jane said finally.

"I can." Eva's face had lost its usual glow. "I have four older brothers. All of them are amazing athletes. When I was a child, it seemed as if one of them was coming home with some new trophy every other day, while I was the kid who tripped over her own feet."

"Did you play any sports?"

"I tried out for volleyball and basketball and field hockey and softball at various times. I ran cross-country and distance track events, and I joined the swim team. But I was so bad at all of them that I either didn't get onto the team at all, or I was given a spot just because they had space to fill. At the track meets, I always finished last. I'd be so far behind all the other runners that sometimes they lapped me. My brothers thought it was hilarious."

"That's mean," Jane said instantly, offended on behalf of the youthful Eva.

"Oh, they were kids," Eva said. "As my mother says, 'Boys will be boys.'"

"I always disliked that saying," Jane said. "Would anyone ever say, 'Girls will be girls'? It's as if people are prepared to have to excuse bad behavior from boys."

"That certainly was true in my house," Eva said glumly.

"Boys can be so difficult," Jane said, recalling her own childhood. "I didn't have brothers, but I remember some of the stupid things the boys in my classes did and said."

"My brothers really were just teasing," Eva said. "They've grown into very nice men, and I'm sure they would be horrified if they knew how bad they used to make me feel." She sighed. "They still make me feel bad, and they don't even know it."

"Do they still tease you?"

"Oh no." Eva almost smiled. "But every single one of them has become enormously successful. They're all doctors, you see. The eldest is a pediatrician. The middle two went into family practice together and my younger brother became a surgeon."

"Wow!" Jane tried to imagine how she would feel in Eva's shoes.

"You said it. Becoming a schoolteacher—even one who went on to get a PhD—doesn't quite rate that reaction, you know."

"It should," Jane said stoutly. "If it weren't for teachers and administrators and all the other professionals who staff our educational facilities, people wouldn't have much chance of becoming doctors. Or anything else important, for that matter."

"I know." But Eva's tone didn't sound as if she believed it.

"You have your own strengths," Jane argued. "Look how great you are at Scrabble. I bet all word games are a breeze for you."

"Not if I'm playing with my brothers," Eva said. "They're all much smarter than I am." She cleared her throat. "I'm sorry for being such a wet blanket. I may not join in your competition today, but I'll enjoy watching. I can cheer for you."

"They have a doubles competition," Jane blurted out. "We could sign up as a team." All the unkind thoughts she had been having about Eva crowded her mind, and she actually felt the sting of tears. How petty she had been!

"I'd hold you back," Eva said.

"No, you wouldn't," Jane said. "And besides, it will be fun just to experience the competition."

"It will?"

"Let's forget about winning. Look at it this way," Jane said. "There can only be one winner in any competition. That means there are a whole lot of other people who gave it their best shot and weren't quite good enough. So most people don't win. But they don't consider themselves losers. They participate to have a good time."

"You're right," Eva said, her tone that of one discovering a new truth. She paused. "Do you really want me to be your partner?"

"Of course," Jane said. She was on the verge of telling Eva how she had felt after the Scrabble game, but she feared that might make Eva feel even worse about herself. "We'll have a high old time trying this game."

Eva was smiling. Not beaming, but at least the unhappiness seemed to have faded. "Thank you, Jane," she said gratefully. "Reserving a room at Grace Chapel Inn has been one of the best decisions I ever made. You've been wonderful."

Jane was gratified to see Eva showing interest in her food. Slowly, Jane rose, her mind reeling. "I'll let you know when I'm finished with breakfast cleanup, and we can leave right after that," she said.

"Great." Eva waved her off with a fork. "These are really tasty, by the way."

"Thanks."

Jane escaped to the kitchen, so disturbed by her talk with Eva that she just stood in the middle of the room, trying to collect her thoughts.

"Jane?" Alice looked at her curiously. "Are you all right?"

Jane shook herself as if coming out of a daze. "Yes, I'm fine. Just have to get finished up here so Eva and I can go to the quoits tournament." She took a deep breath. "Did you know they have a class and then a small competition for novices?"

"No." Alice looked wary. "What are you planning?"

Jane smiled. "Eva and I are going to enter the team competition as partners."

"Oh!" Alice clapped her hands. She was holding a dish towel in one of them, and it made a funny, muffled noise. "That's a wonderful idea. I'm proud of you, Jane."

"Proud of me?"

"Yes. And Father would be too. Resisting the temptation to 'get even' is difficult."

Jane felt her face heating with embarrassment. "I don't deserve any credit. I'm ashamed to say that I was struggling with letting go of that Scrabble incident—fairly unsuccessfully struggling—until Eva shared a story with me this morning that put her behavior in context."

Alice smiled. "You have a good heart, Jane. You would have conquered your desire to get even. I'm sure of it."

Chapter 🐢 Seventeen

E va and Jane spoke mostly of inconsequential topics during their ride northeast to Pottstown, where the tournament was being held. Jane discovered that Eva loved flowers, just as she did. Eva enjoyed a wide variety of crafts, just as Jane did.

"But I can't cook. Or bake." Eva's chuckle was sincere. "I can't even boil water, as they say. Actually, it's probably true. I tend to get distracted and walk away in the middle of things. The water probably would bubble right out of the top of the pot. Or evaporate."

Jane had to laugh at that one. "I have enjoyed my work as a chef. I didn't go to school intending to cook for the rest of my life. But fate put restaurant work in my path, and I discovered I love to cook."

"You're fortunate. I always feel so bad for people who don't like their jobs. Can you imagine doing something you don't enjoy, or even actively dislike, every day of the work week? Ick."

Jane shook her head. "I honestly can't. You like what you do, don't you?"

Eva nodded. "Very much."

"How did you get involved in that? Were you ever a teacher?"

Eva nodded. "Oh yes. My undergraduate degree is in elementary education. I taught first grade for three years and fourth grade for five more after that. Then I took a year off and finished my master's work in special education."

"Why did you switch?"

"When I was in a regular classroom with children who learned at a normal pace, I often found myself gravitating toward the child who was having trouble with a concept. More than a teacher normally would, I mean. The principal began assigning special needs children to my classroom because he knew I enjoyed working with them. So it was a logical transition."

"Did you teach special education after you got your master's degree?"

"Yes, I taught for four more years. I was a learning support teacher, which meant that I went around to other people's classrooms and helped special needs children succeed within the framework of the larger class."

"Why didn't they just put those children in a separate class? Wouldn't they learn more that way?"

Eva smiled. "There's quite a contentious debate on that very issue, as it happens. Some people are in favor of self-contained classrooms only for the children with special needs. Some prefer pullout programs, where a resource teacher takes children out of the regular class for certain subjects and certain periods of time. Other people would prefer that a learning support teacher come into the classroom and work with a child there. Some claim it is harmful socially and psychologically to a child to be placed in a different class. Others claim it is equally harmful not to give special needs children the one-on-one time and attention that they need to succeed."

"Whew. That is quite a contrast of opinions," Jane said. "Is there any research to support one position over another?"

"Oh yes. Unfortunately, each position has research that supports it, and there is not a clear-cut answer."

"Which do you favor?"

Eva did not need to think. "I believe a combination works best. Children cannot be completely separated from their peers if they are to have any shot at developing appropriate social interactions. But sometimes they do need a quieter environment with a much smaller teacher-to-student ratio."

"Makes sense to me," Jane said. "So how did you get interested in your specialty?"

"It was an offshoot of my work in special education," Eva said. "Even then, I believed a combo approach was good for a child. When I did my graduate thesis, I explored the ways in which children interact with others, the way they learn appropriate and inappropriate behaviors, and what part of the process breaks down most quickly when a child is removed to a self-contained classroom. When a position for an evaluator in my school district opened up, I applied for and got it. I worked there for five years before moving into the state position, which is similar but covers a much wider area."

"You travel like this a lot?"

Eva nodded. "I do. The program reimburses me for my lodging, up to a certain point."

"Do you often stay at inns?"

"As much as possible." She laughed. "It's a public school system, so of course they try to be frugal with their expenses. They will only spring for the most modest of Spartan hotels. I found that I adore the adventure of staying at a bed-and-breakfast, so I contribute when I need to to make up the difference."

"Why do you like inns?"

Eva shrugged. "I suppose for the same reasons any of your other patrons do. The friendliness, the conversation, the personal touch. It's so much more *interesting* than staying in some generic hotel."

"I agree." Jane nodded. "One of the reasons we decided to try running a bed-and-breakfast is that we thought we could provide a personal, friendly atmosphere that folks would enjoy."

"And you have succeeded admirably," Eva told her. "You and your sisters do a wonderful job. I can't even imagine trying to please so many different people week after week."

"It can be challenging," Jane admitted. "Occasionally we wonder why on earth we thought it was a good idea, but most of the time we really love what we're doing."

∽

As they drew near to the fire station on the grounds of which the tournament was being held, Jane began to feel butterflies of excitement darting around in her stomach.

She followed a line of other cars into a parking lot, where she paid a fee and was directed to a spot two rows away from the quoiting grounds. Eva was nearly as excited as Jane, and the moment the engine cut off, she depressed her seatbelt clip and swung out of the car.

Jane did the same, and the two women walked away from the parking area. The fire station backed up to a wide, grassy lawn in a sort of natural bowl surrounded by forest. The bulk of the field was taken up by long rows of quoits pits in above-ground boxes that were filled with a soft sand-and-clay mixture. In the center of each was the hob, or pin.

At one side of the field was a large wooden pavilion jammed with picnic tables. Several portable food concessions were parked there, including ones selling funnel cakes, snow cones, popcorn and soft pretzels. A small cinder-block building with a wooden awning that had been lifted to reveal a food concession window carried a modest selection of meal items. Jane noted "steamers," which she knew was a regional term for Sloppy Joes, chicken corn soup, pizza, hoagies and hot dogs, along with a variety of drinks, snacks and candy.

Around the edges of the field, more picnic tables were scattered. Some people had claimed these as a sort of home base, and there were grills, coolers, folding chairs and pop-up canopies everywhere.

"It never occurred to me to bring chairs or food," Jane said.

Looking around at the little nests people had created for themselves, Eva said, "Some of these folks look as if they're planning to be here for a week."

Jane laughed. "It's sort of like a tailgate party, isn't it?"

Directly behind the fire station at the edge of the parking lot, was a blue and yellow striped canopy with a large sign that read, "Registration."

"I suppose that's where we should go first," Jane said, pointing at the sign.

"Oh, good idea," Eva told her. "I bet they have a sched-ule of events too."

"I know the class that precedes our novice tournament begins at ten-thirty," Jane said.

"Good. Then we have time to walk around and watch some of the games."

The two women walked over to the registration tent. Jane noticed that there were quite a few more men than women standing around.

A rotund fellow wearing a white shirt with a huge, bright yellow smiley face on it nodded when they approached the table.

"Hello," he said jovially. "Played quoits before?"

"Ah, no," Jane said. "I've pitched once or twice but never in a game."

"You have?" Eva turned, her eyes wide. "You didn't tell me that."

Jane shrugged. "I barely figured out how to hold the quoit. There was nothing to tell." She looked at the registrar again. "I was told there's a novice class in the tournament. We'd like to sign up for that."

"Singles or doubles?"

"Doubles, please."

"Are you sure you want to pair up with me?" Eva said to Jane. "Just remember: I warned you."

Jane laughed. "Of course I want to be on a team with you. We're both beginners. Stop worrying."

They paid their fee and Mr. Smiley Face wrote down their names. They received tickets that showed they were in the novice class and a second pair that entered them in the tournament. Next they were provided with USQA rule books, T-shirts emblazoned with the USQA logo and the tournament date, and, as Eva had hoped, schedules of the day's events.

"Ever seen a game before?" the man inquired genially.

Jane and Eva shook their heads as one.

"They're just getting a group started down near that red canopy. If you want to see a match from beginning to end, that would be a good place to go."

"Thank you," Jane said. She and Eva turned and made their way around the perimeter of the field to the pits near the red tent.

It appeared that there were four games beginning. They chose one at random and stood back to watch. Fortunately, the pits were laid out at a right angle to them, so they were able to see both sets of competitors equally well.

Eva had her nose buried in the rule book while they waited for the game to begin, and Jane smiled. It was so typically Eva to ensure that she knew every rule.

Jane herself was much more of a people-watcher. She noticed immediately that there were not a lot of children around. One teenage girl sat in a chair with a woman companion, watching a match farther down the field, and a few pits over, one of the competitors looked to be about fourteen.

But there were no screaming babies, no little ones darting to and fro. The few children Jane saw were playing near RVs that had been parked along the edge of the macadam parking lot, and the children were being watched by groups of adults, largely their mothers.

Jane supposed that made sense. Not only was it a distraction for the players, but it was far too dangerous for children to be running loose. If one of the heavy quoits tossed by a grown man struck a child, it could do serious harm.

Jane also spared a moment to scan the field looking for Buck Dabney. Her quoits mentor was quite far away from where she stood, apparently engaged in a singles match. She hoped she would have a chance to say hello.

The match began. Eva closed her rule book and focused intently on the game, as did Jane.

There was a wooden pole that vaguely resembled a short parking meter behind each pit at the right end of the individual court. A device that looked to Jane a bit like an electronic scale was mounted on each, and after each team took its turn and the score for the round was announced, the two team members at that end of the pit walked to the device and recorded the score. Since in a team competition, each member of a team stood at the opposite end of the pit, the two individuals recording the score always included one competitor from each team, ensuring a fair tally.

Jane and Eva were watching a team event. A father and son made up one team. Both were tall men in red T-shirts tucked neatly into belted jeans. One shirt said, "Robinson Sr." and the other, "Robinson Jr." across the back in large white lettering. One man's hair was silver, the other's blond.

The second team also was composed of two men. The first was a mountain of a man with a florid complexion and a beer belly that made Jane wince and automatically think, *Heart attack waiting to happen.* His thick, bushy dark beard had flecks of gray liberally sprinkled through it. He wore a loud Hawaiian shirt in pinks, greens and yellows over bright green shorts, and he sported a golfer's cap with "Hi-Lows" printed across it in neon green.

The second man was shorter than his partner by several inches. He might top five-feet-six on a good day—in boots with heels. He was dressed in an oversize black T-shirt carelessly untucked over blue denim shorts, and his skin was starkly pale in contrast to his clothing. He wore a cap identical to the mountain man's, and Jane suppressed a grin as the significance of their team name, the Hi-Lows, struck her.

At her side, Eva whispered, "Interesting pair."

Jane laughed, then quickly turned it into a cough as the men stepped up to the pits. Mountain Man and Red Sr. occupied the left end; his son and the "Low" half of the Hi-Lows walked to the other.

Play commenced, and Jane immediately realized the importance of what Buck had been trying to tell her. The ability to stick a quoit in the ground at an angle was vital to success.

The men were good, floating ringer after ringer over the hob for three points, sticking leaners into the mud to block their opponents for two points, and using reliable closest-to-the-pin pitches to earn one point. Each match was the best of three, and the first team to twenty-one was the winner, as long as they won by two points.

Jane was fascinated by the different pitching styles. Mountain Man lobbed them high, while his shorter teammate sailed them neatly into the opposite box. Red Sr. was the only one of the four to stand outside the box when he pitched, although Jane noted that many players around them *did* stand outside, as Buck had taught her.

The games were tight. The first match went to the

Hi-Lows twenty-one to seventeen; the second, to the Robinsons twenty-one to sixteen. During the third game, Jane and Eva watched in awe as the men pitched ringer after ringer over the hobs, blocking each other and "settling" for the occasional one-pointer. The Robinsons were up twenty-two to twenty-one when Low stepped up to pitch his last quoit. The hob already had several quoits adorning it, and there was only a tiny bit of the top of the hob showing. Jane doubted a quoit could be made to stay atop the tower.

Low, however, had no such doubts. His pitch sent his quoit straight onto the pile atop the hob. It slid, caught and held for a three-point score that put his team up by two to win the match.

There was a spontaneous burst of applause with a few hoots and whistles interspersed. Low ran toward his partner and to everyone's astonished amusement, Mountain Man tossed his partner right up onto one massive shoulder where Low perched, grinning and making boxing-champ motions.

Eva turned to Jane. "My goodness. This is so different from what I was expecting."

"I'll bet," Jane answered. "And don't expect me to hoist you on my shoulder if we win."

Eva giggled. "You really never have seen a game before?"

Jane shook her head. "No. I visited a friend with a quoits pit who let me try it a few times. He gave me pointers but it's a difficult skill to master."

"I can't wait for our class to start." Eva practically bounced up and down. "I feel so much better knowing there is no pressure to win."

"You don't have long to wait," Jane informed her. She glanced at her watch. "We probably should start walking over there now."

"Over where?" Eva pulled out her schedule and consulted the layout directions on the back. "Oh. It's that first couple of pits at the far end of the field."

"Good," said Jane. "I'm going to feel self-conscious enough without every person in the picnic pavilion critiquing my form. Or lack thereof."

Eva groaned and laughed. "I know the feeling."

They walked briskly to the far end of the field, arriving just a few minutes before a redheaded man in a white T-shirt with the tournament logo began to talk. Jane glanced around. There appeared to be about a dozen people congregated for the instruction, including Eva and her. There was a wide range of ages and about half were men, half women.

"Welcome to the tournament," the redheaded instructor said. "We're always delighted to introduce new folks to the sport of quoiting. How many of you here have seen a match before today?"

About half the people raised their hands.

"That's pretty typical," the man said. "Quoits was brought over from England and was pretty popular here until about the 1930s, and then horseshoes kind of edged us out after that." He made a face and everyone laughed. "Luckily, the game was preserved in a couple of small pockets around the country. We here in Pennsylvania have been the leaders in reintroducing the game, and while it's still not well-known, more and more people are learning about the game every day."

He took a deep breath. "Now I'm sure some of you have pitched a few quoits, but I'm going to proceed as though everyone is brand-new to the game." Each of his assistants began passing out quoits, handing one to each person.

Eva nearly dropped hers, as did several others. One woman in a camisole top said, "Holy cow, these things are *heavy*," and everyone laughed.

Chapter 🐢 Eighteen

As the lesson rolled on, Jane was glad to hear all the things Buck had explained to her for a second time. Eventually, the group was split into three sections and directed to a court with one of the three instructors. There were four people in Jane's group. Eva had gone with a different instructor, on her theory that "you never know what we might learn from different people that will give us an edge when we compete."

Jane just shook her head. She supposed some attitudes simply took time to change.

Initially, the four simply took turns pitching the quoit, receiving basic instruction on the grip, the way to pitch and some tips for accuracy. Jane found that she was able to keep the quoit in the pit most of the time, but any further direction of the round steel disk was far more difficult.

The instructor moved on, showing them how they might stick one into the clay at an angle to block an opponent, but no one in Jane's group mastered the trick. Most of the people in the group were not even able to keep the quoit from bouncing or rolling out of the pit. At one point, the instructor had to leap into the air to avoid getting a leg hammered by a misdirected playing piece.

When the class was over, Jane felt as if she had accomplished as much as she possibly could given the time constraints. She walked over to Eva, who just was breaking away from her group.

"So how was it?" Jane asked. She had been too busy trying to follow her own instructor's directions to do more than glance at Eva's group during the session.

Eva rolled her eyes. "Just as I predicted. I'm terrible. Compared to those men—"

"Stop." Jane held up one hand like a traffic cop. "You can't compare yourself to the men we watched earlier. They've probably pitched quoits thousands of times. Just tell me what you feel you accomplished with the instructions you were given."

Eva took a deep breath. "Okay. Sorry. What did I accomplish . . . ? Well, I got a decent feel for how hard it is to pitch the quoit to get it in the pit. I clanked against the pin a time or two, though."

"That's great! In my group, most people had trouble even getting it in the pit."

"Mine too." Eva shook her head. "That's about it, Jane. I couldn't master that little wrist trick that helps to stick a leaner in the clay. I couldn't judge how high to throw it to get it to go over the pin. Hob. Whatever."

"Whatever." Jane smiled. "I couldn't do those things either, but nobody else seemed to be able to, so we're in good company. I think we're as ready for that competition as we're likely to be."

Eva nodded, her face growing serious. "Do you think we stand a chance to win?"

"I don't know, and I am not going to fall into competition craziness," Jane said firmly. "And you shouldn't either. Remember our talk this morning?"

Eva nodded. "I am having fun. And I promise to try not to think about competing."

"Good." Jane figured that was progress. "Me, too, but now I am starving. Those steamers are looking pretty tasty."

"I've got my eye on the soup."

Laughing, Jane tucked her arm through Eva's and eased her toward the food pavilion. "Let's eat."

They were almost to the lunch pavilion when Jane heard a masculine voice calling her name. She turned to see Buck striding toward her.

She waved. "Hi, Buck. How are you?"

"Great. My first match starts in fifteen minutes." He rubbed his hands together. "I'm ready for 'em this year."

Jane chuckled. "Buck, this is my friend Eva Quigley. Eva's a guest at Grace Chapel Inn, and she has agreed to be my novice partner today." She smiled at Eva. "Eva, this is Buck Dabney. Buck is the one who showed me what a quoit is."

Eva held out one of her dainty hands. "It's nice to meet you, Mr. Dabney."

Buck's hand was so large that Eva's disappeared completely within his palm when they shook hands. "It's nice to meet you too," he said. "Good luck with your match. If I'm not playing, I'll come and cheer you on."

Jane grimaced. "That will make me even more nervous than I already am."

Buck laughed. "Aw, you're going to do just fine. Enjoy yourselves, ladies." He bobbed his head and then moved on.

"How did you meet him?" Eva looked after Buck curiously.

"He knows a friend of mine," Jane said as the pair continued walking toward the food pavilion. "When I first became interested in quoits, he explained the game to me." She thought it prudent not to mention that she only had become interested in quoits after their cutthroat Scrabble game. It was funny, but the memory did not sting like it had before she learned about Eva's bruising experiences with her brothers.

∞

The telephone rang at Grace Chapel Inn shortly after Alice had finished lunch. Louise had gone to visit old Earl Padgett at Francie Litmore's house at the other end of Acorn Hill, so Alice rushed to grab the phone before the answering machine kicked in.

"Alice." A male voice spoke in response to her initial greeting. "This is Dane Rush."

"Dane!" She couldn't imagine why Dane might be calling again so soon. He'd said he was going to his sister's, hadn't he? "Do you have news for me?"

"I do," Dane said in a glad tone that conveyed his pleasure at being able to say that to her. "I got a call on my cell phone a little while ago from a rehabber in just over the Maryland border."

"Really? That's about an hour south of us."

"Right. And it's amazing a tortoise would make it that far. But I must say I've seen stranger things. Anyway, the rehabber got the e-mail just yesterday. Apparently he had been away too. He says he knows who owns her."

"Are you sure? Was he sure? Did he call them?" Alice was so excited she was babbling, but she didn't care.

"He's pretty sure," Dane said, laughing. "He says he kept the turtle last year while the couple was on vacation. He knew about the initials."

"Oh my goodness!" Alice sat down. "How wonderful! For the family and for me. How do I contact them?"

"You don't need to. I took the liberty of giving them your telephone number. They are out of town, too, but they said when they get back tomorrow, they'll call you right away. I guess they're eager to see her."

"Did they say how she got away?" Alice suddenly had her doubts about sending M.P. back to people who had managed to lose her.

"Yeah. They have a good enclosure with inside and

outside access. The floor is even heated in the winter. But a bear came down the mountain where they live and tore the fence apart. Luckily, the tortoise was in the barn or whatever it is, and the bear couldn't get in."

"Wow! I didn't know we had bears so close by." Alice glanced out the window, wondering how far bears traveled. And if they could turn doorknobs.

"We're not going to be seeing any of them around our area," Dane assured her. "These folks live in the hills, I was told. There's some rugged terrain down there. I imagine it wouldn't be hard to find a bear if you really went looking."

"Thanks, but no thanks." Alice laughed. "I have my hands full with one tortoise."

"Not for long," Dane assured her.

"What wonderful news," Alice said. "My sisters will be so happy. I'll look forward to hearing from M.P.'s family tomorrow."

"Great."

"Thank you so much for all your help," Alice said, making herself a mental note to send a donation to Dane's wildlife center. "I hope your jet lag isn't too terrible."

Dane laughed. "Thanks. And remember, you're always welcome to volunteer with us."

∞

Louise was frustrated. It seemed she had felt that way at least once a day ever since Herb Hoffstritt had brought that letter to the library.

She had phoned Francie Litmore that morning, and they had agreed on a time for Louise to visit. Francie assured Louise that Earl loved to get visitors and that he would talk her ear off.

And he had. The only problem with Earl's loquacious ramblings was that nothing he told her had anything to do with the Civil War information she was seeking. She had heard about how Earl met his wife. She had learned the names, occupations and family size of all of his five children. She now knew the names of several of his long procession of faithful hound dogs, the last one of which, Ol' Blue, had passed away a short while ago.

And she was fairly certain he was leading her in circles on purpose. She had tried repeatedly to steer the conversation around to his findings about the events of the summer of 1863. And each time, Earl had managed to slither on to some other topic. The gleam in his eye suggested he knew exactly what he was doing.

Francie stuck her head into the small sitting room where Earl was enthroned in a recliner, and Louise was perched on a nearby loveseat. "Hello, you two. Would either of you like a drink?"

Louise had refused refreshments thirty minutes earlier, assuming she would only be there a quarter hour or so. "I would love something," she told Francie. "Just ice water, perhaps."

"Grandpa? How about you? I just got a new type of tea from Time for Tea."

"I'll try it," Earl said. "What's it called?"

Francie hesitated. "Sorry, I can't remember the name of it. Mr. Wood said it was his favorite."

"Can't remember? You know that's one of the first signs of senility, little girl." Earl cackled at his own wit.

Francie just smiled. "Grandpa," she said fondly. "I'll bring your drinks in a minute."

"That's fine," the old man said. "Just don't make mine too sweet. You like that sugar, don't you?"

"I do." Francie eased out of the doorway and out of sight.

And just like that, Earl picked up exactly where he had left off in the middle of a story about the tornado that took down his barn and killed his mule back in '57. He spoke on that subject until Francie reappeared a few minutes later with their drinks.

Louise took advantage of the momentary break in Earl's monologue. "So, Mr. Padgett, do you remember the other day when you spoke to me about the Civil War? You said there was no battle, but you didn't say why."

Earl cast a mischievous look her way. "Nope. Sure didn't. Bet that's bugging you, huh?"

Oh, he had no idea. Louise prayed for patience. Then she had a thought. "I would like to know," she said, rising. "But if you would rather keep the knowledge to yourself, it certainly isn't that important. I'll just tell them at the meeting that you have some information that you aren't willing to share."

"What meeting?" Earl's faded blue eyes fastened on Louise with a look as keen as an eagle's.

Louise feigned surprise. "Oh, didn't I already mention that to you? I must have forgotten. Just forget I said anything." She took one last drink of her water and set down the glass. "Mr. Padgett, it's been lovely visiting with you. I must go soon, though. I have chores to do at home."

"Don't you want to hear what I found out about that Civil War stuff?" The old man set down his teacup with a clatter.

"Of course," Louise said. "But I assume you'll talk about it in your own good time."

"I'll tell you now." Earl sounded grumpy but resigned.

Louise tried hard not to smile as she sat back down. "That would be nice."

⌒⌒

Jane and Eva's competition was scheduled for two o'clock while the semifinal matches were being conducted. The instructors had told them that their match should finish up in plenty of time for them to watch the championship match. So at two o'clock, Jane and Eva reported to the field where the novice matches would be held. Out of the group of people who had participated in the beginner's course with them, only Jane and Eva and one other team were playing doubles. There were two sets of singles, and the other four had not signed up to compete at all.

Jane's butterflies were back.

Relax, she told herself. *This is just for fun, remember?*

Finally, the time arrived. Jane went to one end of the court, and Eva walked to the other. The other team was composed of two young men who introduced themselves as Chuck and Leroy. Chuck was tall, thin and already balding, while Leroy was slightly shorter and wore his hair in a bowl cut that reminded Jane of Prince Valiant in the old adventure comic strip from her childhood.

The competitors shook hands. Jane and Chuck received the quoits marked with *A*'s while Eva and Leroy took the *B*s, and the game began.

Jane stepped up to pitch first. She tried to remember everything she had learned: foot position, bending her knee, the pitch and follow-through, the use of the wrist—but to her utter humiliation, her first toss fell short. Her second landed in the pit and promptly bounced out.

Her face red, Jane watched as Chuck took her place and pitched his quoits. His first fell short just as Jane's had. His second went wide and landed to the left of the pit. No score for either team. Jane felt a little better.

Eva and Leroy, at the far end of the court, collected the quoits and took their turns. Each of them also failed to produce any score.

As Jane and Chuck picked up the scattered quoits for their second round of pitching, Jane broke the tense silence. "Gee, I hope we aren't still playing this game after dark tonight. Twenty-one points is looking awfully far away."

Chuck laughed. He wore a T-shirt emblazoned with the Nittany Lion logo that read, "We are ... PENN STATE," and he seemed a pleasant young man. "It's a possibility," he responded. "I haven't gotten the hang of this game yet."

"Me neither," Jane said. She stepped up and took her pitches. This time, she landed both quoits in the pit. Neither of them was particularly close to the pin, but Jane was happy with her effort. Chuck's first pitch again fell short, but his second landed in the pit midway between Jane's two. Still, Jane's was closer, and she won a point for her team.

The game continued, and both teams improved. Leroy actually threw a ringer once. Since his other quoit was closer than either of Eva's two, he received three points for the ringer plus one additional point.

Eva looked crushed. "Sorry," she mouthed to Jane.

Jane shook a finger at her, grinning. "Fun, remember?"

Eva's expression lightened and she smiled back. "Fun."

Jane and Eva were down twelve to eight at that point, but they came back with a series of consistent two-point rounds, and eventually the score was 18–16, Jane and Eva.

On her next round, Jane pitched a leaner. Chuck's two pitches each landed closer than her second quoit, but she still received two points. Eva and Leroy pitched. Each of them had a quoit very close to the hob, and a referee came out with his calipers to measure to see whose pitch had landed closest. Ultimately, Eva received one point for closest to the pin.

The referee walked over to the scoring machine and entered the number. "Match concludes. Twenty-one to sixteen, the ladies," he called.

Jane blinked. "We won?"

Eva looked as shocked as Jane. "Really?"

The referee and several spectators laughed. "Really."

"Congratulations," Chuck said, holding out his hand to Jane, as Leroy and Eva also shook.

"Thank you," Jane said. "I can't believe it."

Chuck grinned. "It was fun, wasn't it? I can see how people get addicted to this."

"It *was* fun," Jane agreed as Eva and Leroy joined them. "Now I want to watch that championship match."

Chapter 🐢 Nineteen

Alice had dinner almost ready to be set on the table when Jane and Eva walked in that afternoon.

Jane rushed back to the kitchen. "I invited Eva to eat with us. Is that all right?"

Alice's eyebrows rose. "Scrabble Eva?" she whispered.

Jane laughed and nodded.

"It's fine with me, as long as she doesn't mind a casserole with a store-bought loaf of bread."

"And with me," Louise said.

"Thanks. We'll be back as soon as we've cleaned up."

"Five minutes," warned Alice.

Both of the quoits players were back in just under five minutes, with clean clothes, brushed hair and thoroughly washed hands.

Eva inspected her nails as she and Jane walked into the kitchen. "I had quoit dirt under there," she said with a shudder.

"Clay," Jane corrected. "Me too. Yuck!"

Louise chuckled. "Is it safe to say you won't be playing quoits again?"

"Oh, I don't know about that. It was a fun day." She slung an arm around Eva's shorter frame. "You are looking at novice champions of the USQA," she announced.

Alice's mouth fell open. "You're kidding!"

"That's not very flattering," Jane said as she and Eva laughed at Alice's expression.

"I didn't mean it that way," Alice said. "But I thought there might be some more experienced players who sneaked in there."

"No, all of them looked as if they just had been introduced to the sport," Eva said. "Like us."

"We saw Buck Dabney, Viola's friend," Jane said. "He made it to the semifinals of the singles matches before he was eliminated."

Louise said, "So tell us about your game."

"Match," Jane and Eva corrected her. They looked at each other and laughed.

"Match," Louise repeated as she took buttered and broiled slices of Italian bread from the oven and placed them in a basket.

Alice already had placed a casserole on the table, and there were salads at each place as well.

The four women sat down, and after Alice offered a brief grace, Jane and Eva recounted the day's experiences.

"So we enjoyed it immensely," Jane said in conclusion. "What did you two do today?"

Alice said, "Oh! I have wonderful news."

Louise said, "You found the tortoise's family," in a dry, joking tone.

Alice's face fell. "How did you know?"

Jane's head snapped up. "Seriously? You really did find out who owns M.P.? That's great! When are they coming to get her?"

Alice smiled and shook her head, saying wryly, "Your reluctance to see her leave warms my heart, Jane."

All four women laughed. Then Alice went on to relate the highlights of Dane's phone call and to reveal her expectation that she would hear from the tortoise's family the following day.

Louise cleared her throat. "I have news also."

"Let me guess," Jane said, "You found something that reveals what happened with that supposed Civil War battle?"

"I did," Louise said with relish.

"What Civil War battle?" Eva asked, which prompted the sisters to give her an abbreviated explanation of the recent goings-on.

"Francie Litmore's grandfather has copies of newspapers and letters from that era," Louise said at the conclusion of their minisaga. "I went to visit him today and after a long period of reminiscing, he finally let me in on his secret information."

"I imagine he loved having someone to talk to," Alice said diplomatically.

"And I don't mind talking to him," Louise told her. "Truly I don't. However, in this particular instance, I was dying to learn what he knew, and the old fox kept dodging my questions."

Jane snickered. "I bet you were ready to strangle him."

"If he weren't ninety-three years old, I might have considered it," Louise said.

"So what did you learn?" Alice asked. "Was there or was there not a battle in or near our hamlet?"

"Not," said Louise decisively.

"Then what does that letter of Mr. Hoffstritt's refer to?" asked Jane, her brows drawing together. "What about the fracas and the . . . what was the other term?"

"*Dustup*," supplied Louise.

"That's it." Jane waved her fork at Louise. "What really happened?"

Louise smiled. "I can't tell you."

"What?"

"Why not?"

Louise smiled even more broadly. "I promised Earl Padgett that I would keep the information secret until Monday night."

"What's happening Monday night?" Jane wanted to know.

She had not been in the house the evening before, when Louise had told Alice about her morning discussion with Ethel.

"Lloyd is having a meeting of the planning committee for the reenactment and memorial ceremony."

"A planning meeting for. . . ?" Jane appeared too stunned to complete the thought. Finally, she said, "But now we know there is nothing to reenact. Lloyd's going to look ridiculous to the whole town if he pursues this."

"I know." Louise sighed. "The meeting is going to be small. Just Lloyd, Aunt Ethel, Florence and a few of the other battle-believers. I thought the best way to handle it might be for me to present the information."

"But will Lloyd believe you?" Jane asked. "After all, you've been sort of the de facto leader of the 'no battle' movement."

Louise chuckled. "I wouldn't call myself a leader, but yes, I think Lloyd—and Florence and the others—will have to believe me when Earl shows them the papers he has."

"You're taking Earl to the meeting?" Alice patted the table. "Excellent idea."

"Yes indeed. Francie agreed to make copies of the important items to hand out to each person," Louise said. "And then I plan to give Carlene a set so that she can write about it in her next edition of the *Nutshell*. I've already told her to save space."

"You should invite her to the meeting," Jane suggested.

Louise hesitated. "I almost did. But I don't want to embarrass Lloyd publicly, and I'm afraid if he reacts badly at first, Carlene might feel obligated to report that."

"Good thought." Jane dabbed at her mouth with her napkin. "That's kind of you, Louise."

"Well, I love Lloyd," Louise told them.

"We all do," said Alice, "and I agree. I wouldn't want to hurt his feelings that way, either."

Eva, who had been listening quietly, said plaintively to Louise, "I'm leaving tomorrow. If I promise not to reveal anything to anyone, will you tell me?"

Everyone laughed, and Louise nodded. "Right before you leave, dear."

✎

Eva departed on Sunday morning, shortly before the Howard sisters left the inn to attend services at Grace Chapel.

Jane had finished cleaning up after breakfast and was waiting in the front hallway when Eva came down the stairs carrying her suitcase and laptop.

"Oh, Jane," Eva said, setting down her things. "I am going to miss you." She stepped forward with her arms open and Jane embraced her in return.

"I'll miss you too," Jane said, realizing it was true. The two of them had many things in common. "I won't miss playing Scrabble with you, though," she added, smiling.

Eva's own face sobered. "You know, I have to apologize to you. I was so thoughtless and smart-alecky that day. I treated you the way my brothers used to treat me. It's a wonder you ever spoke to me again."

"It was close there for a little while," Jane admitted, grinning to take the sting out of her words. "But look what a good quoits team we made."

"We did, didn't we?" Eva said, her usual glow returning. She stepped back, raising her right hand as if taking a pledge. "I promise you, Jane Howard, that I am going to try very hard to live by our new motto: 'fun!' I am going to do my best to let go of the need to compete, and I'm going to focus more on enjoying the journey and the people with whom I am playing."

"That's an excellent promise," Jane said, impressed by Eva's sincerity. She raised her right hand as well. "And it's one I echo. A little more humility and thoughtfulness would do me good."

The two women regarded each other fondly for a last moment before Eva picked up her things. "I guess this is good-bye," she said.

"But it doesn't have to be for good," Jane said. "Come back and stay with us again."

"I'll have to do some research and see if I can't find other schools around here that need to be evaluated," Eva said, winking.

Jane laughed, holding the door for her guest. "I'll walk out with you."

Moments later, Jane still was standing on the porch as Eva's car turned left out of the driveway and motored away. Jane didn't move. She was dressed for church already in a tiered floor-length skirt of green, brown and gold paired with a simple gold, jean-style jacket in lightweight corduroy. The fresh, chilly autumn air was bracing and pleasant as it rippled her skirt.

Alice came out the door. "Are you ready for church? What are you doing standing out here?"

Jane turned and smiled. "Just seeing Eva on her way."

Alice nodded wisely. "You were good for her, Jane."

"She was good for me too," Jane returned. "I was never aware of just how competitive I can be. It's good to recognize one's own weaknesses, don't you think?"

"Very good," Alice confirmed.

Behind them, they heard the telephone ring.

"Oh dear," Alice said. "I'd better answer that. I'm not sure if—"

"Aaa-lice!" Louise evidently had been close to the telephone.

"Coming," Alice called. The skirt of her simple navy shirtdress flapped around her knees as she hurried inside.

Louise stepped onto the porch a moment later. She looked as efficiently Louise-like as always, dressed in a taupe sweater and a muted plaid skirt in shades of beige and brown. Her pearls were neatly in place around her neck, and her short, silver hair was flawless. "Good morning again," she said to Jane, whom she had seen just before at breakfast. "I see we're all ready to go. As soon as Alice concludes her call, we can set off."

Jane smiled. Only Louise could get away with saying "set off" without it sounding remarkably hokey. "All right," Jane responded. "I'm eager to talk to Viola this morning. She was the one who knew Buck in the first place, and I know she wants to hear how the tournament went."

The words barely were out of her mouth when Alice reappeared, her face animated. "That was M.P.'s owner," she announced.

"Oh, wonderful," Jane said. "What did he say?"

"He is terribly grateful to us for caring for her," Alice reported. "He and his wife had to leave town to attend a funeral quite suddenly, and a neighbor was taking care of the tortoise. The man went over one morning and found the paddock torn apart. He thought a bear had done it. M.P. was inside the barn for the night, safe and sound. The neighbor went back home to round up some fencing materials to fix up something makeshift, and when he returned, he realized he had left the barn door open. M.P. was gone. How she got so far north is a mystery."

"Interesting, but what did he say about taking her back?" Jane prompted. "Is he coming today?"

"He can't," Alice said. "He's a pastor, and they have a

congregational meeting and dinner after church. The earliest he can get here is tomorrow morning about ten."

"Great," Jane said with relief. "We don't have new guests arriving until Wednesday."

The three sisters set off for Grace Chapel. As they neared the church, Ethel and Lloyd, who were not far ahead of them, turned and saw them.

"Guess what?" Alice called. "We found the tortoise's owners."

Ethel's eyes widened. "Oh, that's good, dear. I know that thing was an interesting guest, but after all, don't those animals represent a hazard?"

"It's a moot point," Jane said hastily. "M.P. leaves tomorrow."

The little group moved inside. Louise went off to meet with the choir before beginning her organ prelude. As Alice and Jane took their seats in the pew alongside Ethel and Lloyd, Alice heard snatches of conversations here and there.

". . . has a lovely pattern for a hoop skirt. I am sure they wore those back then . . ."

". . . red, white and blue bunting, of course . . ."

"Say, Liza, didn't Henry's great-grandfather serve in The War? Do you think he might have an old uniform packed away somewhere?"

". . . The high school band could play a selection of songs from that era . . ."

Alice suppressed a sigh. It sounded as if everyone in the congregation was involved in planning the yet-to-be-confirmed commemoration festivities. She wondered how people would react when Louise's news came out. One thing was very likely—those people who had been most outspoken were going to have egg on their faces, and it would take some serious diplomacy to pacify them.

Louise began to play the prelude, and Alice settled back to enjoy her sister's considerable keyboard skills. Louise had chosen to play a beautifully arranged organ piece based on a song from the musical *Godspell*. As the melodious harmonies of "All Good Gifts" swelled, Alice closed her eyes and savored the music.

Rev. Thompson opened the service shortly afterward. When he asked if anyone in the congregation had any blessings or prayer requests to share, Jane nudged Alice. "Tell them about the tortoise," she whispered.

Alice looked at Jane questioningly.

"A lot of people here have been very interested in her," Jane continued. "You should share your news."

Alice nodded and smiled, then raised her hand. "I have a blessing." The pastor nodded at her to continue. "Many of you know that we—my sisters and I—found a large tortoise. I'm happy to report that just this morning, I received a call from a man just over the Maryland border about her. She walked away from home when a barn door accidentally was left open, and he's coming to pick her up tomorrow."

"Wonderful news," Rev. Thompson said as people nodded and smiled. "I know some members of this congregation have prayed about your tortoise experience. It's wonderful to see that prayer in action. God is good indeed."

⬯

On Monday, the inn was quiet. The Osbourne family and the older couple on their second honeymoon had departed, and no new guests were to check in until Wednesday. Jane took the opportunity to turn out all the guest rooms and clean them from top to bottom.

Alice and Louise both pitched in to help. Alice took down the draperies and carried them outside, vigorously shaking them free of any dust. They all had been dry-cleaned earlier in the year and did not look as if they needed it again quite yet. Louise washed down woodwork and checked on linens. When Alice returned, she rehung the drapes after dusting every exposed surface, including the tops of door and window frames. Meanwhile, Jane polished each of the floors before she used a steamer to deep-clean the rugs.

In the midst of all this, Alice took a telephone call. It turned out to be the man who owned M.P., and he told her he could be there within the hour to pick up his pet. Alice gave him directions, and he hung up after thanking her profusely yet again. When Jane heard this news, she barely could contain her delight. She did everything but kick up her heels and dance around the room while Louise and Alice laughed at her.

Shortly before noon, a battered, blue Ford pickup pulled into the driveway and parked in the lot next to the inn.

"Alice," called Jane, who had been looking out the window when the truck rolled past, "I believe M.P.'s person is here."

Louise chuckled. "M.P.'s *person?*"

Jane shrugged. "Well, I know the fellow owns the tortoise in the eyes of the law, but I'm not sure any of us can really own another life. I even feel uncomfortable when we are referred to as Wendell's owners. I'd rather think of us as his people. Or his family, maybe."

Alice came into the kitchen. "I'll meet him and bring him in through the back door, all right?"

When her sisters nodded assent, Alice hurried through the back door.

A surprisingly young man of medium height with wavy brown hair had gotten out of the blue truck. "Hello," he called. "Are you Alice Howard?"

She nodded, walking to him and extending her hand. "I am."

"I'm Pastor Bennett Sharp, but please call me Ben," he said. "Are you the one who found Miss Priss?"

Alice began to giggle. "That's what M.P. stands for? We thought perhaps it was your initials."

Ben looked sheepish. "Nope. It's just a silly name. My oldest sister named her when we were little, and we never changed it."

"When you were little?" Alice echoed. "How long have you had her?"

"We got her when she was about ten years old," Ben told her. "Someone gave her to my father. I was seven at the time, so we've owned her twenty-one years. I got her after my folks passed away."

Doing some quick math, Alice concluded that Pastor Sharp was twenty-eight, about the age she had pegged him for when he arrived. That also meant that the tortoise was thirty-something, as Dane had guessed. "So were you the one who drew the short straw when you were deciding who was going to take the tortoise?"

The young minister laughed. He had a nice laugh, not too loud, but full and ringing with good humor. "I volunteered," he said. "I was the one who cared for her when I lived at home, and my sisters were not real excited about taking on a great big ol' tortoise, so she came with me. Luckily, the girl I was dating liked Miss Priss, and now she's my wife. The girl, not the tortoise," he clarified, chuckling again. Then he sobered. "We both were pretty torn up when we found out she'd gotten away. We were afraid that a bear got her. Even if that didn't happen, we knew she wouldn't survive long on her own with the weather turning like it has. I wonder if some good Samaritan helped her to get here."

"We may never know, but she's just fine," Alice told him. "A little spoiled, probably. We've been keeping her in the laundry room right next to the kitchen and I suspect my sister Jane has been sneaking her plenty of treats. Come in, please."

Alice turned and led the young pastor through the

back door of the inn and on to the laundry. Louise and Jane were standing alongside the barricade and Alice introduced them.

Ben eyed the barricade. "Did that work?"

Jane nodded. "Mostly. When we remembered to put some weight against it so she couldn't push it out of the way."

He smiled. "She's really strong, isn't she?" Then he caught sight of the tortoise. She was lying on her heat pad in the far corner, basking beneath the lamp. Wendell lay right beside her, equally content in the warmth.

"Well, what do you think about that?" Ben said.

Alice laughed. "That's Wendell. We were surprised at how well they got along."

"We have two big white rabbits that she shares her quarters with," Ben told them. "So she's used to other animals. I suspect if your kitty didn't bother her, she was happy to have the company."

He stepped over the protective chair, got down on one knee and pitched his voice a bit louder. "Hey, girl, don't you recognize me?"

The tortoise slowly turned her head. Then she began to move, trundling out of the corner to bump against Ben's knee. "You know me, don't you, Prissy-girl? You gave me a real scare, I'll tell you."

"I read that they can recognize faces," Alice said.

He nodded. "She knows my wife and me, although I suspect we're her favorites only because we come bearing food."

The sisters laughed.

The young man rose and held out his hand to Alice again, then shook Jane's and Louise's as well. "I can't thank you enough for taking care of her," he said. "I would like to repay you."

"Heavens no," Alice said. "We couldn't take anything for rescuing one of God's creatures."

"I insist." He made as if to remove his wallet, but Alice

shook her head firmly. "If you really want to repay us, make a donation to some organization that cares for animals."

Ben Sharp shook his head. "You ladies are angels," he told them.

Louise chuckled. "If you knew us better, you'd be under no such illusion."

Everyone laughed again, and then, after good-byes, Alice held open the back door so that Ben could carry Miss Priss out to his truck. She watched in amusement as he placed the tortoise on the seat next to him and adjusted the seatbelt in an effort to hold her securely.

"Have a good trip, girl," Alice said before Ben closed the door. "It was nice meeting you."

"I'm sure she thinks it was nice meeting you too," Ben said. "I know I do." He shook her hand once again. "God bless you, Alice."

As the blue Ford slowly backed out of the driveway, Alice turned back to the house. Jane and Louise already had dismantled the barrier. The heat lamp and pad had been unplugged and were set on the porch.

"Well," Alice said. "Wasn't that an adventure?" She was pleased to have found the tortoise's owner, but she knew a little part of her was going to miss the intrepid creature.

"Poor Wendell," Louise said, pointing.

Alice turned. Wendell had leaped on top of the dryer and was looking in vain for the recently removed items of comfort. "Poor Wendell," Alice repeated. "He's going to miss that heat pad."

"Maybe I'll give him mine," Jane said. "And he won't even have to share it."

Chapter 🐢 Twenty

L ouise picked up Francie and her grandfather at six thirty Monday evening. The meeting was scheduled for seven o'clock in the conference room of Town Hall and she wanted to be sure Earl got there safely and had plenty of time to settle in.

She had not told Lloyd or Ethel that Earl would be attending, although Ethel knew that all three Howard sisters had expressed interest in going to the meeting.

Louise stopped in front of Town Hall and put on her emergency flashers. She and Francie helped Earl out of the car, although once he was on his feet, he shook off both of them.

"I'm not dead yet," he said to his granddaughter. "I'll tell you when I need help." He turned, then stiffly swiveled halfway around again. "I need help on the steps," he informed them.

Louise hid a smile. She left Francie to assist Earl while she took the Cadillac around and parked it in the lot behind the building. She caught up to Francie and Earl in the hallway outside the room where the meeting was to be held, moving ahead of them to open the door for the old man.

"Thanks," he said gruffly. "That's somethin' else I do need help with." Louise caught Francie grinning behind her grandfather's back as she helped him to a seat.

There was only a short time remaining until the opening of the meeting, and most people were in the room already. Alice and Jane had caught a ride over with Lloyd when he picked up Ethel.

Florence Simpson sat across from them at the table. From the way Florence occasionally glared at Ethel, Louise surmised that the tiff they had had in the Coffee Shop had not been resolved. Florence's husband Ronald sat beside her, probably dragged along for moral support, Louise decided. Others in attendance included Duane Van Dinkle, Hope Collins, and Loueda Ullman, who had come down on the side of common sense during the first discussion in the Coffee Shop. Nia Komonos was there from the library, seated next to Herb Hoffstritt, the man whose family letters had created all the stir.

Before Louise could take her seat, Lloyd hurried toward her. "Louise," he whispered, "what is Mr. Padgett doing here?"

"He came along with me," Louise said. "He was very interested when he heard about this meeting."

"This was not meant to be a large meeting," Lloyd said. "I only wanted to discuss a few possibilities with key people."

"I heard about it through the grapevine," Louise said, "and I imagine some of these other folks did too. You didn't specify it as a private meeting, so you can't very well throw them all out."

Lloyd all but wrung his hands in a completely uncharacteristic gesture. His gray hair was neatly combed, but Louise noticed that his bald spot shone as if he were too warm or quite nervous.

Then she noticed something else. "Is that Abraham Lincoln on the pin you're wearing?"

Lloyd was well-known around town for his devotion to

collecting political buttons and similar memorabilia. He brightened at her question.

"Yes. Do you like it?"

"It's interesting," Louise said, peering at it more closely through her glasses. The pin consisted of a rectangular piece of metal with a small hole in the top through which a red, white and blue ribbon was strung. The center of the metal rectangle had an oval cutout, and there was some scrollwork decorating the corners of the little pendant, which was perhaps an inch wide and only slightly taller. In the ring was a photo of Lincoln. Not a photo, really, but what she believed was referred to as a tintype. "How old is that?" Louise asked.

Lloyd beamed. "It's an 1860 ferrotype button, although as you can see, it technically is not a button at all. The only fastening that occurs is the pin that attaches the ribbon to the wearer's clothing." He had assumed the tone he often used when discussing his collection, that of an information-imparting tour guide. "It's quite valuable," he went on. "A flawless specimen can go for more than six hundred dollars. I have one of those at home. This one is considerably more battered, and I thought it was the perfect accoutrement, given the topic of tonight's meeting."

"I see."

Louise tapped her watch. "It's seven. Good luck, Lloyd."

Lloyd hurried to the head of the table while Louise took a seat beside Earl. "This meeting is called to order," he said. "This is merely an informal meeting to discuss the possibility of forming a committee to oversee a memorial ceremony and reenactment for the Civil War battle that probably occurred here in Acorn Hill. As most of you know, Mr. Herb Hoffstritt, who is with us tonight, discovered evidence of such a battle in correspondence that came down through his family."

Herb, Louise thought, looked supremely uncomfortable when all heads turned his way. He cleared his throat. "It, ah, never actually says anything about a battle."

"Of course it means a battle. What else could the words *fracas* and *dustup* be describing?" Florence broke in, her eyebrows drawn together into an ominous line. Florence looked ominous all over tonight, dressed in a black sweater over black houndstooth trousers. Even her jewelry was black.

"You want to know what else those words could mean?"

Louise was startled enough to move slightly in her seat when Earl Padgett spoke out. His aging voice was surprisingly strong, and his tone was just as combative as Florence's had been. Enough so that Florence looked completely taken aback.

"I'll tell you exactly what went on here in Acorn Hill on July twentieth of 1863," Earl said. He pointed a gnarled, shaky finger toward Francie, who held up a manila envelope. "Right in here are copies of newspaper articles written in this area in the 1860s."

Someone snickered, but Louise could not see who it was. She was supremely thankful that she had not invited Carlene Moss to tonight's meeting.

"There're also copies of a letter my great-granddaddy wrote to my great-grandma. Only she wasn't my great-grandma yet," he clarified, causing a few smiles to break out around the room.

Lloyd ran a finger around the inside of his collar as if it might be feeling tight. "And what do these items say, Mr. Padgett?" he asked politely.

Earl cackled. That was the only word for it, Louise was certain. "There *was* a fracas in town on the twentieth of July. A dustup, if you like that word better. But a drunken brawl over a woman is what it really was. Two Rebel soldiers from a small group that had sneaked north to steal supplies came into town. Both fellers had tried to catch the attention of a Miss Cicely Simpson a few months before when the Confederate Army was tromping all over southern Pennsylvania."

Florence sat up straight, her eyes wide. "That's my name!"

Beside her, her husband Ronald cleared his throat. "Actually, dear, it's *my* family name. Don't forget, my family has been in this county for at least as long as yours."

Florence turned and shot him a withering look, but Ronald only shrugged and smiled, his freckled face slowly acquiring a flush.

Louise gave him a reassuring smile. Ronald rarely stood up to Florence, but he did go quietly his own way and let her domineering manner roll right off him much of the time. To Louise's amusement, Ronald slowly and deliberately winked at her.

"Anyway," Earl went on, "these two cavalry soldiers rode into town one morning. The newspaper article kinda delicately mentions that they were . . ."

"The worse for spirits," Francie said, grinning as she glanced down at the folder.

"But the letter says they were drunker'n a squirrel in a barrel of moonshine."

Louise, caught by the imagery, pictured a squirrel doing the backstroke in something that looked like a big rain barrel.

"So they ride right up to the Simpsons' house, just about fall off their horses and walk up on the porch. And they holler for her to come out and choose which one she wants. Miss Simpson don't come out. The two fellers git to arguin' about which one she wants to see, and they start a-fighting, swinging at each other but not doing much damage. The fight moves off the porch into the yard, and the one knocks t'other into the water trough. That one's so drunk he don't come up for air. So the other reaches in to haul him out, and he falls in too."

The faces around the table were comical to behold as Earl told his story. Some were laughing, some were incredulous. One, Lloyd's, just looked upset. Florence looked as if she had bitten into a lemon.

"About that time," Earl went on, "Miss Simpson comes

out of her house with a broom. She hollers at them soldiers to stop being a nuisance, and she starts a-swingin' that broom, knocking them upside the head and in the—uh, the behind. They start a-runnin' down the road to git away from her, and she unties their horses from the post and sends 'em off in t'other direction without their riders."

Ronald laughed and slapped his knee. "That's a Simpson for you!"

Earl's eyebrows went up as he turned to look at Ronald. "Guess them Simpsons used to have some spunk, anyways."

"One of 'them Simpsons,'" said Florence acidly to Earl, "became your great-grandfather."

"Well, I'll be. I guess it's true then," Earl said.

Ronald said, "Welcome to the family," with a grin.

Florence opened her mouth with a ferocious frown.

"Grandpa!" Francie rose to her feet before any possibility of a latter-day Simpson dustup could break out. "Why don't I pass out these copies of the things we found, and you can read them for yourselves. I only made ten copies," she said apologetically. "I didn't realize there would be so many folks attending."

Francie passed out the pages she had copied. Louise shared her set with Jane, while Alice moved closer to Ethel to look at hers. The room was silent as everyone read the short article that mentioned the fracas. The second sheet contained a letter to a Union officer in the Pennsylvania Tenth Regiment, one William Henry Taggart, who was commissioned as a second lieutenant. A neatly printed note across the top informed the reader that the Tenth was formed in April of 1861 and recruited volunteers from the area. The letter was sent by Taggart's sister Mary. It went on to note that the subject of the letter was Taggart's betrothed, Miss Cicely Simpson, and that the pair had been affianced before his departure in 1861.

A mild gasp escaped from Jane as she read. She looked

up at Francie. "So Miss Simpson already was spoken for when the dustup occurred!" She began to laugh.

Louise chuckled along with her. A few moments later, as others read the same thing, everyone began to chuckle.

The body of the letter, dated July 20, 1863, included one long paragraph about the fracas. It took some time to decipher, as the copy was of the original letter in the ornate, flowing cursive script of the times. Further complicating it were differences in spelling, which tended to distract one from the content. The meaning, however, was plain: The events that old Earl Padgett had just described were clearly documented by Miss Mary Taggart of Acorn Hill, Lancaster County, Pennsylvania.

It was not lost on anyone that Herb Hoffstritt's letter had been written by and sent to entirely different individuals, thereby removing a certain element of fiction if anyone questioned the single source as historically sound.

There was a long silence in the room as everyone read the letter. Finally, Lloyd cleared his throat. "Well," he said, "I suppose there is no need for a committee now that we have established that the incident in question was not a battle, but a comedy routine."

Everyone chuckled.

"Thank you all for coming. I appreciate your interest in our community." And with that, Lloyd pushed back his chair and stood, signaling an end to the meeting.

Florence immediately swept out with Ronald in tow. Louise noticed that Ronald discreetly pocketed his copy of the newspaper article and letter, although Florence's still lay on the table.

Ethel, Alice and Jane stood talking to Lloyd. Glancing at Earl, Louise noted that he and Francie were with a separate cluster of people. She walked toward the former group. As she arrived, she heard Jane say, "There still are many things that are special about Acorn Hill."

Lloyd looked rather dispirited. "I suppose it's all for the best that we do not have a significant Civil War battle site here. It would change the town immeasurably."

"And we don't want it changed," Ethel said stoutly, clearly trying to cheer him. "We love it just the way it is."

"Perhaps that should be our town's focus," Alice suggested. "What's that you always say, Lloyd? 'Acorn Hill has had a life of its own away from the outside world.' Well it has for a long time, and I think that is something to celebrate. I think we should continue to plan a summer event, but focus on the things that are special about us and have been so for years."

Lloyd was looking a bit happier. "Perhaps you're right, Alice," he said. "I think I'll call Carlene tomorrow and see about getting all this talk straightened out for good."

∽

On Tuesday, Alice and Louise had just come into the kitchen for dinner when there was a knock on the back door.

"Come in," Jane called.

Lloyd entered, his green eyes twinkling. Today he wore a three-piece gray suit with a very pale pink shirt and a bow tie in an interesting pink and gray paisley design. He carried a newly printed edition of the *Acorn Nutshell* in one hand, and he waggled it at the sisters as he closed the door behind him. "I thought you might like to see this," he said. "Carlene gave me an early copy."

"We would," Jane said, grinning as she greeted him, "and I bet the price of a peek is dinner with the Howards."

"Well, now that you mention it . . ." Everyone laughed. Alice quickly set another place at the table while Louise poured chilled tomato juice for all.

Alice, Louise and Lloyd took seats while Jane placed braised lamb chops onto a platter. The table already held bowls of vegetables, and a dish of mint jelly had been placed in the center.

After Jane took her seat, she looked at Lloyd. "Would you like to offer grace?" she asked him.

"Certainly." Lloyd bowed his head. "Dear Heavenly Father, thank You for the loving bonds of friendship and family. Bless the food prepared by Jane's capable hands. Use it to strengthen our bodies for Your work in the world. Use us as well, Lord. Make us instruments of Your boundless compassion and caring. All these things in Your name we pray. Amen."

The sisters joined him. "Amen." Then all raised their heads, and Jane began to pass around the platter of sizzling chops.

"I know it's considered rude to read at the table," Jane said, "but I am dying to know what Carlene wrote about the letters Earl Padgett found. Did you read it, Lloyd?"

"I did, and Ethel's the only other person I've shown it to." He grinned. "It's an obituary."

"An obituary?" all three sisters chorused.

"Oh, now you've done it," Jane proclaimed. "Excuse me." She rose from her chair and plucked the paper off the counter. "Impolite or not, I have to read it."

"Read it aloud," suggested Louise, "so that Alice and I don't have to be uncivilized also."

Jane snickered. The paper rustled as she unfolded it. Then she began to read:

CIVIL WAR NO MORE

By Carlene Moss

The town of Acorn Hill announces that any further speculation about a Civil War battle in or near our community is dead. The speculation died a sudden death on Monday, September 23, in the conference room of the town hall. Mayor Lloyd Tynan presided over funeral services officiated by Mr. Earl Padgett, who provided documentation that showed no battle ever occurred.

The speculation is survived by an article from an area newspaper and a personal letter from an Acorn Hill citizen to a local Union officer. Another personal letter from the period was provided by Mr. Herbert Hoffstritt.

The funeral was attended by Mrs. Ethel Buckley, Miss Hope Collins, the aforementioned Mr. Hoffstritt, Miss Nia Komonos, the Misses Alice and Jane Howard, Mrs. Jason Litmore, Mr. and Mrs. Ronald Simpson, Mrs. Louise Smith, Mrs. William Ullman and Mr. Duane Van Dinkle.

There will be a viewing from October 1 through October 31 by the main desk of the Acorn Hill Library.

Memorial contributions may be made to the library, which will be preserving the remains.

"'Which will be preserving the remains'?" Jane threw down the paper and doubled over laughing. "That's priceless. Oh, Carlene, who knew you had it in you?"

Alice, Louise and Lloyd laughed, both at the "obituary" and at Jane.

"What a clever summation of the events," Louise said. "The stilted reporting and the correct use of titles is what I remember from the papers when I was young. I bet there will be oodles of people viewing that display."

"The preserved remains?" Jane sputtered, still chuckling.

Lloyd smiled at her, then looked at Louise. "I owe you an apology," he said.

"No you don't." Louise waved a hand as if wiping his words away.

"I do," Lloyd insisted. "You were the one who tried to put the brakes on my runaway train. And I know that it was no small matter to locate tangible evidence of the actual events mentioned in Herb's letter. Kenneth told me about all the hours you spent at the library."

"And with Earl the Eloquent," added Jane. "He talked her ears off."

Louise smiled. "He's very interesting, and he has some wonderful stories. Especially if one is not trying to squeeze specific information out of him."

That provoked yet another round of laughter.

A perfunctory knock on the back door followed by the door's opening had them all turning to see who was joining them.

Ethel came bustling in, wearing a loudly rustling raincoat and a clear plastic rain bonnet tied beneath her chin. "Hello, everyone. Hello, Lloyd. I bet you came to share the paper." She stopped to begin untying her bonnet, then looked up. "So what did you think of the obituary?" she asked, a mischievous smile on her face.

"We loved it," Alice said. "Won't you please join us for dinner?"

"No thank you. I already ate." Ethel walked over and peered at their food. "Although now I wish I hadn't." She hung her raincoat on one of the hooks near the door, then accepted the chair Alice had pulled up to the table for her. "Just a glass of juice, if you please."

"Of course, Auntie." Alice walked to the counter for a glass.

"I heard from Florence this morning," Ethel announced.

"You did?"

"What did she say?"

Ethel smiled. "She asked if I wanted to go to the Harvest Craft Fair in Cobalt on Friday."

Silence greeted this revelation.

"And?" Louise asked cautiously. "Did she apologize to you?"

Ethel shook her head. "Of course not. It takes more than a few sharp words between us to get Florence to admit she was wrong."

"That's it?" Alice looked taken aback. "I was afraid the two of you were going to be mad at each other for a long time."

Ethel chuckled. "No. We're like Lucy and Ethel from *I Love Lucy*. Occasionally we get annoyed with each other, but we always get over it."

Louise's lips twitched. She did not dare look at Alice or Jane, who doubtless was imagining their redheaded aunt and her heavyset friend stomping around in a vat of grapes just as their TV counterparts once had done.

Lloyd reached over and patted Ethel's hand in a sweet gesture that brought a surprising lump to Louise's throat. "I'm glad you two have made up. It's never easy being at odds with the ones you love."

"It's never easy being at odds with anyone," Alice said.

Louise looked around the table at these people with whom she lived, for whom she cared. She thought of the uproar Herb Hoffstritt's letter had caused. It was a miracle that everyone involved still was speaking to all of the others. It was a testament to the essential goodhearted nature of the people of Acorn Hill.

God had blessed them in so many ways, she thought, not the least of which was the very special town in which they lived.

Honey-Nut Fruit Salad

SERVES SIX

1 large red apple, sliced thinly
1 large pear, sliced thinly
1 large orange, peeled and sliced
⅓ cup vegetable oil
3 tablespoons white wine vinegar
1 tablespoon honey
½ cup chopped pecans
Lettuce leaves

In a large bowl, combine sliced fruit. In a small bowl, combine oil, vinegar and honey. Blend well. Pour oil mixture over the fruit, tossing to coat well. Arrange fruit on six lettuce-lined salad dishes and sprinkle each with a heaping teaspoon of chopped nuts. Add curled apple skin garnish for color.

About the Author

Anne Marie Rodgers has published nearly three dozen novels since 1992. She has been a finalist for the prestigious RITA award and has won several Golden Leaf awards, among others. In addition, she has been a teacher of handicapped and preschool children.

Anne Marie has been involved in animal-rescue efforts for many years, and her family is used to sharing their home with furred, finned and feathered creatures in need. After Hurricane Katrina, she volunteered at the Humane Society of Louisiana, caring for animals left behind during evacuation efforts. She and her loved ones also have raised puppies for Guiding Eyes for the Blind.

Anne Marie and her family live in State College, Pennsylvania. Her favorite activities include ice skating, needlework, amateur theater and dance, canine training, and scrapbooking. She considers irises, beaches and babies of any species some of God's finest creations.

A Note from the Editors

We hope you enjoy Tales from Grace Chapel Inn, created by Guideposts Books and Inspirational Media. In all of our books, magazines and outreach efforts, we aim to deliver inspiration and encouragement, help you grow in your faith, and celebrate God's love in every aspect of your daily life.

Thank you for making a difference with your purchase of this book, which helps fund our many outreach programs to the military, prisons, hospitals, nursing homes and schools. To learn more, visit GuidepostsFoundation.org.

We also maintain many useful and uplifting online resources. Visit Guideposts.org to read true stories of hope and inspiration, access OurPrayer network, sign up for free newsletters, join our Facebook community, and follow our stimulating blogs.

To order your favorite Guideposts publications, go to ShopGuideposts.org, call (800) 932-2145 or write to Guideposts, PO Box 5815, Harlan, Iowa 51593.